The
Last Dreamseer

Katy Haye

The

Last Dreamseer

More by Katy Haye

Princess Witch series (Firethorn Kingdoms fantasy)
Dragon Thief
Dragon Flight
Dragon Fury
Dragon Stone

The Four Kings series (fantasy)
Awakened by Magic
Inspired by Magic
Shattered by Magic
Drenched by Magic
Ignited by Magic
Courted by Magic

A Clockwork War series (steampunk)
The Clockwork War
An Airship from Ashes
The Tinker Queen
The Immortality Device

The Crown of Fane duology (fantasy)
The Last Gatekeeper
The Last Dreamseer

Standalone (post-apocalyptic)
Rising Tides

Chapter One

I'd foreseen my mother's death so many times it was strange I wasn't there to see it for real. But then, I always knew it wouldn't be dramatic. Compared to all those who had lost their lives fighting in the war, my mother simply slipped away.

I sat on the bed beside her watching her still, calm face. My fingers skimmed close to her skin, down her cheek to the curve of her jaw, and after a moment's stiff indecision, I pressed my fingertips to her neck to check her pulse. Nothing. Her skin was cool which removed any last threads of doubt, but I'd known she was dead before I'd walked in. I'd known as soon as I'd woken and felt, for the first time I could remember, that I wasn't being watched.

She looked peaceful, like she was sleeping, but close to her, I could see the fan of lines around her eyes, the creases beside her mouth. She was worn and tired. Worn down by the old queen; tired out by what was demanded of her because she was the dreamseer.

A role that I had now inherited.

I looked past her to the doors on the other side of the room that gave a clear view of our garden, neat rows of vegetables and herbs edged by fruit bushes with birds hopping through them, seeking the last of

1

the berries. Beyond the wall that trapped the sun in the garden was a short break of heathland and then the forest began, dark and peaceful, even in the bright sunlight.

I could run. I stared at the still forest and listened to my heart beat a steady thud. I could run and it might take years before anyone found me.

But they *would* find me. My skin was as dark as the heart of an *iska* tree, the colour marking me apart from the rest of the milk-pale fane race on our world. I was the dreamseer. It was impossible to hide what I was, and someone would always come for me. I couldn't escape my fate by running. Seeing the route my mother had taken, it looked like I couldn't escape my fate at all.

I shifted on the bed. The scent of *somnaya* tincture rose from my mother's body, leaking from her pores. My stomach turned over and my palms prickled, as though the smell called to the tincture still flowing through my veins from the dose forced on me the night before. I wiped my forehead where sweat was already beading.

That was the last dose I would ever be compelled to take.

The bottle my mother had used to send herself into dream-filled sleep every night stood on the cupboard by her bed, the leftover tincture inside glimmering iridescent in the sunlight. I scooped that up and crouched down, reaching beneath her bed to the box that held her supply. I pulled it into the middle of the room and looked around for something to break the lock. I was never sure whether she kept it locked because she didn't trust me or because she didn't trust herself.

Grabbing a book, I tried to smash the lock, but the loop of metal stayed intact. I glanced around for another tool. If I'd thought it would prove worthwhile I would have looked for the key, but I'd often hunted for it without success and didn't want to waste time now.

I tried to wedge her comb behind the lock and snap it open, but the comb broke instead. Hefting the box into my arms, I crossed to the garden doors, lifted the latch with an elbow and stepped into the already-hot morning air. I found a stone about the size of my fist, nicely flat and lacking sharp edges. Kneeling on the path, I pounded at the lock. Sweat beaded on my forehead again, prickling across the back of my neck. My fingers grew slippery and I had to keep adjusting my grip, but finally the lock gave and I could throw the lid open.

It was full of tiny glass bottles, all brimming with *somnaya* tincture, enough to last even my mother for months. I tipped them onto the soil and worked methodically, prising out the stoppers and tipping the contents onto the ground with a murmur of apology to the soil and plants, who probably wanted it even less than I did. The smell of it rose up and I pressed my nose to my shoulder to stifle the impulse to retch. I couldn't control spontaneous visions, but without the *somnaya* I could never again be forced to have a vision on command.

I kept glancing up, distracted by the forest, which was so close – and so big. Much of our world, Fane, had been turned to desert by the destruction caused by the gates to Earth, but not here. We were far away from the gates that linked the worlds and nothing had changed for centuries. The forest stretched for leagues, dense and beautiful. I could run away. They would eventually find me, but I could have years of freedom before that happened.

My sweating got worse and my hands shook as the smell of *somnaya* grew stronger. My heart beat loud and fast all the time I worked, urging me that time was running past, chances slipping and sliding towards and away from me. Or maybe that was just the final effects of the *somnaya*. I would do it. I emptied the final bottle and rose, stretching as I faced the forest, dark and cool and tempting. I'd do it, I'd run.

I swept the bottles back into the box and returned to the house. I grabbed a bag and tried to think what I needed to take, what wouldn't be provided by the forest. There wasn't much.

"Marra? Deena? Are you there?"

Moons! I dropped my bag as a voice called from the seeing-glass in the next room. The record keeper called from the palace most days, but never this early. I wiped the sweat from my forehead and forced a smile as I walked through to the water-filled bowl used to keep in contact with the rest of Fane, trying not to look like a *bozar* cornered by hunters. "Good morning, Honourable Lady."

Sweat poured off me, and not just because of the *somnaya*. The old dreamseer was dead, and there was protocol to follow. If the record keeper knew the truth she would tell the queen, and any chance of freedom would be gone.

"I need to speak with the dreamseer, Deena. Is your mother asleep?"

4

I peered into the water that filled the seeing-glass. The record keeper watched me through the distance the seeing-glass made irrelevant. She looked cross, but then she always did. She frowned, reminding me I hadn't answered her question. "She... she's not well." That had been the case for ages now. The record keeper usually spoke to me in her stead. I told my heartbeat to calm – the question didn't mean she'd guessed my mother was dead. She couldn't know that anything was wrong.

"I'm sorry to hear that. We are all sorry to know that the dreamseer is fading." The record keeper didn't sound sorry. She didn't look it, either. Her sharp gaze darted past me as though seeking my mother behind me. I could imagine her in a room at the palace, peering into the pool of water she'd poured to make the window to me, craning closer as though that would allow her to see more. "Moonsfall night grows closer and the new queen must be officially confirmed. We need our dreamseer for the ceremony."

As though I didn't know that. Now the war was over, we had three candidates who wished to rule, and the dreamseer was required to foresee which would be Fane's best queen. By tradition, the new queen had to be confirmed as the sun rose after moonsfall night – light following darkness, order from chaos, blah blah. My mother had asked me to foresee the new queen at least once a week since the old queen had been killed. The only problem was – I saw nothing.

"Will the dreamseer be fit to travel to the palace?" the record keeper asked. "Or must we send someone to her?"

There were only two weeks to moonsfall. The trip to

the palace on the Gillabar Plains would take most Fanes less than a day, but dreamseers could only *bound* short distances. And if the journey were undertaken on foot, it might take a week. My mother wasn't going anywhere, but I didn't want to take her place. Not for this. Not for anything.

I'd taken too long to find an answer. The expression in the record keeper's eyes sharpened while her voice went soft. "Where is your mother, Deena?"

"She's in her bed." Panic slid through my veins with every beat of my desperate heart. The record keeper knew something was wrong and I had to allay her fears, but with *somnaya* burning out of my pores, I couldn't think what to say to her.

"Wake her, please, Deena."

"She's asleep. I don't want to disturb her." Another rush of sweat that I mopped with my sleeve.

"I understand, but I need to see her, Deena." Her tone remained soft, but there was iron in it.

I looked into her eyes, leagues away but so close she could be beside me, and I knew I'd lost my chance. I should have run the moment I found my mother. I shouldn't have stopped for anything.

"Deena?"

I covered my face, speaking through my fingers. "I can't wake her. I think… I think she's gone."

"I'm sorry to hear that, Honourable Dreamseer." She immediately used the title that had belonged to my mother moments before. "I'll be with you in an hour."

Her face vanished, leaving me alone. I glanced at the bag I'd half-packed. An hour wasn't enough of a head start. If I ran now I'd be dragged back in disgrace before nightfall. I'd lost my chance. My fate settled around me, heavy and more suffocating than the robes the dreamseer used on formal occasions. I kicked my bag into the corner of my room and sank onto my bed. I was trapped. Trapped by the abilities that ran in my blood, passed from mother to daughter. Trapped by the queen who would use me to foresee whatever she wanted, whatever would help her advance her own aims. The would-be queens hadn't bothered the dreamseer yet, in deference to my mother's ill-health, and because they didn't quite have the authority to command her before being confirmed in the role. I couldn't expect that to last; as dreamseer I was too useful. Once the queen was confirmed, she would have a list of demands to trouble me with. I sank my head into my hands again, breathing steadily, listening to the sound and feeling the air push against my palms. My mother had escaped, using the only route open to dreamseers: death. I was stuck here, at the mercy of the new queen.

I stared at the wall opposite, listening to my blood rushing in my ears. My despair would pass. I could bear this. I'd borne worse.

I stayed that way, breathing steadily and repeating the words to myself, until the record keeper arrived.

Chapter Two

Crowds. I hate crowds. Being gawped at by a couple of fanes waiting to hear what gems of insight would blurt from my lips was bad enough. Being gawped at by more than two hundred of them was unbearable. I shifted in my formal robes under the mid-morning sun, tried to imagine they weren't there, and counted my slightly-too-fast heartbeats instead, but the crowd was too noisy to drown out entirely. They'd been too noisy, too *there*, since they'd started arriving on my doorstep three days before, summoned by the short, fussy record keeper who'd confirmed my mother's death and not let me out of her sight from that moment on.

A funeral should be a day of mourning, but a dreamseer's funeral was a state occasion. Especially now. Moonsfall was two weeks away. The would-be queens were all in attendance, jostling for power.

From my place beside my mother's bier, I watched the crowd. I could make out three distinct factions: the gatekeeper spontaneously declared queen when Issaenaptra had been killed two months earlier, and two members of the Council of Twelve, Saldamia and Gallia. Both councillors had clusters of fanes around them, plotting and politicking for leadership. The gatekeeper stood slightly aside from the Council of Twelve. She didn't seem to care about forging alliances. Two others stood with her, attendants or bodyguards. Judging from their clothes, they were ordinary fanes, not councillors. The gatekeeper didn't seem to want to speak to anyone else, her hands resting over her stomach as though protecting the baby everyone knew was in there. Perhaps she didn't understand the use she was supposed to make of today's gathering if she wished to be confirmed queen. When you were first thrown into a role it could be hard to understand what was expected of you.

I wondered which faction would be best for me – or least bad. Dreamseers live to serve the rulers of Fane. That's always been the case for as long as there have been rulers and dreamseers. So far as I know, no one's ever thought to ask the dreamseers whether they were happy with a life of service. No one was asking me now, they were all too busy hatching their own plans and assuming I would do whatever was demanded of me.

They were fools. We'd only recently found peace after civil war had torn the fanes apart. We should be working to strengthen shaken relationships and return the planet to the fertile, harmonious place it had once been. But most of the fanes in the crowd didn't care for that. They assumed the fragile peace would continue – all they were worried about was gaining as much benefit as they could from the day's ceremony.

And I was stuck in front of them all, standing motionless beneath the hot sun in my stupid, stuffy robes that itched beneath my armpits, watching and waiting to see whose ambitions I would be forced to support. I couldn't resign. The dreamseer didn't have that option; no ruler would accept that. Our talents were born to us, one mother bequeathing her abilities to one daughter, and they stayed with us for life. My visions wouldn't go away just for the wishing of it. And I would never be free while I could see things that other people found useful.

For now, I cultivated my dreamseer indifference, staring over my mother's body in matching robes lying on top of the piled wood. I tried to keep my eyes fixed towards the horizon, but they kept drifting.

The gatekeeper glanced up and her gaze met mine. I saw the brown of her eyes, soft like those of a *chibbok*. She smiled, a warm gesture. That was out of step with the machinations of the council members.

Shaking away my thoughts and looking deliberately in the other direction, I settled my gaze instead on the record keeper, tending the small fire from which the pyre would be lit when the time was right. I was beyond tired of the sight of her. Short, nosy and full of herself, she was tiresomely obsessed with making sure everything was right, meaning it had to match what had happened at these occasions for the past 500 years. If we did it wrong, she gave the impression Fane would cease to turn on its axis so dire would the consequences be.

A hollow sensation pushed my stomach aside. I swallowed and stared hard at the Northern Mountains that marked the horizon. I hoped the sensation was nerves, or something I'd eaten, but I knew it wasn't.

Not now. Not here. For the love of everything I held dear... no, that wouldn't work, there wasn't enough in all I held dear to tempt any spirit. I closed my eyes, blocking out the wide blue sky and the dark mountains for a long moment. My hands clenched, fingernails biting into the skin of my palms. Not now, not now, not now.

Beside my mother's funeral pyre wasn't the time or place for a vision to arrive, but visions never cared for convenience or dignity. I re-opened my eyes, staring hard above the sea of faces who didn't yet know that anything was happening. My stupid, ornate dreamseer's robes that I'd been bullied into wearing dragged at my shoulders as heat climbed up my spine. The silver diadem slipped and I put a hand to straighten it. My long, curly hair was doing its best to cast the stupid thing off, feeling the same as I did about the ceremony we were forced to endure. Clenching my teeth, I breathed slowly, counting the seconds and willing the vision building at the back of my head to go away. I heard a murmur in the crowd gathered before me – perhaps someone had spotted a change in my face. I took a step back so I was better hidden behind the bier on which lay my mother's lifeless body. The susurration of murmurs grew and became a ringing in my ears. I clenched my teeth so hard tears gathered in my eyes but it made no difference. All the colour washed out of the world, leaving the scene before me monochrome and dull. Every face turned to me – and then there was nothing.

*

"It's not over yet," came out of my mouth before I was in control of it – the last of my vision as it fled, leaving only odd sensations and fleeting impressions that sent shivers down my spine. War and death. Again.

I opened my eyes to see the vast, cloudless blue sky that told me I was back in reality. I tried to push my hair back off my face and twitched with shock – someone was holding my hand. It was so long since anyone had touched me that the heat felt strange, pouring over my skin like a warm tide.

I tried to pull my hand away, astonished when the warm fingers around mine tightened reassuringly instead of releasing me. The one who was touching me made the sort of noise you might use in proximity with a frightened, cornered animal and he helped me sit, keeping his left hand firm around mine. He'd positioned himself between me and the crowd, the pyre on our other side, although people beyond him pushed as close as possible, craning to see. I could hear them muttering, "What did she say? What did she foresee?"

"Take your time, they can wait," my hand-holder's voice assured me.

His face came into focus and the world twisted again. I wrenched my hand from his grasp, dropping my gaze in case he saw recognition in mine. Of all the fanes in front of us, the one who had stepped out of the crowd to help me had to be Cal, the exile returned. The rebel. Why hadn't he just stared and muttered, like the rest?

His glittering gaze fell from my face and he shifted away, shoulders square and angry. "I apologise if I've broken some sort of protocol by touching you." I had never heard anyone sound less apologetic. "You looked like you needed some help."

I could have told him that wasn't the reason for my shock – but why should I? The one thing in favour of

12

being a dreamseer was that you didn't have to explain yourself.

"I don't need your help." I rose to my feet, hauteur masking my feelings, trying not to let my gaze track to the young fane who had touched me. My hand was warm and I forced myself to let it hang from my side, not curl and hold the warmth inside. I ignored the crowd a step away from me and faced the record-keeper. "It's time." I met her gaze and held my hand out imperiously for the torch. I acted as though there were no option but to obey my instructions and, after a moment, so did the record keeper. I thrust the flame into the midst of the pyre and held it until the wood caught and flames licked through the stacked wood, reaching to the sky and filling the air with fragrant smoke.

*

The pyre was falling to ash, my mother's remains crumbled to dust, when the crowd began to disperse. The stuffy ceremony was reaching its end and they wanted to move on to the next event – the feast; the fun reward for standing around while the old dreamseer burned. The less important people at the back sidled towards the huge tent erected to hold everyone for the evening's celebrations. The more important – in their opinions, anyway – edged closer to me. I'd fallen into a vision in full sight of the great and mighty of Fane. I couldn't hope not to be quizzed.

The other purpose of today's ceremony was to confirm me as the next dreamseer. I was about to become public property. Well, not quite that, more like the property of whoever could claim me and keep

13

me. Previously that had been Queen Issaenaptra, but matters weren't so straightforward now. I stared into the dying flames as though I would stay there all night and wondered who would have the courage to speak first and stake a claim.

A log shifted, sending up a scatter of sparks. I blinked and saw the echo of light behind my eyelids. From staring at the fire, my eyes were too dry to cry. My mother was gone now, truly gone. I was all on my own. That was the fate of all dreamseers: mother and daughter, then daughter alone, I knew that. I straightened my shoulders and let out a slow breath. My mother had been content with her fate, or perhaps she had simply lost the desire to fight. I hadn't. There would be another chance to run, one day – and I'd take it.

There were three distinct groups waiting to be acknowledged, fanned around me, almost beyond my field of vision. Perhaps they were holding back out of respect, but I read a lack of courage, and continued to study the fire. All the time I had to myself could be counted in the moments until someone grew bold enough to speak.

"Excuse me?"

I stilled. The voice came from the cluster of people further to my right. I gave no reply and after a moment, she stepped forward, into my line of sight. It was the young gatekeeper. I'd never spoken to her before, but I was familiar with her face – how could I not be? The last queen had been obsessed with the half-human teenager who could control the gates between Fane and Earth. "I'm sorry for your loss."

Her voice was gentle. I looked up to her face, and

then away. I intended to ignore her, but something made me say, "Thank you."

Of course, that emboldened her. She took another step forward. "I just wondered – what did you foresee? When you said it wasn't over yet."

I turned away, facing the dying pyre once more. I had foreseen in a vision, and I couldn't expect what I saw to be private – my visions belonged to Fane. I closed my eyes. I remembered nothing clearly, but impressions rushed back to me: a battlefield, chaos and death.

My silence provoked a rustle of whispers in both groups.

The gatekeeper shifted and tried again. "I'm sorry to intrude, but it could be important."

My face didn't change, but the fire of fury licked through me. My visions were important – far more important than I was. I'd learned that time and again in the last ten years, growing into abilities that left me at risk of being torn apart by people who only cared for their own ambitions. The visions were important; the dreamseer was just the vessel.

"Peace is not yet secure on Fane." I looked across all the fanes crowding close without actually looking at any one of them. "But you didn't need me to tell you that."

"What should we do about it?" One of the councillors spoke up, arrogantly expectant – as though I alone should have the answers for everything.

I stared until she found some respect and dropped her gaze. "If you stopped fighting amongst yourselves, that would make a good start."

Someone at the back, out of sight, giggled, the sound

rapidly muffled. The councillor before me, Saldamia, candidate for queen, muttered to the companion closest to her, but nothing clear enough for me to hear.

The fire was reduced to a pile of glowing red embers, edging to black. We were the only people still outside the tent from which flickering lights and soft music drifted. I cast a last, regretful look at the blackening pyre. Then I stepped through the crowd, fixing my gaze above their heads and expecting them to part for me.

Now must come the celebration in praise of the new dreamseer: lucky me.

Chapter Three

After the stillness of the fading day, the feasting tent was too bright, too hot, and too loud. I had to sit in my robes on an ornately carved throne, the diadem making my head itch ferociously. I was once more in full sight of everyone, although now I was utterly ignored while everyone ate the food and drank the drink provided and tried to forge alliances with friends and take the measure of potential enemies. I wanted nothing more than to be in my home, lying in my garden staring up at the moons spinning through Fane's sky and finding some peace.

I picked at the small portion of fruit I'd put on my plate, almost glad of the disturbance when a voice spoke beside me. "I need to speak to you."

It was the gatekeeper. She needed to speak to me, the same way that I needed to be alone away from the press of people, but what we both needed wasn't allowed because ceremony must be followed. The half-human was flanked by the rebel, Cal, and another fane with a scarred face. I didn't know her but I was sure she was another rebel – had been another rebel. I returned my gaze to the male.

"Cal." As I spoke his name, my gaze fell to his hand, remembering what I'd seen in visions, as though I

17

needed to match up the reality with what had only been in my head until then.

His expression twisted cynically and he lifted his left hand to display his fingers, the tips of each cut short, lost to the old queen's violence. "Did you want proof?"

At his aggressive tone, I looked back to his face. Did he know what I'd done? But no. He wasn't angry with me, he was simply angry. I swallowed down my guilt. "No. I was just curious."

I turned next to the scarred fane and raised my brows. "You are?"

"Keba." She supplied her name and nothing more, expression reserved and watchful. I liked her immediately.

"I'm Zan," the gatekeeper added.

I smiled at that. "I know. I've seen you many times." I touched my eyebrow to indicate my visions.

"Oh." She blinked. "Is there somewhere we can speak?"

"We are speaking," I pointed out.

She glanced around as though everyone in the tent might be avid to hear what she had to say. Zan was both queen and gatekeeper. I guessed she didn't get a lot of privacy, either. "In private, I meant."

"Did you wish to consult the dreamseer? I'm sure we can agree a date for an appointment."

More surprise – that seemed to be her default expression. "I just wanted—"

Cal cut across her to snap at me, "This is your queen. You will show her due respect."

I raised my brows. "I am the dreamseer. I believe I am owed respect, too."

Cal glowered, but Keba cut in before he could say anything. "Forgive my friend. Cal has spent too long getting people to do what he wants by throwing things at them." She cast him a look I couldn't interpret. "He's forgotten the niceties of civilised conversation."

Cal made an impatient noise, but he didn't seem angry with Keba. I realised there was friendship there, a connection of trust and respect. I swallowed and moderated my tone as I addressed Zan. "What do you want of me?"

She edged forward, looking around again before she spoke. "I want to make a gate to Talvar. Is it possible?"

My gaze fell to her stomach, but there was no sign of her pregnancy beneath her robes. A gate between the worlds. Not to Earth, which would inflame the war all over again, but to Talvar. And I'd thought I was the only one who wanted to escape. "You want to go to Talvar?"

"Or to let, er, someone from Talvar come here."

"The father of your baby?"

Her cheeks flushed the pink of *gimfruit* blossoms. "That's right."

"Does he want to come here?" My father had vanished once my mother had got what she wanted from him, but perhaps talvarrines made better fathers than that.

She looked startled by the question. "Of course. I think."

"Don't you want to be confirmed queen?"

"No." She glanced at Cal, but if she was expecting him to say something, he didn't oblige, watching silently. "I don't think I'm cut out to be queen." She smiled and half-laughed. "You might not believe it, but I had a quiet life before I discovered I was a gatekeeper." She took a breath. "I was told… There are myths that a gate can be made…"

And the picture that had been starting to form in my head, that we could make a gate to another world and leave never again to be bothered by the cares of Fane, popped out of existence. "Yes, there are myths."

Her face fell at my dull tone. "Can't it be done?"

"Not by me."

Cal stepped forward. "Don't play us for fools. The stories say a dreamseer and a gatekeeper working together can create a gate. You're the dreamseer, here's the gatekeeper – what's the problem?"

His anger provoked the same emotion in me, but I tamped it down, facing him with a calm expression. "Very well." I looked at Zan for permission, then touched my fingers against hers. I looked back at Cal as I declared in a low voice, "The dreamseer and the gatekeeper command that a gate be made between Fane and Talvar." I flicked my hand in a showy manner, then raised my brows. "Oh, it doesn't seem to have happened. Whatever can have gone wrong?"

Cal's scowl deepened, his eyes glittering fury. Zan shook her head. Cal glared at me. Keba was watching all of us, arms folded and an amused expression playing around her mouth. I really liked her, but I tried not to show it.

"Come on, Cal," Zan chided. "You can't have thought it would be that easy."

I dropped my hand from hers. "You need a gatekeeper and a dreamseer, but what you do once you've got them I don't know."

20

"Who—" Zan started, but Cal spoke over her.

"Then why don't you have one of your little visions show you how it's done?" He folded his arms, a cross mirror for calm Keba.

Heat climbed through me, but I wasn't going to show my feelings to this fane. "They don't work like that."

His mouth twisted his cynicism into contempt. "Then what's the use of you?"

"Cal!"

He ignored Zan's protest. "Is it true that creating a gate robs one or both of their life's strength?"

"I don't know. All power demands a price. There must be some sacrifice, but I don't know what. I've never made a gate. I don't know anyone who has. But it must be risky or Issaenaptra would have made her dreamseer create more gates for her soldiers to destroy Earth."

"Who would know what to do?" Zan persisted, unwilling to give up her dream.

My heart felt hollowed out, but my voice was steady when I told her, "Tullan Fabler would know if anyone does. If you can find him."

Cal snorted. "Tullan Fabler? Who knows all the myths we've all forgotten? Isn't he a myth, himself?"

"No, he's real." My heart thudded. I was proof that he was real, but I wasn't going to tell these fanes so. "At least, he was real. Maybe he's dead." Would anyone tell me? Did I care?

Zan sighed and I wished I had been able to help her. A new gate. A new world. And a way to escape my life here. "Never mind." She smiled, although the gesture didn't reach her eyes, and bent her head respectfully.

"Thank you for your time, Honourable Dreamseer."

"I'm sorry I cannot help you, my queen." And I truly was – for her sake as well as mine.

"We'll find this Fabler," Cal swore.

I wondered what made him so determined to give Zan what she wanted. This was more than obedience to a queen. I remembered that they were related – cousins, as unlikely as that was here on Fane where fanes rarely had more than one child. Duty and blood and friendship; a powerful combination, it seemed.

"Perhaps," Zan said.

I wanted to say that I would help them search for Tullan Fabler, but they turned to go, murmuring amongst themselves. I was forgotten already.

I sat back in my ornate seat, watching them as the chance to get what I wanted walked away from me. Beneath the table, my hands clenched. It hadn't really been a chance. I hadn't been any closer to escape than I ever had. But perhaps... Now the idea was in my head I couldn't let it go. Cal didn't seem the sort to give up.

My hands ached, my palms sore where my nails bit into the skin. I relaxed them deliberately and cast a glance over the throng of people feasting in front of us, face impassive in case anyone was watching me.

I didn't move my head, observing from the corner of my eye as Zan and the others returned to their seats. Zan went first, Cal and Keba hanging back in what might have been respect but could just have been caused by the crush in the room. As Cal pushed through the crowd, the hot pain of guilt clawed at my throat and I looked away to lessen the sensation. He'd betrayed the old queen by her terms; any consequences were between the two of them and nothing to do with me.

Keba, the quiet one, went last, glancing around the room as though scanning for threats. The peace following the old queen's death was new and fragile. Keba was right to be cautious. She reached forward and touched Cal's arm, leaning forward to speak into the ear he turned to receive her words. A cold shard of jealousy slid through me. A friend. I'd never had one of those.

Zan reached her seat and sat down. The other two took their places on either side.

I pressed my thumb against a *gimfruit* on my plate. The skin swelled until the flesh burst out on a tide of red juice. I wanted to leave, but custom made that impossible. I wanted the clear sky so I might empty my mind. I wanted my bed and oblivion.

*

A little while later, I escaped for a few short minutes. Even dreamseers were allowed to attend to nature.

Afterwards I walked as slowly as I could back to the tent. The noise, the lights, the smell. They all repelled me. My robes forced me to walk slowly, and I made the most of that. In a stately dreamseer glide, I crept back towards the tent and the seat I had to fill.

"Ghastly, isn't it?"

I turned, and the female who had accompanied the gatekeeper, Keba, was there, leaning against a tree and watching the moons through the branches overhead. I paused. There was no reason to talk to her. I didn't much want to talk to anyone, but I was also, oddly, bored of my own company. In this noisy, argumentative, jubilant crowd, I was dissatisfied with myself. I didn't want to be me.

She filled my pause by speaking again. "I could never stand politics. Fighting is much more honest."

Speaking to Keba gave me an excuse not to return to the ornate seat inside the tent. Except I wasn't speaking much.

She turned away from the moons, facing me fully. "If I wore those robes do you think anyone would notice the difference? I could take your place, give you a chance to escape."

Was my desire to do so obvious, or was she simply more perceptive than most people? "Why would you do that? Why would I want that?"

Keba shrugged. "I made my own choice which side I wanted to fight for during the war. It's always seemed a little unfair that dreamseers don't get to choose. You're not children, but that's how everyone treats you." She had a glass of golden Valderian ale in her hand. Realising I was empty-handed, she held it out. "D'you want some?"

I nearly refused. I don't like intoxicants. The sensation of being out of control reminded me too much of visions and that wasn't something I wanted to bring on voluntarily. But children weren't allowed ale; adults made their own limits. "Thank you." I accepted the glass.

"What's your name?"

I was startled by the question. Dreamseers were always called just that, sometimes with an 'honourable' in front. I hadn't expected ordinary fanes to realise I had a name.

"Or do you prefer to be addressed by your title?"

I shook my head. "I'm Deena."

"Deena. Named for Fane's first ruler, I assume." She knew her history. "That's a strong name."

"Dreamseers are always strong." It wasn't a boast, but a fact. We had to be.

"We've all had to be strong lately." Keba's lips parted as though she might say something else, then she focused beyond me, her weight shifting, pushing away from the trunk of the tree she'd been leaning against.

I turned enough to see that it was Cal walking towards us; well, towards Keba. I stepped back into the shadows to get a proper look at him unobserved. He loped across the ground from the tent towards us, his relaxed gait at odds with the hunch of his shoulders, the watchful way he looked around him. You wouldn't mistake him for anything other than a soldier. I wondered if he was happy with his role. Like Keba, he'd got to choose the side he fought for, at least. His hands snared my attention. They hung naturally at his side, giving no sign of the damage his left had suffered. I glanced at his face but there was no trace in his expression, either. There was no reason there should be, it wasn't like the wounds would still hurt; they were healed now. No matter how much something hurt it always stopped in the end.

His glance grazed my face as he drew near, but he ignored me to speak to Keba. "Problem?"

She shook her head. "I was just chatting with Deena." She stretched, arms lifted high above her head, tunic shifting with the movement. "I'll head back now." Keba walked towards the tent. Cal watched her go, arms folded, observant. I wondered why he didn't accompany her. They clearly didn't like to leave Zan unprotected so it seemed odd that they didn't all stick together, clustered in case of danger.

I tried not to look at him, because that provoked memories from his past that made guilt gnaw at me.

Moments slipped by. Cal didn't speak, but nor did he move away. I didn't break the silence. I had nothing to say to him.

After a minute, my irritation grew, with myself for letting him send me back to the past, and with him for standing there like a great, mute *gobbin*. If he had no purpose in being here, why didn't he leave? "Shouldn't you be inside, guarding the gatekeeper?"

He turned to look at me, as though he'd forgotten I was there until I spoke. His tone matched mine. "Shouldn't you be foreseeing something useful to her?"

"I'm taking the night off." I looked along the path back to the tent. Part of me wanted to move away, but I still didn't want to return to sit down and be gawped at. At least he was honest. I responded in kind. "Are you this rude with everyone?"

He smiled. I was silenced by the change the gesture wrought in his appearance. He was handsome when he wasn't scowling. It was a better sight than my memories gave me of him. His reply pulled me out of my remembrances. "No, it's just you, mostly."

Did he know what I'd done to him? He couldn't. If he did, he wouldn't be talking to me; his hands would be around my throat choking the life out of me. I forced myself to face him. "And what's the matter with me – in your opinion?"

He folded his arms, appearing relaxed as he leaned back in the place Keba had so recently left. I wasn't fooled, I'd seen him in action. His gaze was watchful. If anything happened he'd snap out of his indolence in an instant. "Nothing personal, I just happen to think the crown of Fane would be better off if it didn't pay attention to the incomprehensible ramblings of a reclusive druggie."

Wow, he was direct. No wonder the old queen had wanted rid of him. I kept my tone level. "I can't say I disagree. I'll look for another job in the morning."

He laughed down his nose as though I'd made a joke. Then he stood straight, watchful again. "I need to get back to Zan."

He made no farewell, just walked away. As he vanished into the tent, my feelings of unease were replaced by... jealousy. I was jealous of Zan. She didn't know how lucky she was to have Keba and Cal circling her like moons to her Fane; there was no one to watch out for me.

I drained the glass Keba had given me and followed her and Cal slowly back to the tent.

Chapter Four

I had only just regained my seat when I changed my mind about obeying convention and staying until the end. The people with me in the tent weren't celebrating me, they were serving themselves, bickering and jostling for position and influence, and not even casting a glance in my direction. I didn't have to remain for this. Abruptly, I rose to my feet. I was the dreamseer, and this was my chance to change the role, even just a little. If I couldn't get my own way today I never would. I turned to leave but my heavy robes made it hard to get all my skirts away from the carved arms. I grasped the fabric and wrenched it out of the way.

And a scream rent the air at the other end of the room. There was a crash and someone went flying backwards, hitting the wall of the tent and sliding to the floor.

The tent filled with fane energy. There was a moment like an in-drawn breath as everyone drew on their elemental powers, using their anima keys to draw shields of air around themselves while assessing who was friend and who foe.

Then the air crackled as decisions were made and those violently inclined launched into attack, the power they threw at their enemies colliding against shields in mid-air, air billowing the walls of the tent when the blocked elements had to go somewhere.

"Enough!" I bellowed the word, thankful that everyone froze and turned to me. My voice was the best tool I had – dreamseers don't have the same elemental powers other fanes do. We can't create the bangs and crashes of earth, air, water and fire; our talents turn inwards to our visions. I made my tone as commanding as I could, and the anger vibrating through it came naturally. "This is a day of sadness and contemplation. Your petty arguments have no place here."

There was grumbling and murmurs of dissent, but the elemental power in the room faded.

The injured fane got to her feet. It was one of the Council of Twelve, Gallia, another candidate for queen who had stood surrounded by supporters at my mother's service. She and Saldamia glared at each other. My presence was all that was preventing the violence from breaking out again. Which meant I couldn't go anywhere. Or not until they did.

I looked coldly at the faces in front of me. "This celebration is over. You will all leave."

The fanes closest to the doors obeyed first. They were eager to be far away from the violence they'd played no part in. Once they'd set the example of docility, the rest followed, although I didn't miss the searing looks full of threat that passed between several groups.

My visions sometimes took a while to become comprehensible, but today's had shown its truth already – the discord that had torn Fane apart three years before, and only simmered down to peace two months earlier, wasn't at an end yet.

*

My dreams mixed visions and reality that night. I saw Cal worn and in pain, and the old queen cackling in triumph. I saw Keba before the dagger sliced her cheek, although I knew I'd never seen her before today.

I awoke breathing hard, staring into darkness, my laboured breath loud in my ears. It was the shock of seeing him today, as though he'd come to life from my visions, that was why I was susceptible to the pictures and the emotions they provoked. Now I knew he was here, that he came along with Zan, I would cope better.

I rolled in my bed, curling my hands beneath my chin and staring into the darkness. I was fooling myself if I believed it would all be easy, and I didn't have the luxury to play the fool.

When it grew light, the council would select the new queen, ready for the confirmation ceremony after moonsfall, and whoever was appointed I knew she'd make full use of her dreamseer to shore up her support. If I didn't want to be the new queen's pawn I would have to change matters myself.

That brought my thoughts back to Zan, the one who didn't want to be queen, who only wanted to go to Talvar. I wondered if Tullan Fabler really could tell us how to make a gate. I wondered if Cal would find him.

I pushed off my bed and padded through to my mother's room. At the back of a drawer was a tiny, ornate jewel box. I folded the top back – to find the inside empty. All my hope and expectation whooshed out of me in a disappointed breath. I checked in the drawer, then in the others, but the ring was gone. It had probably been destroyed by my mother in a fit of rage and nostalgia.

I pushed my hair back from my face, picturing the ring. It had been made of my father's hair, plaited into a circle. It was the shade of wet sand, and smooth, as different as it was possible to be from my mother's and my curly, dark tresses. It was also the only thing he'd left behind when he'd abandoned us both. And now it was gone. Like him.

I pushed the door wide and sat on the threshold, looking out to the stars and the moons. Fane's smaller moon had mostly slipped beneath the horizon, only a crescent of silver still visible. The other was bisected by the land. Not long until moonsfall and the new queen and Fane's new era – whatever that would bring.

My mother was gone and the last trace of my father had vanished. Good luck to Cal and Zan finding him.

*

The next day we all had to return to the tent – cleared of all signs of feasting and violence – for the council meeting. I crossed the crushed grass and settled into my place at the edge of the frontmost row of chairs.

I would have preferred for them to decide on the queen during a council meeting at the palace without me, but the dreamseer was always present when a new queen was agreed, so I had to be there.

The record keeper took her seat at the desk in the middle of the tent and proceedings began. Firstly the gatekeeper, Zan, stepped into the space between the record keeper and the audience and renounced her claim.

"I came to Fane to end the war, but I am a newcomer here. Now peace has been achieved, I would prefer to offer my support to the queen chosen by the council today. I have no wish to take on the role myself." There was a moment of silence, then murmurs as she regained her seat, councillors and their supporters in the audience whispering their opinions to each other.

It was a pretty speech and I think she believed it. Much of the council, though, regarded her with suspicion.

Once she was crossed off the list, we had to sit through the declaration of candidates. Saldamia and Gallia stood forward to declare their willingness to serve Fane as queen: last night's warring parties on better behaviour today.

Before the councillors could vote, we had to listen through both the would-be queens and then each of the other council members making a representation. They even asked the gatekeeper for her opinions. I lost count of the number of times she stood up and said she had no wish to be queen (each of them carefully noted down by the record keeper so Zan couldn't change her mind later) and preferred to be impartial in the new queen's selection.

My attention kept drifting. I remembered what Keba had said the previous night, about fighting being more honest than politics. I looked around the crowded room until I found her, sitting beside Cal, both of them behind Zan. She looked up and our eyes met for the briefest moment. Her lips twitched in the shadow of a smile and I looked away before she could, turning my head so I focused instead on the record keeper, scratching away, ensuring every word was kept for history. *Moons*, the council records were still written on carefully-prepared *gobbin* skin, as though nothing had progressed in five centuries. I forced myself to listen to what the current councillor was saying in support of her favoured candidate.

All the councillors despised me, their dislike radiating from them. At sixteen, I was too young to be taken seriously by any powerful, immortal fane, and yet, as dreamseer, they were forced to at least seem as though they deferred to the wisdom of my visions.

I despised them, too. I wanted to stand up and tell them the queen to get my blessing would be the one willing to move Fane out of our rigid past. Burning the dreamseer's stupid robes would be a start. But I couldn't do that, and they wouldn't listen if I did. The dreamseer didn't get to have an *opinion*. She didn't get to *choose* like the councillors chose – she had to *foresee*.

In which duty I was failing. Despite the *somnaya* my mother had forced on me, for the past month I had seen no vision of the new queen. There was no clear candidate whose appointment would lead in certainty to a peaceful, content future for Fane. I wished I could declare for one and get the whole stupid charade over with, but there was nothing to show who was the better candidate and I wouldn't lie. I didn't like either of the candidates well enough to lie for their sake.

At last the interminable speeches were over. Which was a shame, because now I had to make my contribution. All eyes fixed on me. The record keeper was making small but urgent motions for me to move into the space before her where all the candidates and councillors had stood to make their declarations. I pretended not to see her, rising to my feet but staying in my place.

The two candidates were staring at me as though they could force me to say their name through the strength of their will. Saldamia was glaring, as though I'd declare her the next rightful queen if I knew what was good for me. Gallia was calmer, but I didn't like the haughty look in her eyes. Both wanted to be queen for their own benefit, not the good of Fane. I exhaled slowly to delay the moment when I had to declare what I saw. Whatever I said next I would make enemies.

For the first time in my life, I hoped that a vision might strike me down and take me out of the moment. No such luck. I cleared my throat, faced the empty wall of the tent over the head of the record keeper and spoke, "I have not foreseen anyone in this room as the next queen of Fane." A shiver danced down my spine. Something was very wrong. Fane had never been without a queen, not for fifty centuries.

The expressions on the faces arrayed against me hardened. Murmurs broke out. I made out the condemnation, "Too young," from the susurration of discontent.

Saldamia was the one who stepped from her seat, her eyes glittering with dislike as she faced me and spoke in a tone where courtesy barely masked her contempt. "With the greatest respect, Honourable Dreamseer, I think you must be mistaken. A true dreamseer has always been able to see the next queen," suggesting that I was somehow masquerading in the role. I wished. I'd bet she'd be pleased to dispense with the position of dreamseer – just as long as I made her queen first.

I made my glare as hard as hers. "There is no mistake. As you have said, the dreamseer can always see the next queen when Fane is without a ruler. I do not see her in this room."

"Then who is destined to be the next queen?" she snapped.

"I have not foreseen that." I paused, then added for safety's sake, "Yet."

Saldamia's gaze raked my face, then she seemed to accept that she would gain no advantage from me and turned to address the councillors. "Then I suggest we simply vote. We cannot be without a queen."

The record keeper cleared her throat, uncomfortable at putting herself forward, but finding the strength to do so when Saldamia suggested a process that didn't follow the protocol of the last handful of centuries. "A queen has never been decided upon without the guidance of the dreamseer. I suggest we wait. We have been without a formally-confirmed queen for weeks, after all."

"Which is exactly why this directionless limbo cannot be allowed to continue," Saldamia snapped.

Gallia smiled and said mildly, "I am content to wait." Her expression turned sly as she faced her opponent. "For the good of Fane we must be prepared to wait a little longer in order to be sure we get the right queen to lead us forward. There are still nine days before moonsfall, after all."

Saldamia looked as though she'd bitten into a *pannle* berry, then she smiled. "Of course. I am sure the right candidate will become clear."

The record keeper stood up, clearly distressed at not being able to inscribe a new name on her papers. "Very well." She turned to Zan. "I trust our gatekeeper will continue in the role until the next queen is agreed?"

"Actually, I plan to be away from the palace for a few days. I have some private business to attend to." There was a buzz of discussion when she said that. My heart lifted on a surge of hope. She meant to find Tullan Fabler and make a gate, surely. As though she didn't hear the speculation, Zan lifted her chin. "I request that the council work on the basis of consensus for that time. If a decision cannot be made, I can be consulted through a seeing glass."

"Agreed," Saldamia said on behalf of all the Council of Twelve. I didn't trust her. She'd use the time to strengthen her own position — but then she'd have done that anyway.

The record keeper addressed the councillors. "Very well. We reconvene in a week."

"We'll meet in the council chamber at the palace." Saldamia glared at me as she made her statement, which was not phrased as a request, as though I didn't already understand that I was in disgrace for not giving her the answer she wanted. The council would not come to me next time; I must go to them.

The record keeper nodded, too weak to challenge her. "Yes, in the council chambers. Ready for moonsfall."

Zangtaffs the lot of them. They all knew dreamseers can't *bound* the way other fanes do, using their control of the elements to jump ten leagues in a handful of seconds. It would take me days to get there. Unless I

36

didn't have to go there at all...

I glanced towards Zan, but she was already leaving the tent, once more flanked by Cal and Keba. I had to speak to her.

As though she read my mind, Keba turned. I tilted my head to indicate I wished to speak to her, hoping she'd understand. She murmured something to Cal and slipped away from the door. Cal sent a single look towards me then turned back to Zan.

Saldamia watched as Keba drew close. I couldn't do anything about that, but the would-be queen was at least too far away to hear our words. "If Zan wants her gate I will help find Tullan Fabler."

Keba nodded without asking any stupid questions. "She will call on you. Tomorrow?"

I nodded, and bit my lip so I wouldn't give in to the urge to hurry the timescales. I wouldn't plead. Not with Zan and certainly not with her representative. "Tomorrow."

I turned away from Keba, ignored the look Saldamia gave me, and swept out of the tent, finally returning to my home where I could shed my robes and be myself again. I closed the door against the ruckus of the council servants beginning to pack up the tent and everything else they'd brought for the ceremonies and relaxed for the first time in two days.

*

When the bell at my door rang clear and low that afternoon, after the council servants had departed with all the fripperies of ceremony, I actually smiled. I thought it was Zan, too eager to wait, desperate for the gate that would reunite her with her beloved talvarrine. I thought I could take my first steps towards freedom. I had forgotten about the other players and their ambitions.

I opened the door and the dozen fanes standing outside blocked most of the light. I took a step back, instinct when faced with so many. I'd had my fill of crowds. People usually came to visit in pairs: one who wanted the dreamseer to foresee something for them, and one to bear witness.

My foremost visitor was the would-be queen Saldamia. The others she'd brought with her were five councillors – the ones who had spoken in support of her – and the same number of servants or hangers-on. That was a lot to bear witness, more than anyone needed.

"Time to start work, dreamseer."

She had to know protocol, but she seemed not to care for it, stepping through the doorway so I had to take another step backwards or collide with her.

"You want a consultation?" My pulse sped up. Not now. Not so soon. Could she give me no peace? But no one had respect for a dreamseer, whatever they said, whatever tradition decreed. This woman didn't care for grief, or decency, or anything except what she wanted. I stood as tall as I could but I still had to look up to face her. In bare feet, leggings and a tunic, I didn't cut a very imposing figure. "You'll have to come back another day. I'm not ready." I wished I were wearing my dreamseer robes. They were awkward and impractical and looked ridiculous, but they made everyone keep their distance.

The would-be queen laughed and looked at me as though I were a pet *chibbok* that had bared its tiny teeth at its owner. "Then get ready. I don't intend to make this journey again."

I held her gaze, determined not to be cowed by her. She wasn't the queen. She had no right to command anyone, least of all me. The others she'd brought with her slithered into the room, spreading out around me. Danger clouded my thoughts and spiked my pulse.

Ambition and ruthlessness poured off Saldamia. In that moment I knew without any doubt that the fight at the feast had been at her instigation, and she was furious to have been stopped – she'd been aiming to remove her opponent. I was about to make her more furious still because I wouldn't foresee anything for her. She would never be queen and I would never help her, not someone who stood in my home and looked at me like that. "I can't foresee for you, not today. Nothing will come." I spoke with absolute conviction, grateful I'd destroyed my mother's *somnaya*.

Her hand shot out, gripping my arm. I was too slow to fend her off, but I wasn't entirely feeble. I threw what elemental power I had behind me, tugging one of the books from the shelves and letting it fly towards her. She ducked and dropped my hand, but someone else grabbed me so I couldn't move, and the fanes around her used their power against me, creating a barrier of air that held me in place and stopped me using my own feeble strength. Saldamia grabbed my arm again. I tried to pull away but her fingers tightened to the point of pain. More of the books cascaded around us, but none of them struck her or her pet councillors, their shields were too strong. The books clattered to the floor, forming a circle around us.

Saldamia glared at me and squeezed spitefully

tighter. My arm grew numb beneath her rigid fingers. I looked around the room seeking help but her supporters watched me steadily, shields held against me. The would-be queen raised her free hand and slapped me hard across the face. No one made any move to stop her. They were her people; I hadn't expected they would. "Don't think you can oppose me," she snapped.

While I ran my tongue over my teeth, wincing when I found the wound inside my cheek, tasting blood where it had jarred against my teeth, she tugged at my other hand, stretching my fingers and yanking off the ring containing my anima crystal. Fanes were powerless without their anima keys. "I'll keep this for the time being."

The shields around us lowered now I was disarmed. The councillors and their hangers-on stood in a circle around me and the would-be queen. Eleven of them in all, to subdue one feeble dreamseer. Their faces were utterly impassive.

Saldamia leaned close. "You insulted me this morning. I advise you not to continue doing so. I am your queen and I will have your obedience. Do you understand?" Her eyes gleamed with anger, so close I could barely focus on her. Her grip tightened even further. She was enjoying this. I longed to repeat what I'd said yesterday but I wasn't fool enough for that – I wanted to be free to live my life, not free *of* my life. "Do you understand?" she hissed. Spittle landed on my face.

"I understand." The pain around my arm lessened very slightly. "But I can't foresee anything for you today. I can't force a vision."

40

The pain returned and I clamped my lips together, determined not to give her the satisfaction of showing hurt. "I told you not to insult me – take a dose of your medicine. I know how these things are done." The properties of *somnaya* used to be a secret known only to dreamseers, but these days everyone knows our business.

"I can't. I don't have any." And how grateful I was for that. A drop of the tincture induced a dream-like state and opened our minds to visions. It also removed what little control we had over our hallucinations. I was glad I wouldn't have to be defenceless in front of this fane.

"I see."

She released me. I stepped away and found the fanes she'd brought with her had clustered tighter around us while we'd been speaking. Several stood behind me, preventing me from moving away. Unease pricked at me – what would she do now she was thwarted? "I'm sorry." I didn't mean it, but I thought it might pacify her.

I was wrong.

"No need to be sorry." She nodded to the councillors behind me and two grabbed my arms before I could avoid them. Pain shot through my already bruised arm.

"Let me go!" I tried to sound outraged, demanding compliance, but I heard fear in my voice.

"I did say I would make this journey only once, so I came prepared."

My eyes widened as she pulled a small bottle from a pocket, holding it to the light so I could see the iridescent contents swirling inside. *Somnaya.* I struggled

41

pointlessly against my restraints. "No. Not like this."

The would-be queen advanced on me. "We could have done this like civilised fanes, but you had to try to make a silly point. Perhaps next time you'll know better than to attempt to defy me."

She uncorked the bottle. I retched at the smell.

"I will be Fane's next queen. You will foresee, and you will tell me who stands in my way, and you will tell me how to defeat them."

"No." I twitched my head from side-to-side as she lifted the bottle so she couldn't place its lip against mine.

Another nod and one of the fanes behind me grabbed my hair, winding his fist through the length of it and yanking my head back. Tears sprang in my eyes. I couldn't move. I could barely breathe.

"No," I managed, but it was barely a whisper. I had no hope that I could avoid my fate.

The bottle touched my lips. "You will foresee, and you will tell me," she repeated. She frowned down at the bottle. "Now, how much of this do I need?"

Terror turned me cold. "A drop, only a drop!" I gasped.

She smiled, and I've never felt such malevolence emanating from another fane in my life. "Let's be sure, shall we?" She pinched my nose and tipped the entire contents into my mouth.

Chapter Five

I was flying through the sky, keeping pace with the moons as the ground slipped by underneath me, silent with night and tiny with distance. I was lying on my back in a forest, springy moss beneath me. The sound of a stream slipping over rocks woke a thirst in my throat. I turned towards the water and fell off the edge of a cliff. I saw a thousand bodies on a battlefield, eyes pecked out by carrion birds. Faces swam in and out of focus, some I recognised, most unknown. I spoke, but none of my words roused me from my stupor. There was noise for too long and silence that was endless, and heat and cold that were unbearable by turns. And then, finally, there was nothing.

*

When I woke – properly woke – I was in my bed. Every muscle ached, my mouth was dry and my hair was matted with sweat and dirt. I sat up and wrinkled my nose. I smelled, of sweat and vomit. I tried not to identify anything further in the air around me.

Water. My head pounded and my throat was as rough as tree bark. I could still taste *somnaya*. Some ordinary fanes took the drug voluntarily for the dreams it induced. I'd never understand the attraction. A cup of water stood on the floor beside my bed.

Gratefully, I scooped it up and drank the contents in two greedy swallows, ignoring the unease that tugged at my awareness. Perhaps I had had a particularly lucid moment and donned a clean night tunic and put the cup beside my bed before I fell into oblivion. It wasn't likely the would-be queen had taken such care of me, and the thought of her undressing me made me shudder. My anima ring lay on the floor close to the cup, disregarded. I pushed it back home on my finger and felt immediately stronger, even if I knew it couldn't help me against Saldamia and her followers.

I sat back down on my bed and listened. My senses returned as though water were draining from my ears. I heard birds outside my window, the chimes beneath the trees shifting in a slight breeze. Inside the house... there. A sound from the next room. Someone moving, not particularly stealthily. But why would they think to be stealthy, they'd already treated my home as though it were theirs, already treated me... I got off the bed. I needed to be dressed and decent to confront them. I pushed my long, tangled hair out of my eyes and shuddered at a fragment of memory that rose with the movement. My scalp was sore, my neck strained from struggling against the councillor's grip. Scissors. I needed scissors.

There was a work basket with fabric scraps and pins and threads in the back of my cupboard. I pulled it out and found the scissors, then fumbled my hair into a single hank which I held tight as I worked the blades through the strands. It was harder work than I expected, or perhaps it was too long since the scissors had been sharpened. They slipped against my hair, gnawing against it rather than cutting cleanly through.

I persevered, flattening my hair as much as I could to make it easier to cut.

At last it was all sliced through and I dropped the hank onto the floor. The rest of my hair fell around my cheeks. It was short to my head at the base of my skull, but there was still enough to get hold of at the level of my ears. I worked more slowly after that, lifting sections away from my head with my fingers and snipping the strands bit by bit. The scissors made a satisfying snick as they worked and the floor around me grew dark as the strands fell from my fingers. I hardly noticed when the noise in the next room increased, but when the door cracked open I was quick to respond.

"Get out!"

The door shut immediately and it was only after it had done so that I realised the face that had peered in wasn't one of Saldamia's councillors, but the gatekeeper, Zan. The slam of the door was followed by a timid tap and a voice. "Are you all right? Do you need anything?"

"I need nothing."

I paused before continuing my haircut. If Zan was here – and I presumed Cal and Keba with her – the would-be queen and her followers must have left. I was slightly surprised the gatekeeper wasn't dead. I had no idea what I'd said to Saldamia to further her ambitions. I hoped whatever I'd told her had been entirely incomprehensible, but if that had been the case she would doubtless still be here.

And if Zan was here, if she'd waited, that meant she was determined to find Tullan Fabler and make a gate to Talvar. And I'd do whatever I could to help her –

and myself – reach another world.

*

When my hair was finished, I stripped off my night tunic and put on fresh clothes. I wanted to wash, but I would have to venture past my door for that, so I'd wait. Leaning from my window, I grabbed a sprig of *tyyr* from the bush in the garden to chew, ridding my mouth of the unbearable taste of *somnaya*. Then there was nothing to do but face my visitors.

I strode into the main room, standing in the middle of the bare wooden boards, adopting a mask of cool and calm that made me want to weep with its familiarity. The rug that usually covered the wood had disappeared. The fallen books had been returned to their shelves, out of order but tidy. I was right about my visitors; Zan and Cal sat close together, their eyes lifting to watch me as I walked in.

"What have you decided?" The sooner Zan and I agreed to make the gate the sooner this would all be behind me.

Zan blinked as though surprised at the question. "Are you all right?"

That was none of her business. "Have you made a decision?"

"I wanted to talk to you about the gate..." she trailed off. "Your hair."

"You wanted to talk about the gate and my hair?"

"No, just, I mean – you've cut all your hair off."

As though I might not have realised. I lifted a hand to touch the short strands on my scalp. My head felt oddly light. "Yes." It was still none of her concern.

"What happened here?" Cal demanded, sharp eyes resting on me.

I looked down my nose at him, glad they were sitting so I could do so. "I don't answer to you."

He bristled visibly. "No—"

"We were worried," Zan said softly. "Your door wasn't locked, and when we looked inside you'd collapsed."

My hope of having had a lucid interval when I'd taken care of myself faded. I didn't want to ask, I didn't want to put myself in their power, but it seemed it was too late for that. "When was this?"

Cal and Zan shared a glance then Zan spoke. "Three days ago."

"What day is it today?"

Cal told me. I kept my face blank. Four days in all. Because of that *zangtaff* who'd left me once she'd got what she wanted, not caring if I lived or died afterwards.

"We, er, put you to bed," Zan said, killing my last hope. "You were, er, sleeping, so it seemed like the best thing to do. Are you all right?"

I waved a hand impatiently to dismiss her concern, anger roiling in my gut. I knew I should thank them, but the words stuck in my throat. I shouldn't have needed help. "Of course," I snapped. I took a slow breath. "And you've been here since?"

Cal's expression didn't change. Zan looked embarrassed. "Yes," she admitted. "I didn't like to leave you. I'm sorry. You seem like you value your privacy. I… we didn't mean to intrude."

"I don't mind." I could bear this. I'd borne worse. I took a breath and turned away.

Perhaps because it had heard I'd been fasting for four days, my stomach was suddenly ravenous. I left

47

them and walked toward the kitchen.

As I passed the hallway, I saw Keba lurking inside the front door, watching everything silently so I hadn't known she was there until I passed. Was she guarding us from intruders, or preventing me from leaving? She nodded acknowledgement in her usual calm way. Guilt washed through me. She wasn't Saldamia. I wished I hadn't thought ill of her. I nodded in return and continued on my way.

I focused on my anima ring and pulled all the heat in the room into a flame to light the oven. The small domestic task was harder than it should have been, even for me, and I pushed my fatigue aside while I prepared grain porridge, all I could face.

I ate alone at the small table, listening to the shifting and muttering in the next room. I waited for them to knock on the door and push their demands at me, but they didn't.

After I'd finished I washed the pots, then there was nothing for it but to face them again.

Entering the room from the hallway, I saw that the rug which should have covered the *iska* wood boards had been moved outdoors, draped over a bush. I shuddered at the idea of why it would have needed cleaning; what state they had found me in.

My visitors looked up when I walked in. Zan looked worried, Cal seemed cross. Perhaps he was annoyed at the time they'd wasted waiting for me to wake up. I hadn't forced him to wait. Perhaps Zan had. He seemed like he was willing to do anything she asked of him.

"Do you want a gate to be made?" I sat opposite them and came straight to the point.

"Yes." Zan glanced at Cal as though expecting disagreement. He shrugged. She met my eye, her brown gaze steady. "Yes. If it can be done."

A weight I hadn't known I was carrying unfurled inside me. The chance to be free of all this. I'd never wanted it more. "If it can be done, we'll do it."

Cal shifted. "Where do we find Tullan Fabler?"

"I don't know."

Cal made an impatient noise. "We've just wasted three days," he muttered to Zan, loud enough for me to hear.

"We couldn't just leave her, could we?" Zan chided.

Keba spoke for the first time, leaning against the wall where she could see us all. "Did you have a pressing engagement elsewhere?"

Cal made a rude gesture that made Keba laugh. An ache grew in my chest. Jealousy. I wished I could be inside the circle of that warmth.

"Shall we try a window to find him?" Zan suggested. "I don't have a particular connection, but it might work."

Keba nodded. Cal lifted a shoulder indifferently. I could mention my connection to him, but I stayed silent. It hadn't helped me find him before.

"It's worth a try." I looked at the corner of the room. The seeing bowl had been overturned when Saldamia was here, then set back to rights by my visitors. "I'll fetch water."

When the seeing bowl was full of fresh water, we were ready to start. Zan stood forward, the rest of us arrayed either side.

Zan breathed deeply, then dipped her fingers into the water. I held my breath and craned forward.

49

Time fell away. It could have been three years before, me at the window instead of Zan, reaching out to my father with a single plea in my heart: *Take me away from here.* I blinked. The water clouded over as it had back then. It cleared – slightly, which it never had before.

"Tullan Fabler, are you there?" Zan asked.

Hazy shapes appeared in the water, but nothing distinct.

"What is that?" Keba murmured.

"A village, no, a town," Cal muttered back.

"It's Ronar," Keba said in a tone of triumph. "See, the town's nestled in the bend of the river Sar. That's Ronar."

I stared harder. I could make out houses, the gleam of the river Keba mentioned. There was no sign of Tullan Fabler, but the gatekeeper had brought me closer to him than I'd ever managed. I stepped back, swallowing hard.

"If we can't see him, does that mean he's dead?" Cal demanded.

Zan removed her hand from the water, shaking it dry as she looked from Cal to Keba for an answer.

"It probably means he doesn't want to be found," I replied, licking dry lips after just those few words. It was the conclusion I'd come to three years earlier. He didn't want to be found – or at least not by me. Maybe he didn't want to be found by anyone.

"Why not? What's he got to be scared of?" Cal demanded.

"He knows how to make a gate. Issaenaptra would have been delighted to meet him, I'm sure," Zan said.

"Maybe he thinks everyone's still fighting," Keba

suggested.

"We'll make his day, then."

"Is that enough to find him?" Zan queried. "Just the name of a town?"

"Someone in Ronar will know where he is," Keba assured her.

"Take me with you." They all swung to look at me. I cleared my throat. "I mean – I'll go with you, so we can make the gate as soon as we find him."

"Of course," Zan said.

"What happened here?" Cal's eyes narrowed as he watched me. He was annoyingly inquisitive. "Who wrecked this place?"

If he couldn't guess I wasn't going to tell him. "I had a party," I snapped. "I was celebrating becoming dreamseer."

"And you wrecked your own home?"

"I'm leaving. It doesn't matter."

"Don't be so nosy, Cal," Zan instructed him. He ignored her, eyes on me.

Finally, he spoke. "I wish I'd known. We wouldn't have bothered tidying up."

Keba smiled. Zan rolled her eyes. Was that a joke? It was a tone quite different to his usual complaints. I didn't know what to make of Cal, who was mostly angry, then beautiful when he smiled; who would do anything for his friends, but looked at me like he'd throw me to a *snarvell* if I gave him a chance.

I turned away. I didn't need to make anything of Cal, I just needed to put up with him until we made the gate.

"So we're going to Ronar." Zan brought my musings to an end. "When do we leave?"

51

I glanced out at the garden. It was well past noon, and the days weren't long at that time of year. "In the morning." I looked at them and added reluctantly, "You can stay. If you want."

A sudden thought occurred to me. "Where did you sleep? Last night? The last three nights?"

"In here. I'm sorry – is that all right?"

"Yes. You can stay in here tonight, if you want." I wouldn't sleep – I'd slept enough for a week already.

"No, that's all right. Now we know you're okay we'll come back in the morning."

I nodded. "Be here an hour after dawn."

*

I watched the door for a moment after it shut to be sure they were really gone. I had a final job to do if I was going to leave Fane.

The ability – the talent or the curse, however you wished to view the matter – to see visions was passed from mother to daughter. I was the only dreamseer on Fane, last of the line. But just in case the abilities might one day manifest themselves in some unsuspecting child not yet born, I would destroy my mother's diaries that detailed the training she'd put me through, so there would be nothing that could be used to guide others in how to exploit a new dreamseer's abilities.

I built a fire in the shallow pit in the back garden and when the kindling was burning well, I added the books. There was a whole stack in the cupboard in her room, but I guess it had been a long process, from six to sixteen, detailing every vision and what my mother had done to hurry them along.

They made a pretty fire. The books shifted as they

burned, spines arching and pages fanning wide, twitching in the heat as though they wanted to escape their fate. I wouldn't allow that. The flames licked hungrily at the paper, turning the pages orange, then white, then black, heat tightening my skin as I pushed the diaries further into the flames to make sure they'd be consumed. My eyes stung as the smuts of darkened paper lifted and drifted into the air, curling high towards the clouds in wreaths of smoke.

I fed the books to the fire one at a time, to be sure they would burn to ash. It took all the remainder of the day and most of the night. I went inside after a while and alternated tending the fire with packing for the days ahead.

Dawn was breaking, both moons sunk beneath the horizon while the sun's glow turned the sky pink when the last book crumbled to nothing. There was one more thing to burn. I fetched my ceremonial robes, the embroidered hems trailing in the dirt as I lifted them onto the fire. The fabric with its ornate stitchery and crusted gems nearly stifled the flames. I had to rearrange them so air could get through and keep the fire alight. I stayed to watch, pushing the edges into the middle of the dancing flames as the fire consumed the robes from the inside out.

Finally, it was done. I made the fire safe, washed, and put on clean clothes, comfortable ones for travelling. Then I took my bag and waited for Zan, Cal and Keba.

Chapter Six

When the doorbell sounded, I tightened my sash, hefted my knapsack onto my back and walked out to them. "You'll have to go at my pace."

Zan smiled. "That's okay. I don't bound as far as I used to myself." She patted her stomach. I wondered at how happy she was to risk her immortality to give her baby life. I knew humans lived differently from fanes, perhaps talvarrines were different again and there was no risk to her. Perhaps the end of her life wouldn't be signalled by the start of her child's like my mother's had been, watching the days pass until I reached maturity and her life faded away.

"Ronar is east from here, isn't it?" I took two steps away, facing the sunrise and our destination.

"That's right," Keba said.

"Wait."

I turned.

Zan was frowning. "You haven't locked your door."

I shrugged. "I'm not coming back."

"You're really sure you want to go to Talvar?"

"I'm really sure."

Cal cast her a glance. Everything he felt for me was disapproval, but he couldn't stop me making the gate, not if Zan agreed.

"It's just—"

I folded my arms. "Do you want this gate, or not?"

"Yes, I do."

"Then that's what we'll do. If we can find Tullan Fabler."

"Of course. I'm sorry. And – thank you."

"No thanks are needed."

*

For the first eight or ten bounds, the three of them landed leagues ahead of me each time, underestimating how very slow dreamseers are. I wondered how things were on Ţalvar, whether I'd be stronger, or if I'd lose what little elemental power I had when I was in another world. Even that didn't deter me. If I had to crawl across the ground like an insect for the rest of my long life I'd still do it.

Finally we all fell into step, landing at least within hailing distance of each other, not that we had a great deal to say. Cal and Zan chatted now and then but they didn't address me. Keba worked hardest to match her pace to mine but we remained silent, simply exchanging a nod each time to indicate when we were ready to bound again.

When the sun was high, we stopped to eat. Cal, Keba and Zan sat on a rock. I stretched out on the ground and looked up into the sky as I ate the grain and vegetable salad I'd packed in my bag.

"Are you all right? Are you tired?" Zan called after a few minutes had passed.

"Yes. No." Why was it her concern?

Cal spoke to her, but his words carried clearly to me across the still air. "I told you, there's nothing wrong with her. It's just the way they are."

If I'd had energy I might have been riled by his careless dismissal – but he was only saying aloud what people muttered behind my back. I rolled over so the sun warmed my back and squinted at Zan, who was watching me as she ate. "Dreamseers are feeble, did he warn you?" I called. "Not capable of anything much, only good for one thing."

There was a long moment when she just looked at me, then she smiled. "We know that's not true – I've already seen you're a mean hairdresser. For all we know there's nothing you can't do."

I touched the cropped strands. Zan's eyes sparkled, reflecting her smile. Silence fell. I closed my eyes and enjoyed the sun.

"How old are you?"

I opened my eyes again. Zan was still looking at me. Or she was looking at me again. "Sixteen."

"I'm seventeen. Everyone on Fane seems so old to me, and yet here we are – the three youngest all together." She glanced to where Keba was eating silently. "And Keba. She's ancient."

"Three hundred and twelve isn't ancient," she said mildly. "I've hardly started yet."

Zan rolled her eyes. I knew that humans were short-lived. Not as short-lived as dreamseers, but very much so compared to most fanes who were close to immortal unless they were killed or gave up their life to have a child. I watched her. She was half-fane, her gatekeeper abilities coming from the mix of human and fane blood in her veins and I wondered at the difference between her and the rest of us.

Cal was looking across the landscape rather than at his companions and Keba had fallen silent to eat.

"All the councillors were at least ten times my age."
Zan sighed. "It's a good job I didn't want to be queen,
since it was never going to happen." She looked at Cal
but he didn't respond. Then she turned to me again.
"At least you get some respect as a dreamseer."

I sat up. That's what lots of fanes thought. If they
were stupid. Was respect what she thought had been
happening to me before they found me insensible in
my own dirt?

But I couldn't – wouldn't – tell her all that. I stared
past her towards the horizon. The land between was
mostly orange soil, the occasional stand of trees visible
from where we were. It was more damaged than I was
used to seeing at home, but not as bad as it was closer
to the old gates. Not as bad as I'd seen it in visions.
Cal and Zan began bickering about age, trying to draw
Keba into an argument.

"My mother was forty-two. When she died." I
interrupted their arguing and silence fell.

Zan looked stricken. "Oh, I'm sorry, that's very..."
She trailed off with a frown and glanced towards Cal,
who wasn't looking, and then Keba, who was
watching us both silently. Finally she returned to me.
"That *is* very young, isn't it? I'm so sorry."

"Dreamseers always die young. The burden of what
we see becomes unbearable."

Cal sat up, transferring his desire for an argument to
me. "You're hardly worn down, though, are you – you
stepped into the role a week ago. That's not arduous
beyond bearing."

"Cal!" Zan turned, appalled at his honesty.

I opened my mouth to tell him – and closed it again.
There was one fane living I couldn't tell the truth to,

and he was sitting in front of me now. "You said yourself that dreamseers are feeble," I managed. "I suppose I'm just proof of that." I turned to Zan, who was still frowning at Cal. "I just wanted you to understand I'm not making some great sacrifice. I want to leave as much as you do."

Cal yawned and lay down as though he might sleep.

Zan smiled. "You'll forgive me for thinking your motivation isn't quite as strong as mine." Her hand moved restlessly over her belly, as though she was caressing the baby inside. I watched the hypnotically repetitive action. At least if I went to Talvar I wouldn't have to have a child to be rid of my talents. At least I didn't have to pass on the curse to be free of it myself.

Zan caught my eye. "I know this must seem weird to you. Babies aren't much of a thing here. They're far more everyday on Earth."

"Dreamseers only have a child when they're ready to die." I turned and stared into the fire, unsure why I'd said that. It was none of her business.

"You've got plenty of time yet."

I shook my head. "I'm never going to pass on my abilities. I wouldn't condemn anyone to this."

Cal sat up. He'd stopped resting and was regarding me sourly now. "Yeah, because your life is such a hardship."

I should have left it, but I was tired of him. If he was looking for a fight he could have one. "How would you know?"

He glared at me, eyes sparkling nastily. "It's hardly torment, is it? A fat wage from the queen, drugs on tap, and all you need to do is make a few vague statements that anyone with half a brain could interpret any way they liked."

Now we knew where we stood.

Zan's anxious look flitted from him to me. "Deena, I'm sorry, he didn't mean that."

"Yes, I did," he said, at the same moment I replied, "Yes, he did."

I stared him down, as cold as I could be. "If I offend you so much there's no need for you to stay. We don't need *your* help to make the gate."

He smiled unpleasantly. "Oh, you'd like that, wouldn't you? I'm not leaving Zan. I'm not stupid."

Zan gaped at him. "I'm not in danger. Deena won't hurt me."

"No." His eyes stayed on my face while he agreed with her. "Because I'll be watching her."

Spots of colour appeared on Zan's cheeks. "Deena, I am so sorry." She swung on her cousin. "What's the matter with you?"

"I'm flattered if you think I'm capable of harming the gatekeeper," I told him, hiding my hurt beneath anger.

"I don't think she'd do anything deliberately," Cal said, talking about me as though I wasn't there. "But she's flaky. What if she leaves you stuck between the worlds? Or stranded in the middle of nowhere on Talvar?"

"Zan's the gatekeeper. She's the one carrying talvarrine blood right now. I might be able to make the gate, but she's the one who'll control it."

Cal continued to glare at me. I glared back.

"Whatever's going on here, it needs to stop," Zan said. "Deena is doing a task I have asked her to do. She has my gratitude for that. You should be grateful,

59

too, Cal."

He made a contemptuous sound. "I'm a bit busy wondering what she's done that's so terrible she has to run away – and how it's going to affect the rest of us."

I could have told him that what I'd done was so far in the past that any effects were long gone. But I couldn't. Of all the fanes on this world, the one I couldn't tell the truth to was sitting before me now, glaring at me.

"I just want to stop being the dreamseer, and leaving Fane is the only way I can do that," I said, pulling on my dignity so I could speak levelly.

"Except that the council seem to think the dreamseer is an important role. You're leaving them without one."

"Zan is giving up her role. Have you said all this to her?"

"Zan has resigned her role and alternatives are in place. It's quite different."

Yes – because he liked Zan and he didn't like me. "You think all I do is take drugs and mumble nonsense – what's so vital about that?"

"I didn't say *I* thought it was an important role, I said the council value it. If you don't want the job, tell the council so. Tell them why they don't need a dreamseer."

"They'd never let me go." My pulse increased just at the thought of it. If they knew I wanted to leave they'd lock me up. I'd be even more trapped than before.

Cal made a disbelieving noise. "Have you tried?" He waited for me to shake my head. "My point exactly. You're running away instead. That's the coward's way."

Zan drew in a sharp breath. I didn't say anything. It was true – in a way. I remembered what Keba had said on the night of the funeral, about fighting being more honest. Yes, for those who had the strength to stand and fight. Some of us didn't have that option. Some of us could only run – and hope.

"I have a suggestion – why don't we all pretend we're friends and I'm sure we'll find Tullan Fabler and get that gate made in no time. Then we can go our separate ways and live our lives the way we choose." The words were light, although Keba's tone was sardonic. But she was looking at Cal rather than me.

Cal made another scathing noise. "Fine. Time to go."

If only he would.

Chapter Seven

An hour later, we neared Ronar. I was even slower than usual – although it was hard to know what usual was when I'd never travelled so far before. I felt unwell, as weak as Cal derided me. Colours kept turning surreally bright and then bleaching to black and white, and I was hotter than I should have been at that time of year, while stripping off as many of my clothes as I decently could made little difference. The last of the *somnaya* was still working its way through me. I shook away the sensation, wiped my damp face and kept bounding.

Ronar could have been a showcase for Fane recovering from the environmental damage of the war. The orange soil turned darker brown as we drew closer and then progressed to green as scrubby grasses sprang to life. A few bushes dotted the ground. They had clearly been there for years, stunted by the damage the gates had caused, but now new, tightly-furled leaves greened the ends of the twiggy shrubs.

*

About half a league from the town, we stopped bounding and walked, to ensure we wouldn't collide with anyone or anything in the town. That should have been a relief, except that Cal walked ridiculously quickly as though it was a race to arrive first.

"This will be beautiful again soon," Keba murmured, smiling as she looked around at the scenery.

She wasn't hurrying and I let my steps match hers, giving up the effort of trying to keep pace with Cal. "Where are you from?"

She glanced aside at me. "Originally? The coast, near Lysana. Wild and magnificent. Then the gates let damage through and it became just wild."

"Will you go back?"

Keba shrugged. "It'll be different from my memories. I might go somewhere new when Zan no longer needs me."

When she travelled to Talvar. Excitement spiked in my chest. It might be only a few hours now.

Ahead of us, Cal started running, darting aside from the path and disappearing from view into a small copse of trees.

I frowned. "Why is he in such a hurry? Would it kill him to keep pace with the rest of us?"

Keba smiled as though I'd said something funny.

My irritation grew. "He makes me feel slow and useless."

"Deena, he's doing his job."

I focused on her instead of the trees where Cal had vanished.

She explained, "Zan wouldn't accept the queen's official bodyguard of eight trained fanes. She's just got Cal and me. It's our job to keep her safe. That includes checking for risks."

"You're not dashing about," I pointed out. I was starting to feel stupid, as well as inadequate. It wasn't a nice sensation. I didn't want Cal to be doing something praiseworthy.

"No, I'm making sure nothing creeps up on us from behind." Her voice softened. "And I'm enjoying the walk." We went a few more steps. "He isn't doing it to upset you, Deena."

"I'm not upset. Cal can do what he likes. I don't care." I was glad Keba wasn't looking at me. I could feel the heat in my face making a liar of me. I *didn't* care what Cal did. So why couldn't I stop noticing it?

"Okay, then." Keba increased her pace, face tilted to the sun. I walked with her, Zan a few paces ahead of us. Cal was now back on the path far ahead of us all, all risks safely neutralised, presumably.

Cal fell back so we were a tight-knit group by the time we entered Ronar itself. He kept Zan on his right side as we walked the steps up to the council hall. If Tullan Fabler lived in Ronar or anywhere close by he'd be registered for tax.

Ronar's councillor, one of the Council of Twelve, was at the palace with the other councillors, but her deputy, Pell, was eager to provide a warm welcome when he realised the gatekeeper was asking for information.

A tall, angular man, he insisted we join him for refreshments while the information we needed was found, leading the way up an elaborate flight of stairs to the rooms above.

I fell to the back of the group, wishing I could do anything except sit and make polite conversation for half an hour. I was cold, but heat climbed through me once more, clawing at my spine. I wiped my face and followed Keba into the comfortable room.

Once inside, I took the seat furthest from the centre

where Zan and Pell sat to talk. I hoped to be unobserved while I waited for the symptoms to pass. Shrinking into my seat, I wrapped my arms around myself to hold back the shivering that wanted to join my array of *somnaya* withdrawal symptoms.

Cal stood by the door and Keba by the window rather than taking seats, so I hoped my isolation wouldn't look marked. Drinks were brought: juice and ale. I asked the slim fane serving for water with a voice that croaked. She looked at me, a frown spiking between her brows for a moment before she nodded.

She returned a moment later. "Here."

I accepted the tall cup gratefully. Again she looked as though she might say something, then decided against it, moving away to ensure Zan and Pell had everything they needed.

"Are you all right?" Keba wasn't constrained by the same rules of hospitality. She had strayed from her post by the window to pause by my chair, speaking in a low voice that wouldn't interrupt the conversation in the centre of the room.

I took a long drink, grateful for the slide of the water over my parched throat. "Yes."

"You look like you're getting a fever or something."

"I'm not."

Cal coughed. Keba shot him a look. He shook his head and frowned. I didn't need to ask what he was trying to signal: druggie dreamseer. And thus in need of no sympathy, nor healer attention.

"I'm all right. Thank you."

Keba nodded and moved back to the window.

The conversation in the middle of the room ebbed and flowed around me, loud then soft. I went hot and cold then hot again. Finally I settled back to something close to normality – just as Zan made her farewells to Pell.

"Thank you for your help. I am very grateful." Zan held a small square of paper in her fist. Directions to find Tullan Fabler, I hoped. I felt dizzy, and for once it was nothing to do with the *somnaya*.

*

We left the building, Pell's good wishes echoing in our ears. I couldn't take my eyes from the flash of white tethered between Zan's fingers. I wanted to snatch it and see for myself where he was. I wanted to throw it away so we'd never find him. All those years of wishing for him and now the moment was here I couldn't face it? I'd deserve to be called a coward.

I squared my shoulders. "Where do we go?"

Keba was craning over Zan's shoulder to read the directions. "North. Into the forest. It's about six leagues."

Four bounds for me. I could count the time until we were there in heartbeats.

"Come on, then." Cal, as usual, was first to go.

*

Our second bound took us to the edge of the forest, our next into its heart. We bounded carefully to avoid the trees, but Tullan Fabler's home was on the edge of a lake with plenty of room for us all on a pebbly foreshore. To our right was a stone house: our final destination.

I blew out a breath. Smoke curled out of a chimney in the middle of the building. If he wasn't at home he wasn't far away. Cal was already crunching over the pebbles. I didn't want him to be the first. I didn't want to skulk behind them for this. I ran, hurrying past him to bang a fist on the wooden door.

My heart counted the seconds until I heard a noise from indoors. The door swung open and I set eyes on him for the first time.

I'd thought he'd left nothing of himself in my appearance. Skin, hair, eyes, all were shared with my mother. But when I looked at the tall, broad figure before me, I knew I was wrong. The shape of our faces, the angle of our chins. There could be no doubt that Tullan Fabler was my father.

I saw puzzlement form and then clear, and I knew he'd seen the connection, too.

"Deena! Is it really you?" A smile split his face. "I didn't think you'd ever come." He reached out a hand to me.

I took a step back, distancing myself. I was aware of the others gathering around me, staring at us both. My face grew hot.

"Deena..?" His hand dropped and his tone grew wary, a contrast to his blue eyes which sparkled delight. I was torn, too. I wanted to be pleased to see him, but the time for that had long passed.

"I have come with the gatekeeper," I told him, my voice stiff and formal, my heart aching just to look at him. "We need your help to create a gate."

"A gate?" He glanced at Zan and the others before returning to look at me like a hungry man before a banquet. He could have seen much more of me if he'd made any attempt to do so.

"Yes. The gatekeeper wishes to go to Talvar." I didn't mention my intention to go with her – that was too private for the stranger standing before me.

"I... see." He nodded to the faces before him. "Please, come inside and we'll talk."

Keba and Zan walked past us both, throwing confused glances my way. Cal, of course, stopped. "Do you know the dreamseer?" he demanded of Tullan.

I stood forward. Best to get it over with. They'd hear the truth from me, not from Tullan. "This man is my father." I looked away before I added. "Or so my mother told me."

"Your father?" Cal grabbed my arm. "Why didn't you tell us?"

"It didn't matter."

"Didn't matter? You could have found him in seconds."

"I never have before – and believe me, I tried." I wrenched away from his grip and walked after Zan and Keba.

*

"A new gate hasn't been created for centuries – and for good reason. Are you aware of the dangers?"

Tullan had heard our plan, outlined by an enthusiastic Zan. He wasn't thrilled about it. He leaned against the fireplace in his main room, which seemed very small now all of us were inside, arms folded across his chest so the anima crystal in the torq around his arm seemed to wink at me as he moved. I focused on that so I didn't have to look at him and the face that was strange and yet so similar to my own.

"What dangers?" Cal demanded.

"It requires a great deal of power to produce enough energy to bridge the distance between the worlds. Fanes have died making gates."

68

Cal opened his mouth. Zan spoke before he could say anything. "It's vitally important that we make the gate. I must get to Talvar. How do we protect ourselves?"

He shrugged and the blue crystal on his bicep flashed light and dark. "Be strong enough to survive it. You are both young, which should help. And I will add my strength to yours, of course." He took a deep breath. "But there are no guarantees. Once the process is started it cannot be halted – the gate will either be made or we will die in the attempt."

The determined expression on Zan's face didn't change. "This is worth sacrificing everything for." She turned to me. "But I can't make that choice for you, Deena, nor you, Tullan."

I hoped my face didn't reflect it, but misgiving rose in me. It was easy to say I didn't care whether I lived or died – except that I did. I didn't want to live on Fane as the slave of the new queen, but I wanted the alternative to be escape to a new life, not death. I swallowed. "I will do this with you."

"Thank you." Zan turned to Tullan. I looked up. His expression was steady.

"And I will do this, too," he agreed. He looked from Zan to me and I dropped my gaze quickly, afraid of what I might see in his expression. Or he in mine.

Chapter Eight

Two hours later and I was sitting by the lake with the stone house at my back, staring across the still water as the sun vanished behind the trees. Only the faintest glow of the final moon still showed through the branches.

Tullan had agreed to help us create a new gate. Now he'd said yes, I had grown cynical; requested by the famed gatekeeper who had brought peace to Fane, he was hardly going to refuse. I had slipped out of the house. Zan and Keba hadn't said a word of censure, but the puzzlement in their expressions because I'd hidden my relationship to Tullan Fabler made snakes of guilt twist in my stomach. And Tullan kept looking at me like I was a meal he wasn't permitted to eat. As for Cal... Clearly, I could now add 'sneaky liar' to 'flaky drug addict' on Cal's list of dreamseer character traits. It was all very well for principled and perfect Cal. He'd picked the right side to fight for and stuck with it, even through torture. Everything was black and white for him. He was courageous, loyal to his friends and diligent in his work. Good job he was also sarcastic, superior and oozing with contempt for me or I might have been in danger of admiring him.

I picked a pebble from the ground beneath me and

lobbed it into the lake where it landed with a thunk.

"Deena?"

I froze. It was Tullan's voice. I stared straight ahead.

"May I sit with you?"

I wanted to push him away. I wanted to cling to him. I said nothing, did nothing, and he took that as invitation. The pebbles crunched and slithered as he took two steps then sat down beside me. He was close but not touching. The heat from his broad arm radiated towards me.

"It's good to see you, Deena." I felt him watching me, another point of warmth. I kept my attention on the lake. "You've grown up to be a strong woman, a strong dreamseer." I heard the smile in his voice. "And beautiful, like your mother."

I couldn't bear to listen. "I'm only here because the gatekeeper needs her gate."

Silence met that harsh statement and I was glad I wasn't looking at his face.

"It's still good to see you." He sucked in a breath and sighed it out. "Are you angry because I didn't attend the funeral?"

I laughed, then picked another pebble and flung it into the lake.

"I didn't think I would be welcome."

That provoked another laugh. "No, you wouldn't have been."

I caught his nod. "I guess your mother was right and you don't need me."

My fingers tightened around the next pebble I'd selected for a watery end. I flung it down, clambering to my feet. "I guess she was."

I intended to storm away, but the pebbles slid

71

beneath my boots, slowing me down. Before I'd taken a step, Tullan grabbed my sleeve. "What's wrong? Did you *want* me to come to the funeral?"

I yanked away from him. "I wanted you when I was thirteen! You're no use now."

He was on his feet in a moment, standing before me and blocking my way. "What happened?"

I could have dodged around him but I didn't want to. Furious heat spiralled through me. I wanted him to know what he'd done. "She made me do her work. The war started and Queen Issaenaptra used me to find her enemies so she could destroy them. They drugged me so I'd betray people who'd done me no harm. And you – you weren't there. You were never there for me."

"But your mother—"

"She was the one who drugged me. She didn't care for me, only that if I had visions she was spared the labour of doing so."

He sucked in another breath. "Why didn't you tell me? I'd have helped you."

"I tried to contact you but there was no trace. I couldn't find you."

"Your mother said I had to stay away, that it would destroy your talents if I interfered in your training."

I ground my toe through the pebbles. "And you believed her?"

"She was the dreamseer. Why should I not believe her? I made myself untraceable to you, she insisted. But I left a ring, *I* insisted on that – why didn't you use it?"

"Your ring? Mother never let me near it. She wore it herself, and she destroyed it in the end."

72

There was a moment of silence then he spoke again, soft and full of regret. "Deena, I'm so sorry. I would have done anything for you."

The expression on his face made me want to cry, but tears never changed anything. "Make the gate. That's all I need from you."

He nodded, a smile lifting the creases on his face. "I will. We'll make the gate together. And then I'll spend the next sixteen years of your life being there for you."

"Yeah. Fine." I should have told him I was going to Talvar with Zan. But it wasn't any of his business. And I couldn't bear to see the smile drop from his face.

"We should get inside. It's late, and we need to be rested if we're going to make a gate tomorrow. It'll take a lot out of us all."

I nodded, and crunched back over the pebbles to the house.

*

Us three women slept in the loft overhead, while Tullan and Cal had beds below – which in Cal's case would go unused since he intended to keep guard all night. Sleep, it seemed, was an optional indulgence when you were truly dedicated to the safety of the gatekeeper.

I thought Zan and Keba were already sleeping when I climbed up the ladder. All was quiet and I could just make out humps beneath borrowed blankets on the sleeping mats. I crept to my own place so I wouldn't disturb them.

Out of the darkness, Zan spoke. "I have a difficult relationship with my mum. You have my sympathy."

I didn't reply. I didn't want her sympathy. And yet, as I settled to sleep, it felt good to know I wasn't alone.

*

I woke with the dawn, but I wasn't the first up. From below came sounds of movement, then the murmur of voices kept deliberately low. Keba and Zan were still sleeping beside me. I stretched the fatigue out of my limbs, and crawled to the ladder leading down.

This time there was no warning. Two steps from the bottom, my stomach turned over, colour washed out of the world, and the ground shifted beneath me. I fell off the ladder and into a vision.

*

"Danger's coming." I opened my eyes, shaking off my sense of pursuit and the hollow thrum of fear. "We have to get away from here." I blinked, checking what was real and what was clinging to my mind's eye from the vision.

I was lying on the broad, comfortable seat before the fire in the main room. Everyone was clustered around me. I tried to sit up and winced as a hot knife of pain stabbed my right hip and right elbow.

"Take care," Zan told me. "You landed with a bash."

I ignored her, biting my lip against the pain. "We have to go. Fanes are coming here." I caught Zan's eye. "They won't let you leave. Or me."

As I stood, taking my weight on my left side, Keba moved to my right, looping my arm over her shoulders so she was half-supporting me.

"How long do we have?" That was Cal, always on duty. He'd swung the door open a crack, peering out while he spoke.

"I don't know." I tried to find specifics in the

74

fragments left to me now the vision had gone, but there was nothing. "Not long."

He nodded to show he'd heard. "The terrain's in our favour. They won't be able to bound in the trees. We should get under cover immediately." He turned back to us all, focussing on me. "Can you run?"

"I won't hold you up." I wouldn't let Saldamia's fanes capture me – I wasn't letting freedom slip away now.

"I'll help her," Keba said.

Zan bit her lip. "I suppose we don't have time to make the gate first?" She looked apologetic. "Just … if we go, then we're out of reach once and for all."

Tullan shook his head. "We don't know how much time we have. The process can't be hurried. And Deena's too weak."

I waited for a snide comment from Cal, but it didn't come. "We'll find somewhere safe, then make the gate."

"Stone would be best." Tullan said, grabbing a coat and slinging a bag over his shoulder. "Stable. It'll be easiest to make the gate with a stone foundation."

"Fine." Cal swung the door wide. "We'll stay in the forest as long as we can."

I pulled away from Keba. "I'll be fine on my own. Others might need you. Where's my bag?"

Zan handed it to me. Seconds and we were ready.

As we hurried through the door, Tullan ushered me through before him. "I'll keep you safe," he promised. "I'm here this time."

We slipped around the corner of the house, fading into the trees just in time. There was a high-pitched whining sound. A ball of fire soared overhead, then

75

came a crash and the roof of the house behind us burst into flames. I ducked instinctively, flinching away from the heat.

"Run!" Cal's voice. "If they can see to send that, they saw us." He grabbed my hand and pulled me deeper into the trees. My hip ached, jolting pain at each step but I kept going. Trees ahead of us burst into flame. A roar sounded to our left and I twisted to see a wall of water as high as the trees rolling towards us. The lake was being used against us by our unseen enemies.

Beside me, Cal cursed and dropped my hand. "Keep going." He turned where he was, lifting both hands to direct his elemental power in a shield to force the water back.

"Go!" He scowled at me and I spun around, dashing through the trees, tripping on roots but keeping upright. My breath came in ragged gasps. Cal was behind me. I didn't know where Zan, Keba or Tullan were. Another crash sounded behind me. Twigs and branches whipped at me. I tried to keep my hands up to protect my face. I tripped, sprawling into the rotting leaves and scrambled up, sobbing with pain and fear. I had to keep going.

A tree exploded steps ahead of me. I twisted, protecting my face with my hands and blundered into a thorny bush, gasping in pain, dragged to a stop. There was a sucking sense of energy around me. The air grew thin and I struggled to pull a breath into my lungs. I tried to shield myself but the fane advancing on me was far more powerful than I was. Pressure crushed my head, pain surging through me as though my brain was being squeezed. I screamed, unable to fight the pain. Unconsciousness, when it came, was a relief.

Chapter Nine

I awoke in a small, square room. The walls were stone and there were no windows, only a door on the opposite side of the bed I'd been dumped on, still wearing the clothes I'd run through the forest in. They smelled of smoke and had small holes where they'd been snagged by thorns.

I rolled over to see more of my surroundings and winced. Small holes and a few leftover thorns, I realised, picking two out of the arm of my tunic. The walls were unplastered stone, there was a bucket in one corner, a jug of water by the bed and that was all. I rose carefully to my feet finding that the ache in my hip and elbow had been joined by another in my knuckle. My finger was empty of my anima ring, which had been removed with little care. Rubbing my hand, I crossed to the door and tried the handle. Locked, of course.

I didn't know for sure where I was, but I could guess – the palace. Saldamia wasn't taking any chances that there wouldn't be a dreamseer available to confirm her queen when the sun rose after moonsfall.

I sagged against the door. The biggest ache wasn't my hand, it was deeper inside. Saldamia needed me, a dreamseer for the confirmation ceremony. She didn't need the others. They could be dead. I pressed my ear to the door and listened, but I could hear nothing through the thick wood. There could be other cells containing Cal and Tullan, Zan and Keba – or I could be alone. I could try to shout and see if anyone answered, but that would bring guards. It might bring Saldamia herself and I didn't want to see her.

I looked at the jug of water. Without my anima ring I couldn't even search for Zan and the others so I'd know for sure. Maybe that was a good thing.

My thoughts turned sour. Tullan had promised to keep me safe. I wondered how hard he'd fought to make that true. I sighed. I was being unfair. He wouldn't have been able to stop them. Probably no one could. They'd tracked me down, singled me out and snatched me, and I hadn't even seen them. I should have stayed with Cal. He and Keba were the soldiers, after all. But that didn't make him invincible. The last I'd seen of Cal he was trying to hold back the other fanes' elemental power. I hoped that wasn't the last I'd ever see of him.

I retreated to the bed and sat down, rolling onto my left side so I could rub my aching right hip. Cal couldn't be dead. He was the strongest of all of us. If he was dead there was no hope for any of us.

*

I dozed, jerking awake when a guard shook my shoulder roughly. I pulled away and sat up.

"The Lady Saldamia wants you," she told me.

I'd known that summons wouldn't be long delayed. Evading the guard's grasp, I slipped out of bed and strode to the door ahead of her. I stood as straight as I could manage, looking more like a beggar than a dreamseer in my rumpled, smelly clothes, I didn't doubt. But I was a dreamseer, whatever my appearance. "Then escort me to her," I told the guard.

With a sour look, she obeyed.

*

The throne room was designed to be imposing. And intimidating. Aside from the guard who'd escorted me in and walked a step behind to prevent me escaping – as though I'd make a fool of myself by attempting so hopeless an action – only two others were present. My steps resounded on the wooden floor as I trod steadily towards the far end.

The throne was set on a dais so the queen would always be higher than anyone standing in the room. The throne itself had been made centuries before. It was a wonder of construction – it loomed in the empty room, huge and imposing, and yet didn't dwarf its occupant. Saldamia sat stiff-spined, her expression hard and vengeful as I walked towards her. Around her lips played a smile of triumph. I suppose that was understandable. I wondered what had happened to Gallia, whether she was mouldering in a cell somewhere – or worse.

For a moment I thought of asking Saldamia what had happened to Zan, Keba, and all the fanes I cared about. But Saldamia wouldn't tell me. She'd withhold the information just because she could, I was sure of it.

Beside her was Jettaena, one of the councillors who had spoken in her favour at the meeting after the funeral. And one of those who had crowded into my house the next morning. They made a pretty pair, staring down their noses with matching sneers and smug, smug smiles.

The smugness was understandable but it was misguided. I still hadn't had a vision that showed Saldamia as queen. No queen at all. I didn't think such a thing had ever happened in Fane's history.

Saldamia waited, watching me with proud eyes until I stopped before the dais. Her smile and her glare didn't waver but I saw her hands on the arms of the throne. Her knuckles were clenched white, fingers gripping the ornate wood as though she feared being prised away from it. That was the truth of it: she was afraid. I wasn't surprised. If she was truly confident she wouldn't have summoned me, she'd have waited for the council meeting.

Looking up at her, I told myself to lie. If I could bring myself to smile and tell her I'd had a vision that showed her as Fane's new queen I could stop this now. I wouldn't be locked in a windowless cell if I did that. And the *somnaya* Saldamia was undoubtedly carrying could stay in her pocket. I should greet her with a bow and address her as queen. Then she'd leave me alone.

Except she'd never leave me alone. If I proclaimed her queen I'd condemn myself to a lifetime of doing what she told me, of bending my talents to please her, like I'd been forced to do for Issaenaptra.

Our eyes met. I watched her as calmly as I could manage. A spark of defiance made my pulse surge. I wouldn't do it. I wouldn't lie and tell her she was queen. I wouldn't let her believe herself triumphant for even a moment. She should have accepted the word of the dreamseer, like she expected everyone else to do.

I lifted my chin and regarded her steadily. She wasn't my queen. I wouldn't lower my gaze. She had no shame, so she didn't lower hers either.

She made me wait. I was tired of her games, the petty power plays she thought were suitable for a ruler. "You summoned me, Saldamia. What it is you want?" As though I didn't know already.

Her lips tightened, then she deliberately relaxed. She raised a lazy hand and waved a small circle to indicate the room around us. "I summoned my dreamseer to my side, yes. You ran away from your home, Deena, and led my fanes on quite a journey. You must always be available to serve the queen – did you not know that?"

Defiance raged in my chest, as though it would burst free and suffocate her like it was suffocating me. "There is no queen to serve. Dreamseers are never wrong and you are not the queen, nor ever will be."

Her arrogant expression faltered long enough for me to see the fear that held her heart. Then it was masked with anger. "Because of your little holiday, you are not aware of recent developments. Gallia has agreed to rescind her claim on the throne in order to serve Fane as my deputy." Saldamia loosed her hands enough to spread them wide, palms upwards. "There are no other candidates." She lowered her voice to a hiss. "You should be cautious, dreamseer. I will be confirmed as Fane's queen when the council meet for the confirmation ceremony, and I will deal harshly with those who oppose me. Look at me and look into your heart and consider what you want *your* future to be." She sat back, satisfied with her threats. "Now, are you prepared to confirm that I am queen?"

My heart beat hard against my ribs, filling my whole chest. A lie would have been easier. It would certainly have benefited me since it might have stopped what I knew would happen if I continued to oppose her. But my heart was thumping so fast I knew a lie would choke me.

And sometimes defiance is all you've got, and when that's the case you have to hold it to you, even if it bites you in return. I looked straight into her angry, demanding, terrified eyes and spoke the truth. "You will never be queen of Fane."

Saldamia stood up slowly. My heart thudded so hard I thought I could hear it, not just feel the boom in my chest. She'd make me pay. I wondered she hadn't gathered more fanes to witness how she dealt with those who opposed her, then I realised she'd held back because she'd expected this outcome. She didn't want more witnesses until she was truly sure of her power. She stepped down from the dais, one slow step while the skirts of her long robe swished around her, then another and she was level with me, although still taller because that was how nature had made us.

I caught the nod she gave to the guard behind me, unsurprised when my arms were gripped. It wasn't necessary. Where did she think I would try to flee to? But it was typical of Saldamia – for show, to reinforce a point that had already been made.

She watched me for a long moment, her eyes raking my face as though looking for a weakness, a way in. I glared back. All the weakness was in her, not in me. She raised her hand and slapped me hard across the cheek, snapping my head aside. "Too stupid even to lie to me," she commented.

She was turning away when I answered. "You have followers and sycophants who will tell you what you wish to hear. I wonder you trouble to seek the company of a dreamseer if you will not hear the truth."

She stepped forward. I expected another blow, but it didn't come. "Perhaps I should be glad you won't lie to me," she murmured. "If you do not yet see me as queen, someone must still stand in my way. I need to know who that is."

As my heart beat faster, she made an impatient gesture to the councillor. Jettaena sidled down the steps to join her, producing a glass from who knew where which Saldamia took from her.

She lifted the glass so the light caught it. Mostly water, but an iridescent film of *somnaya* tincture swam unmistakeably on the surface. "Just a drop this time." She spoke to the glass, then looked past it to me. "You were somewhat hard to understand last time. Perhaps I should have paid attention when you told me to be sparing with it." She cocked an eyebrow. "Can we behave like civilised fanes this time?"

Fear twisted my stomach, but I tried not to let it show. I glanced between the two fanes and forced myself to smile at Saldamia. "I don't need that. If you wish me to foresee I will do so." Now I was lying, but because I was offering what she wanted, Saldamia didn't recognise the fact.

For a single uncertain moment she scowled at me, then she made her decision. "Very well." At a flick of her hand, the guard released me.

"I just need a little peace and silence." Before she could dictate what form that might take, I dropped to my crossed legs on the floor and closed my eyes. I held my hand out expectantly. "And my anima crystal."

There was a fractional pause, then the ring was dropped into my palm. "Thank you." I pushed the ring home on my finger and returned to my preparations. I breathed deep and slow, tipping my head down so my expression was hidden. Saldamia had never accompanied Issaenaptra when she had visited her dreamseer, so her only knowledge of what a dreamseer in a vision looked like was from my mother's funeral and from when she'd drugged me after that. Noises sounded above me. I suspected Saldamia was dismissing the guard, and when I opened my eyes, only the two women remained. Saldamia wanted Jettaena as her only witness. It seemed she placed her trust wholeheartedly in her favourite councillor. I hid a smile. Perhaps I could shake that certainty. I could offer no proof – but then dreamseers were never asked for proof.

I met Saldamia's eyes, slipping easily into my role. "You wish to know who or what still stands in the way of your becoming queen?"

"Yes."

I nodded. "I will foresee that for you." I closed my eyes again. While I breathed, I tried to recall the scent of *somnaya*. I didn't want a *somnaya*-prompted vision, but just the memory of it made me shiver authentically. I twitched my eyes from side-to-side beneath my eyelids the way I'd seen my mother do years before. I shivered again and pronounced, "Danger lies close to you." A pause, then I added, "You rest your head on a pillow of *quanars*, and you will wake one day to find fangs in your pale skin."

I closed my eyes and slumped over to one side, carefully, so I wouldn't hurt myself on the stone floor. I stated, "Trust no one," a moment before I blinked my eyes open as though the words had driven me out of my vision. I rubbed my forehead as I sat up and echoed my own words, "Trust no one," in case she hadn't heard.

When I looked at Saldamia, she didn't seem half as confident as she had when I'd first walked into the room. I ached to laugh at her, but that would have been foolish and I wasn't a fool. I rose stiffly to my feet and tightened my sash. "I hope that helped, Honourable Lady." I used the title she was entitled to as a councillor and hoped she wouldn't notice that – yet again – I'd not referred to her as queen.

"I hope so, too." Saldamia's tone was uncertain, as though she wasn't sure how to take what I'd said to her.

I darted a glance towards the door but I didn't quite dare to leave before she dismissed me. "If that is all, Honourable Lady?" I prompted.

Saldamia continued to regard me, uncertainty clear around her. Jettaena leaned forward to murmur something in her ear. Saldamia smiled. I shivered. "Of course," Saldamia agreed with her councillor.

She took a step towards me, then paused to reach back. Jettaena placed the glass in her hand, the water with its filmy scum of *somnaya* shivering as it moved.

I couldn't help the step back I took away from it. "You don't need that. Haven't I foreseen for you?" I couldn't tear my eyes from the glass. I'd only just got rid of the symptoms. I didn't want to go back to that.

Not again. "I gave you your vision," I said, half-pleading.

"You gave me *a* vision," Saldamia corrected. "I need to be sure it was truthful and complete."

"Why use me if you don't trust me?" I asked bitterly.

"Because you are the only dreamseer," Saldamia told me calmly. "And I trust no one. Such is the burden of ruling. Drink."

I took as small a sip as I could manage, my stomach turning over at the smell even before I swallowed the tincture. Saldamia might have prompted me to have more, but if she did I didn't hear her – the glass smashing on the stone floor was the last thing I was aware of as I fell into a vision.

Afterwards, I remembered nothing, no pictures and none of the words I must have spoken. I didn't know if I'd backed up what I'd said to Saldamia earlier, or contradicted myself. Saldamia had gone, along with Jettaena. The room showed no signs of violence so I didn't think either had turned on the other. Even the shards of glass had been cleared up and I shuddered at the idea of a palace servant clearing up while I lay unconscious, perhaps shifting my limbs out of the way to be sure they'd got all the pieces. I sat up and straightened my clothes, brushing the horrible sensation away. Now, I was alone but for the guard leaning, bored, against one of the walls. I wondered if the boredom was customary, or if she'd had to wait a long time for me to waken.

"Nice nap?" the guard asked, pushing off from the wall and ambling towards me.

Did she think I'd been sleeping? Then I caught the gleam of malice in her eyes as she neared. She knew exactly who I was and what I'd been doing. She was simply enjoying my powerlessness.

"Can you get up? Or do you need me to help?" She loomed over me, holding out a hand. I ignored that and got to my feet, shaking away the last fogginess from the *somnaya*.

"Come on, then." She waved me towards the door. "I need to get you back to your room. I've got real work to do."

I walked ahead of her, shoulders stiff and my head deliberately high. Dreamseers used to be treasured. Now I was mocked. I wanted to wipe the grin off her face, but I didn't have the power to do that. I had no wretched power at all.

Although, there was one thing. Saldamia had forgotten to remove my anima ring. I might not have had much power, but with my ring I was in a better situation than I'd been when I awoke in my cell. I needed to know where Zan and Tullan were; if they were still alive.

Cal's face came to mind, eyes flashing, scowl grooving his forehead. I wanted him to be safe, too. He'd faced enough already. He and Keba were soldiers; they knew how to take care of themselves. I had to believe that. I couldn't bear to worry about everyone.

Chapter Ten

I immediately discovered how pleased Saldamia was by what I'd said in my vision.

The guard led me to a different destination. When we left the throne room we turned in the other direction and walked up two flights of steps and along a brighter corridor, where the plaster walls were painted with pretty scenes. The guard threw a door open and I walked inside. This was a room, while the other place had been a cell, below ground, dark and unembellished. The new room's beautifully painted walls enclosed a bed, a comfortable chair by the window, and a desk and hard-backed chair.

And a table covered with foods that set my mouth watering the moment the door swung wide. I hadn't eaten since our evening meal at Tullan's house, and I wasn't sure how long ago that was. I glanced out of the window to judge the time from the light. A day, since it was evening again already. I forced myself to wait until the guard closed the door behind her before falling on the meal. Bread and broth, grains baked with fish and vegetables, sweet pies filled with nuts and nectars. I sniffed carefully, but when I didn't smell either the scent of *somnaya* or anything more sinister, I couldn't hold back any longer. Saldamia didn't need to use subterfuge if she wanted to drug me. I'd take the food for the blessing it was.

Once I was sated, I crossed the room and sat by the window. It was day, but it wouldn't be for much longer. The day's shadows were lengthening as darkness fell. The sun was a faint glow to my left while the second moon barely peeked over the horizon, a crescent of light against the black. We had three days to moonsfall night when the darkness would be absolute. And then we'd declare a new queen. I sighed. It would be Saldamia. It had to be. Maybe my vision would arrive the night before. Or the day of the ceremony itself, because I hadn't done enough falling over and spouting nonsense in front of crowds lately.

The view from my window was expansive, but not especially interesting. For leagues there was bare ground, a few rocks, but nothing big enough even for a fane to hide behind. The fane queen's palace had once been set in beautiful gardens that legend said would take you a full day to walk through. But the gate that used to lay at the bottom of the palace, connecting Fane to Earth, had leeched environmental destruction, and then Queen Issaenaptra's fear of rebel attacks made her demand that the ground be stripped of anything still living.

When I looked straight down, I could see the start of greenery close to the palace walls, but only a few steps away from that the ground returned to bare, sandy soil. Nature was still struggling to return here.

With a sigh I turned and took in the room itself in more detail.

The bed was wide and comfortable with clean covers, and there was a chair beside the window in case I wished to relax and enjoy the view. Against the other wall was a desk and hard chair. Maybe palace guests needed a desk to sit and write at, but I was hardly going to pass my time writing letters home. The only other things in the room were the doors, one leading out, which was locked. The other was ajar and I glimpsed a bathroom through it.

This place offered such a contrast to the cell I'd woken up in that morning; it was clearly a reward for services rendered. Unease slid through me and I wished again that I knew what I'd said when I was drugged. Might Saldamia have decided Jettaena wasn't to be trusted? If she had, what had she done about her anxieties? I'd chosen what to tell her with deliberate intent. Was it my fault if they turned on each other?

Pushing that thought away, I reasoned I might as well enjoy the luxury while I had it. I was grubby from sleeping in unchanged clothes, and along my spine and across my forehead I could already feel sweat prickling just from that tiny dose of *somnaya* tincture. I poured myself a deep, hot bath and luxuriated long enough to relax. When I started to tense at every noise outside the room in expectation of someone bursting in so they might drag me back to Saldamia's presence, I got out and dried off. A set of drawers in the room held clothes and I found some leggings and a tunic that didn't fit too badly.

After that, I had nothing to do but think. I needed to find Zan and Tullen. I was shying away from that in case they were dead; better to have hope than none, but I needed to plan. I needed to know.

I sought out Zan first. I didn't need *somnaya* for that, just my anima ring and some of the water from the jug on the table. Crossing to the table of grown-cold food, I snatched up an empty dish and the water. Settling cross-legged on the floor, I poured some water into the dish to make a seeing glass, brought her face to mind and dipped my fingers into the pool I'd made. If she was alive I would be able to find her – and if there was water where she was, the portal would go both ways and we could talk to each other. If not, the portal would only exist for me to see her.

"Zan?"

Her face rose behind my eyelids, blonde hair and brown eyes sliding into my vision. It was Zan and she was alive. "Can you hear me?"

Nothing. No water.

I pulled back my view of her so I could see where she was. Bars. She was behind bars. Was that a cell here in the palace? I looked past her, trying to see where the cage was, but all I could see was the warm stone the palace was built from. She was in the building with me.

I pulled my hand from the water and sat back. She was alive, and probably close. If I tried to contact her at another time of day I might have more success. I'd have to hope we could speak to each other and plan a way out of the palace.

Tullan was next. I had a clear face to bring to mind now, not just a name. But it made no difference. The water clouded and didn't clear. The block was still in place. Frustrated, I pushed the seeing glass away and wiped my damp fingers dry on my leggings.

Cal's face slid into my mind next, his angry expression vivid in my head, then Keba's still, watchful face rose in my memory. Were they still alive? My fingers hovered just above the water. I could look for them and find out for sure, but I tipped the water away instead. I was too much of a coward to bear it if Zan and I were the only survivors and everyone who'd tried to help us was dead.

I closed my eyes and faced the truth. I hadn't tried to contact Cal because I was unpleasantly sure he was dead. He was too stubborn to surrender, and Saldamia had no reason to keep him alive: a troublesome rebel with no love for the new regime, she'd be better off without him. My breathing hitched and I pressed my lips together. To survive all he had, only to end up dead because of me. I snapped my eyes open and stared at the wall. I didn't care what happened to Cal. He was nothing to me; I barely knew him. Except that wasn't true. His face had been seared into my thoughts for years now, since Issaenaptra had made it clear how very dirty her dirty work could be.

I got into bed and tried to push him out of my thoughts, but he wouldn't go. It wasn't fair. If he were alive, I was sure he wouldn't waste time thinking of me. He'd be plotting how to rescue Zan. He'd never hidden the fact that she was his priority. I didn't matter to him. I just wished I could make the opposite true.

Irritating Cal wouldn't leave me alone, though. Even when I finally fell asleep he was there in my dreams.

*

It wasn't a vision, it was an ordinary dream, confused and disquieting. I tried to wake myself up as soon as I recognised the tired figure and the backdrop of Issaenaptra's darkest cell, but my brain wouldn't co-operate, forcing me to watch as Cal's fingertips were removed, one by one, with enough time for his screams to fade in between.

When it was done, he lifted his head, exhausted and defeated, and looked straight at me. I blinked in shock. His eyes weren't Cal's eyes, sparkling and mad, they were my mother's. Her bright, savage face came closer, advancing on me. My head filled with the scent of *somnaya*. I gasped – and woke.

Dawn's pink light greeted me. I rolled onto my side and pulled the covers over my head. I didn't expect to sleep again, but I must have done.

The clear, white light of day greeted me when the sound of the door opening jerked me awake.

"Come along. There's much to be done today. You've slept long enough."

The record keeper bustled into the room. I scrambled to my knees on the bed, my back against the wall. "What now?" I thought I'd seen the last of her after the funeral. I should have known I wouldn't be that lucky.

She tutted. "We need to rehearse today. The ceremony must proceed perfectly." She glanced behind her and gestured to someone waiting outside the door. The smug guard from earlier walked in, arms full. My heart stopped for a moment when I thought she was carrying a dead body. Then my pulse calmed. It was a bundle of robes, not a dead fane.

"New robes have been made for you. Ready for the confirmation ceremony," the record keeper told me.

The guard smiled unpleasantly then dropped the clothes over the end of the bed and left. I reached out and took a corner of the robe between thumb and forefinger and lifted the stiff, heavily embroidered

94

fabric. The colour changed as it flexed in the light, metal threads glinting dully.

My dreamseer robes were ash, but these were as bad – or worse. I pulled at what turned out to be a sleeve, frowning at the weight of it as the long gown pulled slightly off the bed. I couldn't shrink into the background in this. And wearing it wouldn't be optional. This was a grand robe for a public occasion.

"We must check it fits." The record keeper was as fussy as I remembered, frowning at the robe and me. If it didn't fit, I got the feeling she'd blame me rather than it. "You must be properly attired."

I dropped the robe back to the bed, my fingers plucking at the fabric. I wanted to ask, *Or else what?* But I didn't.

"Try it on."

"No." I'd wear the wretched thing for the ceremony. I wasn't going to prance around in it for a rehearsal.

The record keeper's lip tightened. "Stupid child. I need to see if changes must be made." She grabbed the robe and pushed it towards me. "Try it. Or I'll summon the guards and we'll do it for you."

I took it and disappeared into the bathroom, the heavy fabric trailing after me. Leaning back against the door, I thought for a moment of locking it and refusing to come out – but that idea only lasted a moment. The record keeper was so determined to do everything right she really would summon guards and instruct them to hold me down and dress me forcibly.

I removed my night tunic and tugged the robes over my head, twitching them to get them to sit comfortably and walking across the bathroom floor to ensure I could do so without tripping. When I was

95

ready I faced the mirror. I wasn't admiring how I looked; there wasn't anything to be vain about. I wasn't sure I even recognised myself. The fane who greeted me in reflection was narrow and angular, the robe hanging from her in ways its maker could neither have imagined nor desired. I'd lost more weight than I would have thought possible in the days since my mother's funeral; not enough to eat and too much running for my life.

I looked older than sixteen. My eyes were large, shadowed with not enough sleep. I needed a holiday. That thought provoked a hollow laugh. I'd needed a holiday for the last three years. Unless I could find Zan and make a gate to Talvar, I was unlikely ever to get one.

An impatient knock at the door jerked me from my reflections. Before the record keeper could break down the door, I twisted the lock and stepped out.

The room was busier than I'd left it. Two other servants, directed by the record keeper, were removing yesterday's dishes and bringing breakfast. The record keeper turned when I walked in, her lips tightening once more as though she found me wanting.

She strode across and twitched the robe to sit better on my shoulders. I itched to slap her hand away. "You should take better care of yourself." She looked up and pulled a face, reaching for a very short strand of hair. "You have a position to uphold."

"A dreamseer needs to *see*, she doesn't need to be pretty to look at," I murmured back.

The record keeper gave me another hard look. "Given the state of you right now, that's just as well."

"I want to go home," I said to her. She could speak

to Saldamia; persuade her to let me go. Then I could find Zan and we could find Tullan, and make a gate.

The record keeper ignored me. Another servant had entered while she was fussing with the robe and she turned to him, noting what needed to be changed to make the robe fit better.

"I want to go home. Am I Saldamia's prisoner?" I asked, louder.

The record keeper looked up at that. "Don't be silly. You may return home after the ceremony, provided you fulfil your role properly."

So I was a prisoner – to be judged by others and given the freedom any fane might expect only if I gave satisfaction. I stared at the far wall over the heads of the record keeper and the seamstress. They paid me as much attention as you might a statue. I had seen my mother treated with respect, but I'd only known her in her later years. I wondered now if her early years in the role had been like this – if that had fuelled her desire to take the only escape she could.

For the first time ever, I sympathised with her.

"You can get changed now." When the record keeper and the seamstress were done, I was allowed to escape and put on something I felt comfortable in.

But that wasn't the end of it.

"Come along." As the seamstress swept out of the room with the dreamseer's robes across her arms, the record keeper snapped her next command at me. I swear, her fingers moved, only just preventing herself from clicking her fingers as though I were some sort of a pet. She started towards the door, expecting me to follow.

I held my ground. "Where are we going now?"

Hand on the doorframe, the record keeper turned with a huff of annoyance. I lifted my chin and raised my brows, expecting an answer. If my mother had started her dreamseer career like this I was sure she hadn't just been handed respect. She had forced others to respect her. I would do the same.

"To the throne room," the record keeper snapped. "We need to ensure the ceremony proceeds without a hitch. You need to know what to say when."

"Very well." Head still lifted high, I swept through the door in front of the surprised record keeper. Thank the moons, I knew where I was going and didn't have to wait to be guided.

Chapter Eleven

Several guards and palace servants were milling around the throne room where chairs had been set out facing the empty throne. I slowed and the record keeper overtook me, clapping her hands to get everyone's attention.

"Thank you for waiting. Ten of you, please stand in the front rows, where the councillors will be. The dreamseer will stand here." She pointed and I moved to the seat closest to the wall on the front row. "And who has the crown?" She looked around until one of the servants raised a hand, their other occupied in carrying the queen's crown, a delicate glint of silver on a midnight blue cushion. "You others," she gestured to the remaining guards, "You act the part of the queen's bodyguard. Start by the door, please."

When we were all in place, the record keeper made us run through the ceremony. "I will take the part of the queen. All eyes will be on the queen as she takes her place." The palace servants turned obediently to watch as she stalked from the door ahead of the bodyguards, stepping carefully up the dais while the guard fanned out to stand facing the audience, arms folded, looking slightly above the heads of the 'crowd'. I looked around, wondering if anyone was being themselves, apart from me. Servants were playing the part of the councillors, guards were pretending to be the queen's official bodyguard and the record keeper was pretending to be the queen. I hoped the real fanes knew what was expected of them – it would distress the record keeper if I were the only one to get it all right.

Rather than sit on the throne – that was clearly a pretence too far – the record keeper slipped to the side, glancing in my direction to make sure I was still where she had put me. "Now, I will kneel before the queen." She dipped down, reciting from carefully-practised memory. "I will ask the queen if she willingly takes on the queen's responsibilities, if she will serve Fane with the courage of her heart and the wisdom of her mind and the strength of her body, and if she will be guided by councillors trusty and true." She got back to her feet. "The queen will indicate her agreement to each question."

I hid a smile. Of course she would. Saldamia hadn't come this far to fail during the ceremony itself. She would want to be as perfect as the record keeper – I'd bet they were having secret rehearsals, probably at night when the palace was sleeping.

"I will turn to the dreamseer." She did so, fixing me with a hard stare. "And ask, 'Do you foresee a prosperous and peaceful reign under Queen Saldamia?' You will answer…"

She paused, waiting for me to speak, her expression glaring a warning. "I will answer, 'I do'," I assured her.

She nodded satisfaction and turned from me. "I will set the crown on the queen's head." She mimed, not quite lifting the circlet from its cushion and not quite setting it on the invisible head in the empty throne. I thought that was quite fitting; a fake ceremony for a queen who would never be.

Unaware of my thoughts, the record keeper turned to her audience with a smile. "I shall finish by saying, 'Honourable ladies and gentlemen; honest fanes, I give you your new queen. Bow the knee and confirm you will be bound by the new reign!'"

There was a shuffle as everyone complied. I bobbed down so I wouldn't catch the record keeper's eye.

*

The record keeper clapped her hands for silence. "Well done, everyone. You are dismissed."

The guards and servants relaxed, clustering in groups and chatting, some of them edging towards the door. I strode past them. The record keeper had dismissed us all and I intended to take her at her word.

I almost made it. I was tugging at the heavy doors when the record keeper caught up with me. "Where do you think you're going?" I froze, then remembered: respect. I turned and looked her straight in the eye. "To the gardens. I want some fresh air."

Her lips tightened and I thought she was trying to think of a reason to stop me.

"You can find me there if you need me," I told her, heaving the door open and striding out, daring her to stop me. She didn't.

I hurried down the corridor, stopping around the corner to sag against the wall in relief. I listened, but no footsteps hurried after me. Was it really as simple as that — just act with confidence and they'd defer to me? I wished I'd tried it before.

I set off again, striding down the corridor towards

the stairs. I wasn't going to the gardens, that was a fiction to set the record keeper at her ease. I was going to find Zan, if she was here to be found.

Chapter Twelve

At the bottom of the palace, I turned into the final corridor that led to the cells, then twisted back out of sight. A guard was leaning against the wall halfway down, facing one of the doors that edged the corridor, which meant someone worth guarding was down here.

I held my breath but there was no sound of footsteps. He hadn't noticed me. Some guard, although I was grateful. I leaned my head back, staring up at the ceiling while I tried to think what to do. I needed to get rid of the guard, but my elemental power wouldn't be anything like a match for his. And I'd only get one chance — if Saldamia learned I'd tried to help her prisoners I'd go back to being one myself.

I was calculating whether I could use my status as a dreamseer and the confidence I was just trying on to command the guard to let me into Zan's cell — if she was even there — when it all fell apart.

A hand cupped over my mouth while another gripped my wrist. I twisted away instinctively, coming face-to-face with Tullan's blue eyes. Relief slackened my joints at knowing he was alive, and safe. He let go of my wrist and held a finger to his lips as he dropped his other hand from my mouth. He jerked his head and I nodded. Together we retreated back along the corridor and halfway up the flight of stairs.

"You're safe!" Tullan hissed. He hugged me, arms tight around my shoulders. I stood for a moment, shocked to immobility, then relaxed into the warmth and comfort of him. "You too," I murmured, setting my cheek to his shoulder.

His arms tightened. "I'm sorry it took so long for me to get here."

"It doesn't matter." And it didn't. He'd come for me. I could rely on my father like I'd never been able to rely on anyone before. The knowledge, deep in my bones, that I was no longer alone, sent warmth through me and fixed a stupid smile on my face. "You came. That's all that matters."

He smiled. "I told you I'd be there for you. That's my first demonstration. There'll be others."

His embrace loosened enough for him to look past me. There was a clatter of footsteps. I shrank back in alarm but Tullan shook his head. "Keba," he murmured. A moment later, her scarred face appeared. She nodded to me then turned her attention to Tullan. "Status?" she asked in a low voice.

"One guard."

She nodded. "Shall I?"

Tullan waved her on, waiting with me on the stairs while Keba padded silently down the last of the steps and along the corridor, disappearing from our sight when she rounded the corner. A burst of elemental energy surged along the corridor, followed by silence.

"Come on." Tullan hurried down the stairs. I followed. The guard was now lying on the floor, unconscious. Her back to him, Keba was working to open one of the cells opposite. As we drew close, the lock popped open and Keba pushed the door wide so we could all step inside. We'd found Zan.

A row of iron bars spanned the room from floor to ceiling, spaced evenly to divide the area in half, creating a cell within a cell. As the door opened, Zan jumped up from the bench on the other side of the bars. She looked tired, but she grinned when we walked in. "Am I glad to see you!" Then she noted who had come to her rescue and her face sagged. "Cal?"

"Don't worry. He's here. He's next on our list," Keba told her.

"Okay." She gestured to the bars. "If you can just get me out of here I'll help."

Keba smiled. "I can do better than that." She reached into a pocket and lifted out a chain. Dangling from it was a pendant that glinted in the light with the gleam of a red anima crystal.

"Oh, thank God." Zan reached through the bars and Keba dropped the anima key into her hands. Zan slipped it over her head. "I was afraid they'd destroyed it. It was like losing an arm being without it."

Keba folded her arms. "The guards follow exactly the same procedure for dealing with the anima keys of prisoners that they did when Issaenaptra was queen. I'm not sure that's wise. You might think the next queen would have changed things."

Zan flicked her long hair out of the way of the chain so her anima key rested on her collarbone. She pulled a face at Keba. "Then aren't we both glad I didn't get around to changing palace procedure? Stand back." We retreated to the door while Zan drew on her elemental powers and made three of the bars bend and pop out of their sockets in the ceiling to clear enough room for her to step through. I watched with a twinge of envy – I'd give anything for that sort of power.

"Where's Cal? And how long have we got?"

"He's in another cell here. If the guards are still on the same shifts as they were under Issaenaptra, we've got about three hours before the guard outside will be missed."

We spilled out of the door and Keba worked on the lock of the next cell. I watched the back of her head. "Do you have Cal's anima crystal, too?"

The side of her mouth lifted in a smile as though I'd said something funny. "Cal's can't be taken from him."

"How are they keeping him in a cell, then?"

The lock clicked and the next door swung open. I followed Tullan in with Keba behind me. She spoke as we entered. "How to neutralise Cal: knock him unconscious, and keep him unconscious."

Zan pushed past us to kneel by the pale figure prone on the bench, checking for a pulse.

"He swallows his anima," Keba explained. "Being Issaenaptra's prisoner once gave him a strong desire never to be powerless again." My cheeks warmed. It was me who'd put that fear in him. Keba shrugged as though it was a pragmatic response to an unfortunate incident, nothing remarkable at all. "It's not foolproof, though."

Zan looked round. "Can we find a healer?"

"Not one who'll be willing to help us."

Tullan stepped forward. "I'll see what I can do." He knelt down on Cal's other side and pressed a hand to his forehead, his other hand circling Cal's wrist. Tullan closed his eyes and lowered his head. His bicep bulged as his fingers tightened and his anima crystal flexed, sending a glint of blue light through the room.

A minute passed while we watched, waiting to see if whatever Tullan was doing would have an effect.

Cal coughed, his back arching off the bench with the effort, although his eyes remained closed. Tullan altered his grip on Cal's wrist and silence fell again. Another cough, then Cal gave a groan and rolled onto his side, eyes flickering open. He would have rolled off the bench onto the floor except that Tullan and Keba were there to stop him. They helped him sit up.

Zan hovered anxiously close by. "How do you feel?"

Cal lifted a hand to his head. "*Ernith*, what just happened?" His voice croaked, cracking on the words.

Tullan set a reassuring hand on his shoulder. "You've been unconscious more than a day. Take it easy – you may feel woozy for a while."

Cal looked up, eyes glittering with more than his usual fervour. "Woozy? I'll woozy the *zangtaff* who did this to me." He tried to stand up, but dropped back down before he'd managed it.

"Have a drink." Keba had found a cup either in this cell or the other. Cal drained it in a second.

He glanced around, then looked at Keba. "Report?"

"We're at the palace. We're all together and we've got a maximum of three hours before you and Zan will be noticed as missing."

"Right." He stood up, reaching for Keba's shoulder when he wobbled. "Time to go."

"Go where?" If we were running for our lives again, I at least wanted a destination to aim for.

"Ah, we can stay in the palace," Tullan said. We all

swung to face him. "We need stone. We can use the stone in the gate room." He turned to me and Zan. "If you feel strong enough to create the gate now?"

We nodded. My heart surged against my ribs at the idea of escape – proper escape.

"Do we have time?" Ever practical Cal was back on duty.

"It only needs a few minutes. About the same as to activate an anima key."

"So the rest of us will have time to get away afterwards?" Cal clarified.

"Yes." Tullan considered Cal, who looked pale and was more crazy-eyed than usual. "And you'll be able to recover while we make the gate," he said, half-statement, half-instruction.

We stood for a moment, our gazes darting from one to the next, checking that we were all in agreement. We nodded and a thrill of excitement passed through me.

"To the gate room, then," Keba said, sticking close to Cal as they made for the door.

I was a step behind Tullan as we walked to the end of the corridor. He glanced back and smiled. "There's nothing to worry about. We can do this."

I shook my head. "I need to tell you – I'm going with her. I'm going to Talvar with Zan." I had to tell him. But I wished I hadn't when I saw the change on his face. "I can't stay here, at the beck and call of the queen. It's unbearable."

"I understand." He smiled, but I saw the strain behind the gesture. For the first time, escape felt like exile. For the first time, I had someone I didn't want to leave behind. "I'll miss you. I was looking forward to learning more about my daughter."

"You could come, too," I blurted.

He shook his head. "My life is here." He reached for my hand and squeezed. "But perhaps you might visit. In a while. When it seems less unbearable."

I nodded. "I'd like that."

Then we were inside the gate room, with the thick wooden door bolted shut behind us and the bare stone wall that had once been the last gate to Earth in front of us. I shivered. The air was still and cold, as though it were waiting for something. I breathed in and smelled the heat of energy – elements colliding. This was the scene of Issaenaptra's final defeat – and her death. I shivered again and rubbed the goosebumps on my arms.

On the other side of the room, Zan was hunched like she felt the chill too.

Cal was leaning side-to-side as though he was in a stiff breeze, but he still had space to worry about his cousin. "Are you all right?"

"Of course." Zan's tone was determined, but I was sure Cal could see the uncertainty in her eyes like I could.

"Are you sure about this? Are you going to be okay?"

Zan nudged against him, bumping shoulders, a smile wiping the worry from her expression. "I've just escaped from a cell. My life's looking better already."

Cal laughed, but the crease between his brows remained. "You've never been to Talvar before. What if Thanriel isn't there?"

"He'll be there."

Her voice was firm, but the pucker of anxiety that

109

dented her forehead told another story.

"Okay, maybe I put that wrong." He tried again, "Talvar's a big place. You're one person crossing through one gate. What if you can't find him? What if he's a thousand miles away from the gate you cross through? And someone finds you before Thanriel does and they're not as friendly? You remember your arrival on Fane the first time, don't you?"

That was during the war. I hadn't seen when Cal and Zan arrived, but I knew how eager Issaenaptra had been to get her hands on the last surviving gatekeeper – so she could lead her army to destroy Earth.

"Your blood leads you home when you cross a gate. If I go to Talvar, our baby's blood will lead me to Thanriel." Zan's voice was stubborn – as though the blood inside her had better lead her to him or she'd want a good explanation why not.

"And there'll be two of us," I pointed out. "If he's not waiting for her, I'll help Zan find Thanriel."

Cal looked at me. I thought he was going to say something sneering about how little use a feeble dreamseer would be, but he just nodded. "Very well."

Zan stepped up to him, pulling him into a hug. "You've done a great job looking after me, Cal. Thank you for everything." She stood back, smiling. "You can relax now."

Cal huffed. I agreed: Cal relaxing was not likely to ever happen. "Just... take care." He backed away a few steps and sank to the floor, cross-legged while he watched us. Keba stepped away, taking a post by the door so she'd be first to know if someone from outside tried to enter the gate room.

I turned my attention to Tullan, who was staring at

110

the stone wall ahead of us as though he could see the gate we were yet to make. He turned. "Are you ready to do this?"

My mouth dried immediately. I nodded, then cleared my throat. "Yes. Yes, I'm ready."

He turned to Zan. "Ready?"

Her eyes shone at the idea that she'd soon be reunited with Thanriel. "Yes. Tell me what to do."

"We'll make the gate here." He guided us to one side of the gate room. "I want us to be clear of…" He waved a hand as though seeking the right word. "Scar tissue, from the gate to Earth. I want a clear passageway."

Zan and I nodded, and waited for the next instruction.

"You need to be in contact with your anima crystal, and in contact with the gate." Tullan twisted his silver torq off his arm and pressed it so his palm connected with the crystal, the flat of his hand spread against the stone in front of him so the anima crystal touched both.

On my other side, Zan nodded and removed her locket, twisting the chain around her fingers. I turned my ring so the crystal was on the inside of my hand. We pressed our hands against the stone.

"Link your other hands," Tullan prompted.

I reached out my free hand and slid my fingers between Zan's.

"Good." Tullan reached around me so he could set his hand over both of ours, his fingers curling around to hold the three of us together.

The anima crystal beneath my other hand vibrated. I was aware of the elements in the room, the potential power in the air and the stone and the ground beneath our feet. The hairs on my arms lifted, a visceral reaction to the banked energy around me. Tullan's calm gaze met my and Zan's excited ones. "Are you ready to make a gate and cross between the worlds?"

We both nodded. Zan added, "Yes."

Tullan's eyes shone, serious and steady. "Once the process has been started it cannot be stopped. We will all be committed. The gate will take the energy needed to form a connection between the worlds, even if that drains all of us. If you have any doubts, we need to stop now."

"No." Zan shook her head. "I can't wait any longer. I feel strong. We can do this."

I nodded in agreement. Now the gate was almost here I felt stronger than I had for days. Excitement thrummed through me. I felt invincible.

"Ready?" Tullan asked.

Zan's eyes shone, her voice steady as she assured him. "Ready."

He focused on me. My heart beat a firm pulse of hope. "Ready."

From nowhere, a breath of air swept around us, the elements impatient for what was to come. Tullan's fingers tightened hot around our hands. His eyes were closed and his lips moved, saying words too low for us to hear. He'd said the process was similar to activating a fane's anima key – but I was too young to remember what my mother had done to activate mine.

The energy in the gate room picked up. The air shifted. It wasn't a wind or a breeze, it felt more like the air had somehow expanded, swelling in preparation for the space between the worlds that it would soon have to fill.

The temperature in the room increased and sweat prickled across my forehead, my fingers growing slippery where they linked with Zan and Tullan's. My anima crystal vibrated against my skin, and now the stone under my fingers did likewise, trembling faintly, the stone of the floor throbbing in echo.

Heat burned through me as though the stone was hot, the vibrations of it sending shocks up my arms. My bones began to shake like the stone under my hands. My ribs tightened and my spine compressed. On either side, I could hear laboured breathing from Zan and Tullan and I knew the gate must be affecting them in the same way. I gritted my teeth, squeezing my eyes closed as the vibrations grew strong enough to be painful. Something shifted beneath my fingers and I opened my eyes in time to see the solid stone melt away.

Chapter Thirteen

The universe flowed into the space we'd created, a terrifying void of cold emptiness flooding into my body where I was still connected to the space that had become the gate. I tried to move my hands, to pull away from the darkness, but I couldn't move. The three of us were tied together and tied to the gate for as long as it took.

I shivered as cold seeped into my veins, chilling me so I could hardly breathe, my breaths becoming short gasps that barely drew oxygen into my body. I thought the shaking would stop now there was no stone, but the opposite was true. My body vibrated harder, as though it wanted to rip into its constituent elements. I focused on my anima crystal, the one spot of warmth left in the world, trying to hold myself together. Fear gripped me, adding to the cold. When Tullan had said it was dangerous, I'd said I was willing to take the risk. But I hadn't understood what danger meant. I'd just assumed that my desire to escape would make that escape possible. It hadn't occurred to me that creating an escape route might kill me.

Until now.

A keening cry escaped my clenched lips. The cold crept deeper, chilling my bones. My shivering stopped because there wasn't enough heat left in me to move. My heartbeat slowed. For one terrible moment it might have stopped. The cold gathered around my crystal as though trying to find a way into it. I dragged a breath into my lungs, willing myself not to let the cold take over. If my crystal died I would die with it, I was sure.

The pinprick of heat in my anima glowed, then spread – warming my hand. I felt Tullan and Zan's fingers intertwined with mine. I drew in a gasp of breath as the warmth flowed further, driving back the chill. Heat burned through me, reaching the crown of my head and the ends of my toes. My slowing heartbeat increased again as the warmth twisted from welcome to uncomfortable. My temperature soared higher as though the heat generated by my crystal was prepared to burn me up to drive away the cold from between the worlds.

Talvar.

As the word came into my head, a spot of light appeared in the darkness. Zan was thinking of our destination. She held the talvarrine blood; she could link us to our ultimate destination. I told my racing heart to calm – we were almost there.

The spot of light increased, overwhelming in its brightness, filling every shaking, aching cell of my body. I squeezed my eyes shut but the light was inside me, as though the talvarrine sun burned through the gate and straight into us.

Fire burned through my veins. I screamed again. Through the pain, I felt Tullan's fingers squeeze mine reassuringly. I stopped screaming and drew a breath inwards instead. He was with me. I drew in another breath, pulling strength into me along with the air. Together, we could do this.

With renewed determination, I thought about my destination: Talvar and the freedom I'd find there. Tamping down the terror that wanted to claim me, I stopped fighting the light and let it flood through me. Every atom in my body flew apart.

*

The first thing I grew aware of was a band of heat around my wrist. It gave me an odd sense of déjà vu when I blinked my eyes open to once more see Cal frowning down at me.

"Are you all right?"

I answered, "Yes," before properly processing the question, then shifted fingers and toes to ensure I had come through the process safely. "Zan?" Had she gone to Talvar without me – why else would Cal be paying attention to me?

I struggled to sit up, forced to accept Cal's help when the gate room swung around me. I cursed under my breath, then froze when I realised I looked to be in the best state of the three of us. Keba lay beside a prone Tullan, and Zan... I blinked. Zan was surrounded by a bright light that reminded me of the light that had nearly killed me. I blinked and the light resolved into the shape of a figure crouching by her side.

"Is that Thanriel?" I realised why Cal had abandoned his cousin.

"Yes. And we have a problem."

My heart jolted. "Is she all right?"

"I will take care of her." Thanriel spoke without turning. There was something about his calm, certain voice that made me believe him.

"That's not the problem."

I looked past Cal and saw what was. Tullan – and Keba. My heart jumped. "No!" I crawled the two steps to Tullan's side. My hand touched warm flesh and his chest rose on a breath. I sagged with relief, resting my forehead on his chest.

"No, it's not Tullan, either," Cal told me. "Or Keba. They're just unconscious."

Just. I sat back. *The gate will take the energy it needs, even if it drains us all.* The gate had drained us all and I was the first to recover. But that didn't explain Keba. "What's happened to Keba? Why is she unconscious?"

"Yeah. That *is* part of the problem – Thanriel didn't come through alone."

"Algamel." Thanriel spoke the name, then turned. "Algamel came through with me."

I sucked in a breath. Algamel. The talvarrine who had been working with Issaenaptra during the war, who'd been willing to kill everyone on Earth to serve his purposes. Zan had thwarted him in that ambition – did he now want to destroy Fane?

"Why did he come here?" I asked, aware I might not want to hear the answer.

"He is seeking power," Thanriel told us. "Enough to destroy the guardian of Talvar." He looked up at Cal. "I would go after him if I could, but I cannot leave Zan."

Cal got to his feet. "We'll do what we can to stop him."

Thanriel's face was still so bright it was difficult to make out his expression, but his sad tone was clear. "Thank you."

Algamel couldn't be allowed to harm Fane, I knew that, but the gate was still shining wide open behind Thanriel. I couldn't help the words. "What about going to Talvar?"

Thanriel shook his head. "Talvar is not safe. The guardian must indeed be stopped, but not through violence. I can resolve matters there, but Algamel must be contained first. I could not allow you to go to Talvar now."

I wasn't sure how he could stop me with the gate open behind him, but I didn't try to dodge past him. It would be stupid to go to Talvar alone when I didn't know what I'd be facing on the other side of the gate. I wasn't stupid. An ache grew in my stomach. I was... sad. Because once again, the future I wanted had shifted out of reach.

I turned to Cal, who was standing by Keba's unconscious form. "What do we do?" I waited for him to sketch out a plan to contain the rogue talvarrine.

"If you can take care of Zan," Cal said to Thanriel, "Deena and I will go after Algamel." Thanriel nodded and Cal swung to me. "If you're recovered?"

"I... yes, I'm okay." I was so surprised to be included, I didn't point out I'd be no use if he needed fighting skills. "What do we do?"

"Okay. First step: find out where Algamel is right now." Cal headed towards the door.

I followed, grabbing his sleeve. "What if guards are there? What if Saldamia finds us?"

He looked round. "I'll hide behind you. She likes you."

I thought he might be joking, but that seemed unlikely. We shot the bolts silently and slipped out and down the corridor, where he proved he wasn't serious by leading the way past the prone guard Keba had knocked out earlier.

"How long was I out?" I asked as we neared the stairs, keeping my voice low in case guards or servants were close by.

"From a spectator's point of view, it was a little hard to know what was going on, but it took about five minutes to create the gate, and you were out only a minute or two once the gate opened. Not long," Cal whispered back.

"When did Thanriel appear?"

"As soon as the gate opened. These two spots of light appeared. It was only when it spoke that we realised one was Thanriel – and that the other one was Algamel, but he'd gone by then."

"Through the bolted door?"

We edged up the stairs. Cal gave a shrug. "Talvarrines are creatures of *pure energy*." He put on a voice when he said that, like he was quoting Zan – or maybe Thanriel himself. "A door is no barrier, apparently."

"He can pass through doors, but he needs to steal power from us? How strong is their guardian?"

"Yeah, I'm not sure that's something we really want to find out."

Best not to let my imagination loose on that. "What's the matter with Zan?"

His shoulders hunched as he moved up the stairs. "I don't know. Thanriel said she used too much energy making the gate, and she and the baby are in danger. He said he'll keep her safe."

"Do you believe him?" Cal wasn't the sort to

abdicate a responsibility he'd taken on – especially when it came to his cousin.

"He saved her life before. No reason for him to stop now."

"And what about Keba? What's he done to her?"

"I think Algamel knocked her out so she wouldn't stop him leaving the gate room."

"You didn't stop him."

I meant it as an observation rather than a criticism, but Cal's face still tightened. "I was still recovering from what Saldamia's people did to me. I have to assume he didn't think he needed to knock me out."

"Are you all right now?"

"Yeah. I guess seeing my friends collapse or get knocked out had a sobering effect. I'm fine."

We fell silent as we neared the first landing on the stairs, in case anyone was passing.

"Wait!" Cal hissed the warning, throwing a hand back to keep me behind him.

I stopped and tried to peer around him. Keba had dealt with the guards on the way to the gate room, but we couldn't stay hidden from everyone in the palace forever. I followed Cal's gaze along the corridor. I'd expected to see a guard, perhaps with their back to us, since Cal hadn't ducked back out of sight. I suppose that was what we saw – except that the guard was lying down on the hard floor, asleep.

Cal glanced around, then darted out of the stairwell. He knelt beside the sleeping guard, checking her pulse.

By the time he'd done that, I'd caught up with him. "Is she alive?"

"Sleeping." Cal twisted round to take in all the details of where we were, that soldier's watchfulness back in force.

"Someone else Algamel knocked out?" I asked. "Why? How were they standing in his way?"

"I don't know. Yet." Cal drew close, then passed by me and jogged up the next flight of stairs.

I tip-toed up the stairs after him, the soft fall of sunlight through the narrow windows once we got above ground making me feel exposed.

It wasn't until we reached the main floor of the palace that we encountered another fane, a servant, asleep on the floor like the guard had been.

"This is creepy," I murmured to Cal.

Without saying a word, we both hung back at the top, half-hidden by the stairwell as we peered into the corridor beyond to see if anyone else was there.

Cal straightened and strode to the prone servant, as though proving he wasn't worried. He knelt down to check her pulse even though I could see her chest moving from where I stood. I checked no one else was in sight then joined them. "Why's he doing this?"

Cal looked up. "I don't know the detail, but Zan told me Thanriel borrowed energy."

"How?"

He shrugged. "Before Zan came to Fane and sealed the gates, Thanriel went to Earth to tell her what was happening. In order to have a body on Earth, he borrowed energy from a human, who was left lying unconscious while he was on Earth."

"And Algamel's doing the same thing now?"

"That's my guess." Cal got up.

"How many fanes does he need to steal energy from to get a body?"

The expression on Cal's face didn't comfort me.

"Let's find out."

He strode towards the council chamber halfway down the corridor. I lagged behind, my heart beating harder in alarm. The last thing I wanted to do was stride into the room when Saldamia was engaged in a meeting with her councillors and tell her that her prized prisoners were on the loose, and that a pair of talvarrines had come to Fane and one of them had just put her guards and servants out of action.

But I didn't need to worry. Or at least not about that. Saldamia didn't jump to her feet and call for our capture the moment we walked in, because when we stepped into the room she was sleeping, just like everyone else around the broad table spread with maps and papers to help the council with their administration of fane business.

Cal strode inside, checking each of the councillors in turn. I followed more slowly and headed straight for Saldamia herself. She had fallen forward at her place at the head of the table, hair splayed around her. I pushed the strands back to see the bare hand and the side of her face that had been hidden beneath it. Her eyes were closed and her back was moving, a steady lift and drop, the papers beneath her shifting as they were disturbed by her breath.

She was oddly ordinary close-to, when she wasn't standing over me or forcing me to drink *somnaya*. She looked a lot like my mother. I stroked my hand over her bare fingers. While she slept, I could find something heavy and smash the slim fingers that had forced my mouth open and poured *somnaya* tincture into it; find a blade and ruin her looks with a single, fast stroke. I dropped her hair and stepped away,

122

fingers curling as though that would keep them safely out of the way. It wouldn't make any difference. It might hurt her, but it wouldn't make me feel any better. Or not for long. I looked up to Cal. "Someone has taken her ring."

He was checking on one of the councillors on the other side of the table, fingers pressed to her neck. He looked up at me. "What?"

"Saldamia isn't wearing her anima ring." I lifted her limp arm to show him. The finger that had previously been home to her ornate, glittering ring was now bare.

"Algamel took it from her?"

"I can't see her giving it up voluntarily, can you?" I stepped to the side, looking to see if I knew the fane sitting beside her and how she wore her anima crystal.

Cal stood behind a councillor, arms folded across his broad chest. "I really don't like the look of this." He looked around the room, taking in all the occupants. "They didn't even try to fight."

I shivered, then folded my fingers so my own anima crystal was safe and reached out with my elemental powers. Just like usual, they were feeble, but I could shift the papers in the middle of the table enough to reassure myself they were working as well as they always had.

A crash on the other side of the room made me jump. My eyes snapped up to see Cal glaring into the corner where a chair had been sent flying into the wall. He was testing himself, too. And he'd certainly passed.

I walked slowly around the table, checking each councillor for jewellery. Rings, armbands, necklaces. All that I found were pure metal. It seemed that each had been robbed of their anima key when they were knocked out, or perhaps robbed of them in order to knock them out. But none gave any sign that they'd fought over the matter.

"So Algamel can pass through doors, and he can knock out the entire council of Fane – along with servants and bodyguards – before any of them have time to act. How are we going to stop him?"

Cal's face tightened with determination. "We'll think of something."

He spoke so confidently I found myself nodding along before I realised how entirely outclassed we were by the talvarrine. "How long do you think we have before they wake up?" I spoke quietly, as though my voice might be enough to rouse them, although checking their hands and necks for anima crystals hadn't disturbed them in the minutes before.

"I don't think they will." Cal walked around the table until he was by my side. "Not until Algamel has what he came for – and not at all if what he wants is the anima keys."

My stomach hollowed at the idea. I stood up. The councillors were still slumped in their places. "Do you want to see if Keba's awake yet?"

He frowned. "Why would she be awake when no one else is?"

"I don't know, but – wouldn't you rather have her to help?"

His expression tightened. "Are you giving up already?"

His tone made agitation flare through me, even though that was mostly what I'd been hoping for. "No. But what am I supposed to do? She's the soldier."

Cal stared at the floor as he scuffed a foot. "Keba and I can fight but you – you might see something that will make a difference."

That was too big a change of mind for me to let it pass unchallenged. "You told me I was useless – a hallucinating druggie spouting nonsense. Why do you suddenly think a vision might be useful?" I shivered. I didn't like the idea of facing Algamel at all – much less the idea of collapsing in front of him while a vision gripped me.

He cleared his throat. "You're not useless. I got you wrong. I'm sorry."

I didn't understand why he'd changed his mind about me. I was still the same person I'd been yesterday. "Is this because I opened the gate?"

He shook his head. "You gave us warning when we were attacked at Tullan's house. You probably saved our lives."

"Except I didn't. You, Zan and I were captured. That's not much use."

"Those two minutes made all the difference. Keba and Tullan weren't captured. Which left them free to rescue us."

I shrugged. "A vision the night before would have been better. We might all have got away, then."

He smiled, tension leaving his face. "Yeah, life rarely cooperates like that. Something will always screw up what looks like perfection at the planning stage." His eyes glittered while he explained. "Look, it's the sentry's job to give warning of an attack. It's not the sentry's fault if the attacking forces turn out to be overwhelming."

I tried to understand his thought process. "So I was

a feeble dreamseer foreseeing rubbish, but now I've been of use to you—"

"No," he interrupted. "It's not being useful to *me*, it's being competent at what you do." He shrugged. "That's reasonable, isn't it?" Spots of pink appeared on his cheeks.

"But having visions is what a dreamseer does. I've had lots of them. You *saw* me have a vision – at my mother's funeral."

I'd never seen Cal look anything other than confident, even cocky. He positively squirmed. "I thought you were faking, okay? I thought it was all made up." He blew out a breath while I was too surprised to say a thing. "And I'm really sorry I got you all wrong, but right now we need to deal with Algamel."

"Okay, yes. Algamel."

He strode back out of the room and I followed. In the space of a moment, it seemed I'd gone from deserving Cal's contempt to gaining his respect. It was very strange. And oddly satisfying.

Chapter Fourteen

We tried every other room on that floor of the palace and found no one still awake.

Unfortunately, we also found no sign of Algamel.

"They have a myth on Earth that describes this situation perfectly," Cal told me.

"Do they?" I couldn't see how a story from Earth was going to help us now, but I'd try anything.

"A wicked witch casts a spell and everyone falls asleep for a hundred years until they're woken when a handsome prince kisses a beautiful princess."

When he said the words, my gaze tracked to his lips, even though we hardly fit that description. Just because he suddenly liked me, didn't mean he suddenly *liked* me. I wrenched my eyes away. "So Algamel's the wicked witch – are we just supposed to wait a hundred years?" Running away was quite appealing, but that wasn't Cal's style at all.

He scowled. "No, we find out exactly what we're dealing with – and then we deal with it." He started towards the door. I followed.

Then something exploded outside the palace.

We jumped, hunching defensively as whatever it was shook the walls so a cloud of plaster dust puffed from them.

We dashed to the nearest window. A figure, dim with distance but tall and dark-haired, stood in the middle of the grounds surrounding the palace. He was a long way away, but I recognised him from visions I'd had at Issaenaptra's prompting. Algamel, the talvarrine stranded on Earth who Issaenaptra had hoped would help her take over that world. He was oblivious to our observation as he spun around, raising a concealing cloud of sand around him.

He didn't send anything else flying towards the palace, so I didn't think he was trying to destroy it. The curtain of sand dropped abruptly to leave him standing in the middle of the plain, and I understood – just as Cal and I had done earlier, he was testing his powers. The crash we'd heard was because he'd sent a rock flying – I guessed – as far as he could manage. He was testing abilities that were new to him.

"That looks like a skin and bone being, not a creature of pure energy," I pointed out.

"That sounds like what Zan described on Earth: take our energy, take our form." Cal watched him, faced pressed close to the window. "For someone who's just discovered their abilities, he's not doing badly," he said, his tone slightly awed. Algamel had pried a rock the size of a room out of the ground and now lifted it high into the sky. The talvarrine's mouth was wide, showing white teeth, and I thought he was laughing. I guess it would be intoxicating to find out what you could do. If I could lift a rock that big, I'd be laughing too.

"Except he's stolen more than a hundred anima keys to get that strong. It's not really that impressive."

We watched Algamel toss a huge boulder aside using

the strength he'd stolen with the anima crystals that were probably stowed in the knapsack I could see hitched over his shoulders. It didn't land especially close to the palace but the thud still shook the building.

"Hmm, well, it's pretty impressive," I admitted.

Cal sighed. "We've got to stop him."

I backed away. "The two of us against that?"

He shrugged, shoulders hunched as he peered so close to the glass his breath fogged the surface. "Anyone's welcome to join in, but I can't see us fending off offers of help." He swiped the glass with his sleeve. "Do you think he knows we're here?" Then he corrected, "I don't mean *here* as in this room in particular, I mean, do you think he knows there are fanes he hasn't sent to sleep in the palace?"

"He came through the gate. He sent Keba to sleep. Why didn't he stop and steal our power then?"

"You, Tullan and Zan were unconscious. I was slumped on the floor and probably didn't look up to much. Keba must have seemed the only one with energy to steal. With Thanriel there, as well, maybe he wanted to get away as quickly as he could."

I peered out of the window alongside Cal. Algamel had now created another storm of sand and dust that obscured him from our sight. "So what do we do now?"

"We go after him."

I nodded. That's what I'd been afraid he'd say.

Algamel came to a stop, the debris he'd caught up around him settling back to the ground in a small, circular heap. Then he *bounded* straight towards the palace.

We ducked down instinctively, although it was ridiculous to suppose he might see us, tucked away and hidden behind a window as we were.

"What's he want now?" I hissed.

"I don't know," Cal replied.

I didn't really want an answer. My imagination was brimming over with fantastical, terrifying ideas: Algamel knew we were there by some strange interplay of fane and talvarrine powers that meant he could sense our heartbeats; he was going to test his fane powers by tearing the palace down, stone by stone; now he was sure of his strength he was going to kill everyone while they were powerless to stop him.

"We'll slip in behind him," Cal said.

I didn't have time to ask, "And do what?" before Cal wrenched open the window and climbed out.

He jumped twice his height down to the sand below and I followed with much less elegance, legs wobbling as I landed, knees buckling. I hoped that looked like weakness from opening the gate rather than the general dreamseer inability to control the elements elegantly.

Cal stepped forward but I waved him away. "I'm fine."

"Come on, then." He headed towards the ornate main doorway into the palace, gesturing me to follow.

Together, we slipped through the archway. We were just in time to catch sight of Algamel's back as he turned the corner into the stairwell. I wondered for a moment if he had got what he came for and was heading to the gate to return to Talvar. My heart pushed against my ribs for the time it took for me to wonder if we'd let him go without waking everyone he'd sent to sleep. Cal, with his upright sense of right and wrong, wouldn't let the talvarrine vanish without undoing the damage he'd done. If we could even stop him.

But when we reached the stairs we found he wasn't heading for the gate to get home, since he was going up rather than down.

Out of sight, we hurried to the stairwell, glancing cautiously up to ensure we remained unobserved before slipping as silently as we could after him. Algamel's footsteps scuffed above us as he kept moving.

We passed the corridor with the council chamber and he continued upwards, so Saldamia wasn't his target.

At the top, we hung back in shadows while Algamel strode down the corridor. He didn't glance aside or behind, doubtless considering himself alone but for sleeping fanes.

I looked at Cal as Algamel disappeared through the doorway to the record keeper's chamber. Cal kept his body safely behind the newel post in the centre of the spiral stairs from where he could see the door.

Faint noises reached us. "Is he looking for something – or someone?" I frowned, wishing I could see into the room.

Cal sniffed. "You're the dreamseer – can't you tell what he's doing?"

"It doesn't work like that." I remembered all the times I'd sat with a seeing glass in front of me while Issaenaptra breathed down my neck, using the window she'd commanded me to make to speak to Algamel. But all I'd done was enable them to talk – I couldn't read his mind, or see into his future.

The sound of something crashing to the floor made us jump. "That's enough," Cal muttered. "He wasn't welcome in the first place." He strode towards the half-open door. I cast a glance behind me down the stairs, wondering if it would be good or bad for someone to wake up and come and deal with Algamel so I didn't have to. Then I followed.

Another crash resounded in the room when I was halfway across the corridor and I darted forward. I could barely get in the door. Algamel and Cal faced each other, the air shields they'd conjured colliding in the centre of the room. That was the noise I'd heard – at the edges of their power, the wall of air rebounded against the bookcase-covered walls, dragging volumes from the shelves to clatter to the floor.

Cal kept gathering up the books and sending them flying towards Algamel, but as though he'd been using fane powers for years rather than minutes, the talvarrine stopped each one, flinging them back to Cal so they clattered to a stop midway between the two of them.

Cal's back was to me. Algamel, facing him, saw me. He smiled. A shiver trickled down my back. "The queen's dreamseer. Welcome!"

Cal looked back, his concentration on his shield faultless. "Stay back, Deena."

Algamel grinned. "That's right. Stay away from the nasty talvarrine. You don't know what he's capable of." His teeth flashed white. "Or perhaps you do."

Cal was shaking with effort but Algamel had energy to spare for chat. I stared, paralysed by what he might say about what I'd done while Cal was there to hear.

"Wake them up," I managed. "Leave us alone."

Algamel threw back his head and laughed, his pale throat working. He straightened and glared at me. "I don't have what I came for yet."

I was about to ask what more he wanted – then it was too late. Algamel spun around, sent a blast of power towards Cal that sent him reeling backwards, and before he or I could recover, Algamel had thrown the window open and bounded out.

Cal leaned over, hands on knees, gasping from the exertion. I reached the window in time to see Algamel vanish, what could only be his second bound from here sending him beyond the horizon. I'd never seen a fane move like that, and I wondered if I'd be able to do the same if I grabbed a bunch of anima crystals instead of using just my tiny one. Except Algamel wasn't a fane. Talvarrine and fane power together was clearly a potent combination.

I turned back to Cal. "What did he want from here? Did you see?"

He shook his head. "He stuffed something into his pocket, but it could have been anything."

The room – not unexpectedly – looked as though a small storm had spun through it. It could take weeks to put the books and papers back in their places – and even then we'd need the currently-sleeping record keeper in order to have a hope of knowing what was missing.

Cal reached my shoulder and looked out of the window. "Did you see what direction he went in?"

"He was heading north, but there's a lot of north out there."

Cal cursed, then headed towards the door.

"Aren't we going after him?"

Cal shook his head, hurrying down the stairs so I had to nearly run to keep up with him. "Not yet. Thanriel can tell us exactly what we're dealing with. Then we might have a chance of stopping Algamel."

*

Thanriel looked up when we hurried back to the gateroom. He was still so bright it was hard to look at him, but I started to see details of the talvarrine beneath the light. I could make out expressions. He looked past us and his shoulders sagged when he saw we were alone.

Cal summarised the last ten minutes. "Algamel has knocked out everyone in the palace and stolen their anima keys. I'm not bounding after him blind. What do you know about what he plans to do?"

Thanriel settled back down. Zan's hand was held in both of his, cradled in his lap in a pool of warm light. He nodded. "I must tell you some of my past, but I will be as quick as I can."

Cal folded his arms. "That would be appreciated."

"After I went to Earth and helped Zan cross to Fane, I never returned to Talvar."

"Where have you been?"

"Trapped between the worlds. I left Earth, but I couldn't return to Talvar. It took a while for me to realise that was deliberate. The guardian who sent me to Earth did not expect me to come back. Nor want me to come back."

I just watched. Cal gave a tight nod.

Thanriel drew in a deep breath. "He knew I would not fit back because having been set free to go to Earth, I would see what he had done to me. To all of

134

us."

"And what has he done to you?" Cal asked.

"Enslaved us."

"How?" I asked.

"I come to you here as a being of pure energy. That is – I think – how talvarrines have always travelled through the gates to other worlds. But on Talvar we have physical forms. The guardian found a way to split our physical forms from our energy. He hoards our energy and feeds from it and our physical forms become shells."

Cal nodded again, a short, military nod to show he understood. "And Algamel wants to overthrow this guardian and set the talvarrines free?"

"Yes."

"He's stolen our anima keys. Is that how he plans to do it?"

Thanriel shook his head. "He will need more energy than that. The guardian has access to an array of crystals. Algamel will need a crystal of his own. A full, unbroken crystal."

He'd headed north. There was a lot of north out there, but now I was sure where he was heading. "Do you mean he wants to use the Light of Fane?"

"Yes."

Cal made a scoffing noise, then swung to me. "The Light of Fane? That's a myth."

I regarded him in surprise. "It's no such thing. How else did we all get our elemental powers?"

"Oh, come on, it's a story only children would believe. The fabled crystal from which our animas were taken and then it was placed on the Isle of Fire – which doesn't exist either – for safekeeping."

"The Isle of Fire exists. It's in the Northern Mountains." I blinked at the shock on his face. "Is that something only dreamseers know?"

"It's not real," he insisted, then stopped, watching my face as though looking for signs of deception. "*Is* it real? Do the Isle and the Light of Fane really exist?"

Thanriel interrupted. "Algamel has come here to steal it. I have no idea how he knows it is here, but if he believes it, I am sure it is real."

"Of course it is," I agreed.

I could picture the book containing the story that I had buried myself in so many times in childhood – how could I have guessed it wasn't common knowledge?

"Algamel must be stopped before he gets the crystal," Thanriel told Cal.

I shared a glance with Cal then turned to Thanriel. "You didn't see how powerful he's become. We're not going to reach anything before Algamel does."

Cal cleared his throat. "Do we need to get the crystal before him?" He shrugged at my expression. "It's not like we've been using the Light of Fane ourselves, is it?" He turned to Thanriel. "And it sounds like your guardian needs to be stopped." He held out his hands. "Why don't we let him take the Light to Talvar and sort things out there?"

Thanriel shook his head. "The crystals on Talvar have been corrupted. That is why the guardian has been able to use them to ensnare us. Your Fane crystal could be destroyed forever if Algamel takes it."

"Isn't that a chance worth taking?"

"It is a risk you do not need to take," Thanriel said. "Now the gate is made to Talvar, I can return. I will awaken the sleeping talvarrines and we can work together to defeat the guardian. I would not have you risk your Light."

Cal thought for a moment, then nodded. "All right. We'll go after Algamel."

"We'll never catch him up," I pointed out.

Cal made an impatient noise. "You're far too quick to accept defeat, Deena. We're going to have to work on that."

A strange feeling ran through me when he said that, like it was a promise we were going to spend enough time together for him to persuade me to his way of thinking, insane though it was.

"Why don't we just stay here and intercept Algamel on his way back? He's got to get back to Talvar with his new crystal, after all."

"No, he—"

Cal interrupted Thanriel's protest. "We don't have to catch him up, we can get to the Light of Fane before him and hide it somewhere he won't find it."

I shook my head. "You saw him, Cal. We're not going to reach the Isle first."

"Oh, I think we might. Can't you guess what he took from the record keeper's room?"

I shrugged, wondering at the change of topic.

"I can't be sure, but I'd be willing to bet it was a map. Now, given that the Isle of Fire is a myth, I don't think it'll be marked on whatever map he found. Which means he'll have to search the whole of the Northern Mountains. By contrast, you know where the Isle is, don't you?"

"If the stories are true, I do."

"Right. So unless we're incredibly unlucky, we can

find the Light and take it to safety while he's still blundering around in the mountains."

"Where are we going to take it to?"

"I will help you conceal it," Thanriel told us.

"There." Cal spoke as though that sorted the matter. "Are you ready to go?"

"You'll be quicker without me," I pointed out. "You've seen me bound."

"Yeah, but you're the map."

I sighed. I could have told him where to go and sent him off alone, but I didn't. I wanted to go with him. I didn't like to think what that meant.

Chapter Fifteen

Algamel had crossed the Gillabar Plain in seconds. I took eight bounds in all, Cal leagues ahead of me after a couple of bounds because he'd forgotten how slow I was – pretending he wasn't impatient when he had to wait for me.

Once we were past the plains, Fane changed. Threads of green alleviated the dry orange ground where the planet had started to recover from the damage the gates had caused.

Algamel was so far ahead and moving so fast we didn't even see him, but we stuck to our own route and hoped he didn't know exactly where to go.

Out of the dusty brown of the plains rose the vibrant greens of Valderia, where the threads of green grew more prolific. Cal landed on the outskirts of the town a few moments before I did.

"We'll get something to eat here," he said. I nodded and we bounded closer. The farming town had grown up around the spring that fed the river Paengan, and although the river had dried up to nothing during the last century, the spring was sufficient to keep the reduced community alive and fed.

We'd come to a stop on the edge of the town's fields. Some were empty, the black of turned soil waiting for spring, but others held winter crops of *solla* and *vett-roots*, and all were edged with thick hedges heavy with *filla* nuts and cornered with majestic *iska* trees like sentries. On a bright day like this, I would have expected the fields to be full of fanes. The nuts needing harvesting before the birds took them, if nothing else. Instead, they were deserted.

"Do you think Algamel—"

"We'll soon find out." Cal cut me off and strode along a path between the hedgerows that lead to the centre of the town.

That, too, was deserted. A look around the nearest house confirmed our fears. The citizens hadn't had chance to flee. They probably hadn't known they should until it was too late. They were all there, all sleeping. Cal checked for longer than I did – hope; or maybe just thoroughness. His expression grew tauter when he tried yet another building and found nothing to his liking inside.

"Valderia is a usual stop-off if you're travelling from Gillabar to the north. It doesn't mean he knows where to go."

"No. I just wished we knew where he was for certain." Cal's expression grew speculative, like he wanted to suggest I have a little vision and see what Algamel was doing. Perhaps a vision *would* help, but I couldn't force one. I shivered, glad there was no *somnaya* tincture to hand. I wouldn't be tempted, but Cal might.

"We should keep going. We have to get to the Light of Fane before he does." We didn't need a vision to know that Algamel finding it would be a disaster.

Cal was looking at me strangely. I *knew* the idea of a

140

vision was turning over in his head even if he didn't say so. "Then we shouldn't waste time here." He ducked into one of the shops that edged the town square, reappearing a moment later with a loaf of bread and a cup of water. "Eat this. Quickly." Thrusting them into my hands, he made a second visit to the shop to find food for himself.

As soon as he'd finished his meal, Cal thrust the cup into his pocket. He was still wiping crumbs from his mouth as he spoke. "Time to go."

*

The rest of the day passed in endless, silent bounding. The changing landscape marked how far we'd come; green fading to orange and then re-greening the ground once more. I was stronger than I'd been just a few days before, but as the light faded to dusk, I wondered if Cal was going to insist we kept bounding all night.

We reached another settlement, a tiny village of half a dozen houses. Algamel had been here, too. Every fane lay sleeping, although there was no trace of the talvarrine.

I thought Cal was thinking the same as me – that it was time to stop for the night. I thought he was looking for a place to sleep when he ducked into the last house on the road that ran through the middle of the village, and when he came out again with a rolled-up blanket under each arm, I nearly wept.

"We have to rest," I said, meaning that *I* had to rest. Who knew what energy source Cal was using; he didn't seem to feel fatigue.

"We can get a bit further before the light goes completely."

141

"And then what? Sleep under a rock?

"If he doesn't stop for the night, he'll be even further ahead. We can't risk him finding the Light first."

"But if we don't rest, we'll be in no state to take the Light anywhere when we do reach it."

"We can't stop, Deena. We can't afford to waste any time."

I nearly snapped that he could go ahead and I'd catch up in the morning, but the words never formed. I caught an expression in his fiery eyes that only existed for a moment before he blinked it away. Fear. Unfamiliar and unwelcome – to Cal, at least.

I forced a smile. "Okay. A little further." I pushed off first, Cal only a moment behind.

*

When it was so dark it was difficult to see where we were landing, we finally stopped in the shelter of a low cliff. The foothills of the Northern Mountains loomed to the left of us, tops silvered in the last sliver of moonlight, their bulk black against the distant midnight sky. We'd be there early in the morning.

"Where exactly are we heading?" Cal was staring towards the mountains. He looked round when I didn't reply. "Where is the Isle of Fire?"

"It's on Mother Payluria." I named the largest mountain in the range, which filled the sky behind us.

"Where on Mother Payluria?"

I tried to remember the stories. "High up." I could see from Cal's face that he didn't consider that to be enough detail. "I guess we just look. Fire should be obvious on a mountainside. That still narrows it down more than Algamel knows."

142

Cal grunted.

I unrolled my blanket, finding as sheltered a spot as I could. Hunger gnawed at me, although there wasn't much I could do about that. I used my elemental powers to pull water from the air around us to fill the cup Cal had given me earlier. I drank it down and drew another cupful. I'd hoped the water would fill my stomach and dampen the worst of the hunger, but it just changed the sensation from an ache to nausea.

Then heat climbed up my spine and the pain in my belly became a lurch of dismay – in the darkness I hadn't noticed the loss of colour so I hadn't realised what was happening. I closed my eyes, but that was every bit as helpful in driving away my oncoming vision as it had ever been.

*

"Where Payluria meets Challiguran," were the words that brought me back to reality. I was lying on the blanket I'd laid out minutes earlier. Cal was sitting, cross-legged, next to me. At least he hadn't grabbed hold of me this time.

I sat up, stretching to ground myself. "Was that clear enough for you?"

"Perfectly comprehensible. Well done, Honourable Dreamseer," Cal said, his voice dry. He glanced at me, then turned away, returning his attention to the mountains. He cleared his throat. "See? Keba wouldn't have been able to do that."

"I saw the Isle of Fire." I usually remembered nothing but impressions, but that sight hung clear in my memory. I smiled. "It was beautiful."

"That's good. I'd hate to be heading to a dungheap on the say-so of a mad woman."

Cal's voice stayed light, improbably teasing, but I still felt a pang as his words punched my heart. Mad woman. Yeah, that would be me.

"We'd better sleep, it's late."

Cal moved off my blanket to unroll his own. I wrapped mine around me, snuggling into the shelter of the rock. Cal became a lump an arm's span away.

"Has anyone ever tried to understand what your visions actually are?"

"There's a lot of conjecture, nothing definite."

"And? What do you think?"

I studied the arc of dark sky overhead, the darkness prevented from being absolute by the sliver of the only still-visible moon on the far horizon. "The explanation put forward most often is that we can tap into some sort of an energy which Fane itself projects which connects everything in time and space, so we can see things that are far away in space, and we can see things that happened long ago or which haven't happened yet."

Cal said nothing. I was mildly surprised he had nothing scathing to reply to that.

"There is another explanation, of course," I added.

"Hmm?"

"That we're a bunch of addict druggies, all we see are hallucinations, and the people with us when we make our random pronouncements force meaning onto our words for their own benefit." My heart beat fast when I finished that little speech. I knew what people said about us, but until now I hadn't realised how much resentment I carried about it.

"Yes, but I think we can discount that idea now, can't we?" There was a noise and he rolled over to face me. "You haven't had a fix for several days, but you're still falling over and spouting rubbish."

From his tone I thought that was a joke, but my mouth dried any reply I might have made. We weren't friends. I wasn't Zan, who he definitely would be joking and laughing with. I cleared my throat. "I thought you said I made sense."

"Vaguely. I wanted to keep your spirits up."

Again he was joking, but my chest reacted like it had received a blow. I took a breath, tipping my face to the sky. "Don't patronise me, soldier," I snapped, as sharp as I could manage.

"No insult intended. Maybe I was trying to keep my own spirits up, too."

I wanted to scoff at that, but I remembered the fear in his eyes earlier. I shifted, tucking my hands beneath my chin as my muscles relaxed. Sleep wasn't far away. "There's nothing to worry about," I told him. "We'll find the crystal." I lowered my voice, mocking myself as I pronounced, "I have *foreseen* it."

"That's all right, then." I heard the smile in Cal's voice.

I was more surprised to realise, just before I fell into oblivion, that I was smiling, too.

Chapter Sixteen

I awoke with the dawn, but Cal was earlier. A fire was already roasting the bodies of a couple of creatures Cal had managed to trap – lizards, I thought, from the shape of the meat presented to me a couple of minutes later. Whatever they were, they were delicious.

An hour after breakfast and we were in the mountains. Payluria was the tallest mountain in the northern range. Even if my vision hadn't been clear, as we bounded into the shadow of the mountains, I'd have known where we were supposed to go. Cal dropped from his bound beside me, rubbing his stomach.

"You can feel it, too," I said.

He looked at me blankly.

I nodded to where his hand was resting above his navel. "I think our crystals can sense the proximity of the Light of Fane." I splayed my fingers. "My ring hasn't stopped vibrating for the last ten minutes." I looked uphill to where Mother Payluria split from Challiguran, creating a valley halfway up the mountainside.

"Why does no one know about this place?" Cal looked around and I followed his gaze. It was green here, lush and beautiful, more so than anywhere we'd bounded through from the palace. Everyone should have come here once the destruction took hold, escaping dry and blighted Fane.

"Hard to build a town on a slope like this," I pointed out. I ignored the fact that it would provide an ideal home for a couple of dreamseers, well away from prying eyes.

"I suppose so." Cal huffed, looking up at the mountains beside us, rubbing his stomach where he could clearly feel his anima. "I'm still going to be surprised if we really find the Isle of Fire. I thought it was a myth – and that we all had anima crystals just because we did."

I folded my arms. "Maybe we forgot."

"Forgot?"

"Once we had our crystals, we could do anything we wanted. Once you've got used to power, it's easy to forget how you came by it."

Cal humphed. "You don't forget how you came by power if you want to keep it. I'm surprised no one thought of the advantages of possessing this place."

Like Saldamia, or Issaenaptra. "Then we should be glad it got forgotten about."

Two bounds higher up the mountains, we stopped. Mother Payluria was at our backs while the smaller crest of Challiguran peaked on the other side of the plateau that linked them. Greenery clothed the ground beneath our feet and a dozen brooks cascaded down the mountains, creating a cacophony of sound and throwing spray into the air. Bright birds flitted into the sky, jewel-bright sparks of colour against the blue, adding their calls to the rush of water. The air was filled with the sweet scent of the flowering plants that

147

grew along the sides of the cascades. This was Fane at its most beautiful, before the gates to Earth wrought destruction.

The Isle of Fire lay in the middle of the plateau before us, maybe a quarter of a league distant. My anima ring throbbed against my fingers as though it sensed the Light of Fane. I covered my ring with my other hand, breathing deeply while I drank in the sight. The Isle of Fire was the most beautiful thing I'd ever seen.

The Isle itself floated, as its name suggested, in the middle of a lake of fire that filled the plateau. The surface was covered with greenery – bushes and trees that shouldn't be possible with fiery heat only steps away. Somewhere there was the crystal from which all our anima keys had been created.

The flames leapt high in the air, but there was no smoke and clearly no danger to the island – the lush, tall trees in the centre of the Isle were unaffected, birds flitting between their branches carelessly. The dreamseer stories said that the Isle of Fire had been created by fanes thousands of years before, when we first gained power over nature, and I didn't doubt the stories now. It was beautiful – but its very existence was unnatural.

And Cal was unnaturally quiet. He hadn't said a thing since we'd stopped. I turned. He was sitting on a rock, hands on his knees as he breathed deeply as though he couldn't pull enough air into his lungs. Alerted by my movement, he raised his head. He looked exhausted, his sparkling eyes dimmed to dullness.

"Are you all right?"

He shrugged and looked up at the side of the mountain. "How much further?"

If he hadn't looked so bad I would have assumed that was a joke. I stepped aside so his view was uninterrupted. "We're here." I considered the stretch of ground, around a quarter of a league, between us and the fire surrounding the Isle. "Nearly."

Cal scowled. "What do you mean we're here? Where's the Isle?"

Warmth drained from my face. I flung my arm towards the flames. "It's right there."

He followed the line of my hand, gaze questing when it should have instantly landed on the Isle.

"It's there, Cal." My voice was low, robbed by sudden fear. "It's right in front of you." His frown grew deeper. "Tell me you can see it, Cal."

His eyes raked the scene in front of him, then he turned to me. That expression of fear was back. Or maybe it was my fear, reflected back at me. "I see rocks and grass, Deena. What am I missing?" He raised a hand to brush his hair off his forehead, scratching at his skin in puzzlement.

"It's there. It's right there." I realised that wasn't very helpful. "Where the mountains meet is a plateau. It must be half a league across. The Isle of Fire is in the middle and it's just like the name suggests – there's, well, it's a lake of fire, real flames, with the Isle in the middle. The Isle is green and beautiful, as though it's surrounded by water, not fire." I stopped describing it, my words trailing off. "Cal, you look dreadful. What's wrong?"

He huffed a sound that might have been a laugh. "Apart from the fact that I seem to be the one hallucinating now?"

It was more likely I was seeing things that weren't there, than that Cal wasn't seeing things that were. Except that I didn't feel sick, and everything was in bright, beautiful colour. I took a step towards the Isle of Fire. "It's there. I can feel the heat, Cal. It's really there."

"I don't... I can't..."

I turned at Cal's confused reply. He slithered down the rock into a heap on the ground, head hanging forward, chin against his chest.

"Cal!" I crouched at his side. "Cal? Can you hear me?"

He lifted his head. "I'm fine, I'm... tired." He sounded surprised, as though it was a weakness he found difficult to apply to himself.

I glanced towards the Isle of Fire, then back to Cal, whose head was nodding again. I guess we'd just found out why the Light and the Isle of Fire had fallen into folklore – no ordinary fane could come close to the Isle.

"Cal?"

This time, he didn't even raise his head, mumbling into his chest, "I'll be fine. Give me a minute."

I made my decision – the only one possible. I wasn't a healer, and if I carried Cal back down the mountainside, I'd only have to return for the Light of Fane later. That was still our priority. My only option was to get to the crystal before Algamel, like we'd planned.

And it was only half a league. It should have been the work of a moment to reach the Isle and secure the Light of Fane. A single bound should have taken me safely over the flames to the middle of the Isle. Except that when I pushed, all I did was lift onto my tiptoes. I tried again. And went nowhere.

I could no longer bound. The crystal in my ring was buzzing so hard it shivered against my skin. Whatever power the Isle used to keep itself hidden from ordinary fanes, this must be what it could do to dreamseers.

It was a shame Cal was barely conscious, so he couldn't appreciate the sight of me not accepting defeat. If I had to walk, then I'd walk. The ground leading to the Isle of Fire looked level but it wasn't. I stumbled and twisted on hidden rocks and roots. The birds in the trees around me chattered as though they were laughing at my struggles. I kept the fire in sight and didn't let myself look back at Cal. I was on my own, but there was nothing new in that. I could manage alone; dreamseers always did.

And then I could go no further, held back by the ferocity of the flames that surrounded the Isle, my skin tightening in the crackling heat. If I couldn't bound I'd never get past the flames to the Isle itself.

I sank onto the rim of rock that prevented the lake of fire from spilling over onto the plateau and looked across to the impossibly green island in the middle of the lake of fire. How could I reach the crystal? How could I get to the Isle?

I refused to look back. Cal couldn't help. I'd figure this out. I glanced around, checking that I was truly alone. Algamel had to be somewhere in this huge range of mountains, although I hoped he was nowhere close by. I scuffed a foot against the ground, loosening a pebble that I bent to pick up. I threw it up and caught it several times, then I stretched my hand, about to fling the pebble into the fire when I thought better of it. Opening my fist, I used my elemental powers to lift the pebble into the air, slightly surprised to find I could do so. The proximity of the crystal hadn't destroyed my abilities, it had changed them. As I sent the pebble whistling through the air towards the flames, I realised some of my abilities were stronger than before.

Rising to my feet, I held out my hand, concentrating all my strength on pushing the heat out of the flames, driving them away from me. After a long, astonished moment, the flames immediately beneath my hand simmered down to nothing, revealing bare, grey rock at the bottom of the lake. This was my chance.

Forcing my hand to remain steady, I took a breath and stepped into the lake of fire.

The bottom surface of the lake, where it showed between the flames that still danced level with my shoulders where my control ran out, was warm beneath my feet. But it was warm as though it had baked beneath Fane's hot sun all day, not as though it had spent the day burning. It was also bare – giving nothing for the flames to feed off. But the crackle and the heat showed that didn't matter. They still burned, with a ferocity that would keep away all but the most determined – or foolish.

This was power beyond anything I'd experienced before. I wondered at the fanes who'd created it – what had they been protecting the crystal from? I pushed cold air ahead of me, shuffling forward with careful steps when the flames died down.

After a couple of steps, the fire flared again behind

me, springing to life with a roar that made me jump. I carried a circle of cool through the burning lake. Sweat broke out down my back, and it wasn't just due to the flames around me. If I lost concentration... if a vision gripped me, I'd be dead before I hit the ground.

But my visions left me alone. Five minutes later, I stepped onto the lush Isle and relaxed. The flames jumped hot behind my back and I stepped further towards the trees, my anima crystal humming as though excited to be nearing our destination.

My footsteps trod slowly through the low undergrowth, cautious and quiet. This felt like a place that should be hushed. The birds I'd seen earlier had grown still. No animals moved or called to each other and an eerie quiet descended. I shivered and pressed on. It was as though something awe-inspiring – or something plain awful – had happened here, and its trace lingered on.

I pushed through undergrowth towards the crystal. So low as to be almost inaudible was a throbbing hum, echoed by the sensation of tingling from the anima in my ring. The Light of Fane.

The silence that had held so far dissipated, a breeze moving the leaves restlessly overhead. I pushed faster. Branches and twigs grabbed at my clothes and slapped my face. I shivered, trying not to be fanciful and suppose they were trying to keep me away from the crystal. Why would it make itself known to me if I wasn't supposed to reach it?

With a final stumble on a rock hidden beneath the grass, I reached a clearing where the trees and shrubs fell away to leave a rough semi-circle of bare ground.

The crystal lay in the middle of the clearing. It was

the most spectacular thing I'd ever seen, a clear shell about the size of my head filled with shining colours, writhing around each other below the surface like something living.

I crouched down, transfixed by the glowing lustre of the colourful facets. This was what Algamel needed to destroy the talvarrine ruler. Except that he'd never get his hands on it. Cal and I would make sure of that. I tugged the sash from around the waist of my tunic, spreading it on the bare ground beside the crystal. I nudged the crystal into the middle of the sash then gathered the ends, twisting the material and wrapping it back to front to make a bag I could carry back – to Cal and to the palace, and then to whatever hiding place we chose.

I pulled the loop I'd made over my body, resting it over my shoulder so the wrapped fabric containing the crystal settled on my other hip. The faceted crystal seemed to throb very slightly as though it were alive, or it held something alive in its centre. The anima crystal on my finger pulsed in unison. There was no doubt that my crystal and the Light of Fane were made of the same material and had the same powers. Having the crystal close felt right. I wanted to touch it. I wanted to see what I was capable of with a crystal like this instead of my tiny anima key. But there wasn't time for that. We had to get the Light of Fane to safety – then I could examine it.

I returned to the lake. My fingers shook as I extended my hand, fearful that I wouldn't be able to control the flames this time – that the fire would somehow know I'd stolen the crystal and wouldn't let me leave.

But if anything, I could control the elements with even more precision now. The circle of cold calm around me was wider, my composure stronger. The crystal bounced steadily against my hip as I walked. I had the strangest sensation that it was pleased to be on the move, that it wanted to go with me.

Cal was fully unconscious when I reached the plateau. I knelt to check. He was breathing, but unresponsive. I straightened, watching him, blowing out a breath as I considered what to do. Perhaps with my new, stronger abilities, I would be able to carry him and bound back to the palace where we could all decide...

"Thank you!"

I whirled round as the loud voice startled me out of my thoughts.

Algamel stood close by.

I gasped and took a step away from him, crowding closer to Cal. With the whole of the Northern Mountains to search, Algamel had still found us – and the Light of Fane. "Don't come any closer," I told him, my hand resting protectively on the fabric at my hip and the cargo it held.

He grinned, teeth gleaming like a *snarvell*. "I'll be gone as soon as you hand over the crystal." He took a step closer and I instinctively moved back to maintain the distance between us. I was pressed against the rock beside Cal with nowhere else to go.

"I won't give you the Light of Fane. You will have to manage without it," I replied.

Algamel laughed. "'The Light of Fane'? How sweet, you named it." He drew water from the air and flung it at my face, laughing. "That crystal belongs with me more than it does with you fanes. It came from a long way away." He grinned to see my expression. "Your stories don't tell you that, do they?"

I frowned. My hand rested on the Light of Fane, the swirl of its power noticeable even through its fabric wrapping. The talvarrine was trying to distract me so he could snatch it. I noticed the grasses around my feet shift and sigh counter to the breeze. If he couldn't distract me, he'd use force.

"Of course the Light of Fane belongs here." But faced with his jubilant certainty, I wasn't so sure.

"You were nothing until the talvarrine people visited your planet. We gave you the power to control your world – and now you will give me back that power." He sketched a mocking bow. "I regret your loss, but I need it more than you do." He stretched and the trees strained around him, creaking with the strength of his power. He clapped his hands and a shaft of lightning split the sky above his head.

Instinct flung a shield into the space around me and Cal to keep Algamel two steps away. I was pleased with my reactions, but the talvarrine just laughed. "Do you really think that will stop me?" He stepped to the side and I shifted my shield to keep it between me and him. "I know you don't want me here. I agree I don't belong here. Give me the crystal and I'll return to Talvar." His expression darkened and he took another step. My shield wobbled. I forced it to stay steady. "I will not go without the crystal – there would be no point to that. I've waited a long time, and now the power to do what I must is within reach. I will not give up."

"The Light of Fane could be destroyed by what you

want to do. There are other ways. Thanriel—"

Algamel laughed. "Poor Thanriel wants to save everyone. He lacks the stomach to destroy the guardian. He will fail because he is weak. I will do what must be done. And you won't stop me."

"The Light of Fane belongs here. I won't give it to you."

The air crackled against the shield I'd made, its surface rippling as Algamel tried to push through. He watched me coldly, the expression in his dark eyes making the hairs at the back of my neck rise. I held back the impulse to shudder, determined not to let him see a reaction. "Oh, there are many other ways to get the crystal. Will you compel me to destroy things to demonstrate?"

The urge to tremble rippled across my shoulders. I clenched my teeth to hold it back. If I grabbed Cal's arm, would I have the strength to lift him and bound far and fast enough to escape Algamel?

His eyes settled on my sash bag. "I will have the crystal." He took another precise, dancer's step towards me. I moved so as to keep the Light of Fane turned away from him.

"No."

Algamel smiled and the need to shiver twitched at my spine again. His expression became focused. He was directing his new power towards the outcome he wanted. I wasn't sure what that was; I didn't feel any effects.

Then I realised, and I knew why Cal was unconscious rather than delirious the way I'd left him. "You can't send me to sleep like the others. I'm a dreamseer, our powers work differently." I wasn't sure what it was about being a dreamseer that meant he couldn't send me to sleep, but I was glad of it.

He grinned that nasty smile again. "Oh, I only need a glance at you to know I can't control you like I have these weak fanes. But are you sure about your ability to defy me? You didn't even know where your crystal came from. Your ignorance will be your undoing."

"No!" Too late, I realised Algamel had distracted me after all. The talvarrine leaped forward, grabbed Cal's tunic and lifted him as though he weighed nothing, then dodged back out of reach. His careful steps had been deliberate – in matching them I'd moved my shield so that it remained between me and him – but not between him and Cal.

Algamel turned, smiling that nasty, cold smile. "You want him back? Then give me the crystal."

"Never."

He didn't respond, just stood smiling at me with Cal dangling from the cloth gathered in his fist. "This one came a long way with you. He must care a lot. Are you equally concerned about him?" Algamel twisted his hand so that Cal flopped from side-to-side. "If I damage this one, will you care?"

Heat rose in my face. "I care about all of them." I evaded the question, surprised to find it was true. The sleeping group around the grand table in the council chamber came to mind. Even them. I didn't even want Saldamia to come to harm, although I wouldn't care if she was sent to the other side of Fane with no chance of return.

Algamel pulled Cal closer, one arm around him so he could turn the unconscious body towards me, his face pressed cheek-to-cheek with Cal's. With his free hand, Algamel squeezed Cal's face, adopting a strange tone as though Cal were his puppet. "All of them?" He waggled Cal's chin. "Not just me?" He pulled at Cal's cheeks to tug the corners of his mouth down. Then he released his hand and Cal fell to the ground with a thud, limbs thrown wide on impact.

I cried out in alarm. Algamel looked up sharply and grinned. "Soft-hearted. And weak." He took a step closer. I took a step back. He stopped, a smile quirking his mouth as though it amused him to see my distaste. "The difference between you and me is that I will do anything to get what I want. If you aren't so ruthless, you may as well give in to my demands now."

Was I mistaken, or were threats all I'd heard for the last month? No, they were all I'd heard my whole life. "You forgot to say please," I snarled.

Algamel threw back his head and laughed, the sound jolting my pulse and causing a hard knob of defiance to form behind my ribs. The laughter stopped abruptly and Algamel's face twisted in a sneer. "I've never said 'please' in my entire existence."

I folded my arms, the sensation in my chest making me bold – and maybe stupid. "And look where it's got you – stranded on an alien planet, having to borrow power from the locals because you can't do anything on your own."

Algamel looked aside, down at the ground where his foot was standing on a corner of the unconscious Cal's tunic. "Oh, I still have enough power to get what I want. Because *you* can be compelled much more easily than *I* can." He leaned down and lazily picked up Cal once more. Hot fury surged through me again.

He addressed me over his lifeless burden. "I have

left everyone unharmed so far. They're asleep, but they will suffer no lasting damage. I need not continue to be so forbearing. I could tear this one limb from limb. When his life's blood is staining the ground around us, will you still say you won't do as I tell you?"

My breath shortened. "Put him down. Carefully this time."

Those cold black eyes met mine. "No." He lifted one of Cal's unresisting hands. "I could break each bone in his body. Do you know how many bones there are in a fane's body?" He waved Cal's left hand towards me and my breath caught in my throat. "This one seems to have lost four already. How clumsy."

"Put him down," I repeated, my voice cold in contrast to the heat of fury climbing through me.

His dark eyes gleamed malice. He ignored my command. "That still leaves plenty for me to play with. I could break them all and then return him to wakefulness. He might not be delighted by that outcome."

"No!" I shook my head, trying to make sense of him. "What sort of a monster are you, that you would do that to someone?"

Algamel's eyes narrowed as though he was struggling to understand the question. He glanced down at Cal as though ... as though he were a bundle of clothes ready for washing. "He is nothing to me. Why should I care for him?"

"Because he's a sentient creature like you. Because... because there's no *need* to harm him."

Algamel focused on me again, waiting for my next words.

I could hardly see him through the anger that

blurred my vision. The talvarrines were just as bad as fanes. Was there no end to the atrocities we'd commit to get our way?

I looked into Algamel's dark, careless eyes and let my fury ebb. I could bound away, but Algamel would follow. There was only one way to be rid of this creature and his unpleasant threats. "You don't have to harm him because you're right. I can be compelled more easily than you can. You can have the Light of Fane."

He dropped Cal to the ground again with a thud that made me wince. Algamel faced me, but didn't come any closer. I was pleased to see that small sign that he was, if not afraid, then at least cautious of me.

"But I will have something in return."

He raised his brows, his eyes fixed on the Light of Fane at my hip rather than on me. "You must give me the anima keys you stole. Fane must be returned to normal."

I slipped the bag over my head and held the crystal in both hands in front of me. Through the material, I could feel it pulsing. I wondered if it had any idea of what was happening, if it knew the use Algamel planned to make of it. If it knew it was in danger.

Algamel lifted his eyes to my face, a mocking smile tugging the corners of his mouth. He inclined his head in a bow, dark hair falling around his ears. "I agree to your demand, dreamseer. If you give me the crystal you are guarding, I solemnly promise I will leave Fane as though I had never been here." To prove his intention, he shrugged the knapsack off his back and threw it to land on the ground at my feet.

I stepped forward, my foot pressing onto the fabric

so he couldn't snatch it back. "Agreed." I placed my sash bag into Algamel's waiting hand. He curled the parcel into the crook of his arm. Then he pushed off, high in the air within a moment.

I picked up the knapsack carefully, then ripped it open. I'd half-expected a double-cross, but Algamel had kept his word. I was greeted by the glitter of hundreds of anima keys, the rings and bangles and pendants slithering against each other as the bag moved. He'd returned all he'd stolen, as agreed. Perhaps he wasn't entirely irredeemable.

"What the hell just happened?"

If I had any doubt that it was Algamel who had sent Cal to sleep, it vanished when he sat up, then groaned and dropped back down as if he'd thought better of the action.

I closed the knapsack and turned my attention to Cal. "I got the Light of Fane, but then Algamel took it." I lifted the knapsack. "But I got all the anima keys back that he'd stolen. I'm sorry if the Light is damaged when he takes it to Talvar, but like you said, we weren't using it." I watched Cal's face as the truth of that sank in. "Moons, it's really over."

Cal sat up, carefully this time. "We need to get back to the palace and tell Thanriel what's happened. And we still need to get the animas back to everyone." He reached round to rub what was clearly a sore spot on his back. "I feel like I've been run over by a herd of *bozars*."

"I think you'll have some bruises to show for this journey."

He frowned. "I barely remember a thing." He looked around. "Last thing I knew we were further

162

down the mountain than this."

"I think the Light of Fane has a bad effect on ordinary fanes. You – well, it was like you couldn't see where you were. You couldn't see the Isle of Fire." I looked at the plateau between the two mountains. The fire had died down, as though it had been guarding the Light of Fane and knew it was gone. There was a ring of grey stone and then a grassy space. It wasn't as beautiful as before. I turned back to Cal. "Then you fell unconscious, but that was due to Algamel."

"Did I fall onto a pile of rocks?" Cal staggered to his feet, wincing when his hands touched more sore spots.

I looked away. Once more I'd stood by and watched while Cal was hurt. At least I'd been able to stop it this time, although I didn't plan to tell him that. I didn't plan ever to tell him any of it. After a moment, I realised Cal didn't require an answer.

Cal shaded his eyes to inspect the sun, checking how late it was. "We should start back. We've got a long way to go."

"Yes." Hope flared in me. "We should hurry. Zan might be awake and we can go to Talvar."

"You really want to go there with Algamel running amok?"

"If he defeats the Talvar guardian it should be all right. If we get back to Zan, we can decide what to do." I stared away from the mountains, back along the route we'd already come. My chance to escape was running through my fingers like warm sand, but I couldn't let it go. I had to believe things would work out and I could make my escape.

"Right." Cal stretched and winced again.

"We should hurry. They'll all wake up when Algamel

returns to Talvar." The figures around the council table appeared in my memory again. Awake, and powerless. I wondered what conclusions Saldamia would jump to about what had happened to her and all the council. I couldn't stop my lips twitching at the idea that I would now, free from the effects of *somnaya* and with my anima ring safe on my finger, be more powerful than Saldamia and all her followers. And Cal would be strongest of all. Perhaps he would decide to be king. Fane had never had a king before. I frowned, wondering if that was why I hadn't been able to see a new queen. But I hadn't seen him as our leader, either, and surely I would have done if that was his destiny.

"No time to waste, then," Cal commented. He bounded down the mountainside. I followed.

Chapter Seventeen

When we arrived at Valderia to find its inhabitants awake, it was like being the Harvest Queen, bearing gifts that prompted cheers as soon as everyone understood what was in the knapsack. I didn't mind being seen as different when it was for a reason like this. The townspeople jostled around us, although the atmosphere was good-natured and everyone patiently waited their turn. I doubted Saldamia would be as calm when it came to hers.

The townspeople urged us to eat with them while they listened to our stories of Algamel and what had happened, and by then it was nearly dark, so it was easy to accept the hospitality pressed on us and stay the night. We didn't even need our rolled blankets, since beds were made up for us in the town's central meeting hall. A tiny voice at the back of my mind reminded me that I only had Algamel's word for it that he was leaving, but he wanted to create havoc on Talvar, not here – Fane had only been a means to an end. I snuggled into the bed provided and closed my eyes. There would be enough time to worry about what might or might not happen in the morning.

*

In the middle of the night, I woke, rolling over and

pulling the blankets snug around me, drowsy with sleep. A steady sound filled my ears which I identified after a moment as rushing water. Valderia's spring rippled out of the rocks to become a stream, but I hadn't noticed the sound of it earlier. It hadn't seemed big enough to be heard in the middle of the town, but then, everything sounded louder at night.

It was only when a crack of lightning turned the air electric white that I woke enough to realise the sound wasn't rushing water in the river, or at least not only that. Rain was also pounding on the roof, and that was certainly a recent thing.

Pulling a blanket with me, I crossed to the window, the sound of my movements obliterated by the crash of thunder that followed the lightning. I pulled the shutter aside to see out, only for my face to be drenched by the driving rain that burst through the gap. I curled my hand around my anima ring and pushed the rain out of the way, but I could still see nothing. From the size of the drops and the force with which they hurled against the building, I was sure I could push the rain aside for the length of a league and I'd still see nothing but more rain beyond. Added to which, the clouds made it as dark as moonsfall night.

"They got storms on Earth."

I jumped when Cal spoke beside me. The rain had covered his footsteps as he'd walked to my side. "When? What does that matter?"

He leaned closer, staring over my shoulder although I didn't imagine he could see any more than I could. He moved away and I re-shuttered the window while he explained. "When the gates were left unsealed between the worlds, Fane heated up and dried out.

166

Earth got wild – storms, tsunamis and tornadoes."

I didn't even know what the second two words meant, but they sounded dramatic.

"Some of that destructive power was what Issaenaptra had sent through on purpose, but she always said it wasn't all her doing – that she was just using what nature was providing anyway."

"So you think this is because there's now a gate between Fane and Talvar?"

"I think this would have started a couple of days ago if that were the case."

"You mean it's because of the Light of Fane?"

Cal shrugged, but he didn't look in any doubt. "Our anima crystals allow us to have control over the elements. It's not that big a stretch to think that Fane itself needed the Light of Fane to keep the elements in balance."

"Algamel told me our crystals came from Talvar in the first place, so how would losing it make such a difference?"

"He said that?"

I nodded.

Cal stared at the shutters. The sound of rain and the river filled the air. "So, Fane was like this before the Light of Fane arrived." He took a breath. "If that's the case, then it's possible it was brought here for a very good reason, and we might just have discovered what that reason was."

I was sure Cal was already thinking how he could fix everything. "I thought you didn't think it was a good idea to go to Talvar in the middle of a rebellion."

"That was when I didn't want to interfere with Talvar's business. This makes it Fane's business, too.

167

If losing the Light of Fane has caused this we've got to get it back."

The word 'we' seemed to hang in the air between us. I had said I didn't want to go to Talvar alone. And being with Cal was easier now he didn't hate me. That would change if he knew what I'd done, but he didn't have to find that out – it wasn't like I was going to tell him, was it?

"We need to get to the palace." Cal's eyes were already on the door.

Was he seriously considering bounding in rain-drenched darkness? That would be madness. "You know, Saldamia was eager for the responsibilities of queenship. This is her problem."

Cal folded his arms. "We made the mess, we should clear it up."

Heat burned through me. "We *didn't* make this mess, Algamel did. You don't have to be the one to fix everything, Cal. And if you want to go anywhere on a night like this you're on your own." I shut up then, mainly because I'd run out of breath.

I expected Cal to shout at me, or to make some rousing, rally-the-guards speech to persuade me to do what he wanted. I didn't expect him to sit back on his bed and say, "Okay."

Watching him, I walked sideways until my legs met my bed and I could sit, too. "What? That's it? Aren't you going to tell me we must do it because we can?"

"No." The rain drumming on the roof and the water rushing in the river were **oddly** soothing for being so out of place. I was exhausted by not needing to fight with Cal. "Not in the dark. We'll head off at dawn." Cal swung his legs back into bed and pulled the blankets around him.

"I suppose that's the best I'm going to get."

Cal didn't answer. He was already asleep. Or ignoring me.

*

But before dawn the situation changed.

"Flood! The river is flooding!"

Shouting voices woke us, knocking against the door ensuring we couldn't sleep through the disaster. Over it all, still, came the sound of the rain. When I swung out of bed, I found the immediate truth of the call – instead of solid floor my feet met a handspan of chill water. It took a moment of looking to find my boots. Liberated by the water, they'd floated to different sides of the room.

As I was gathering them up, Cal cursed behind me. I turned. He was shaking out his coat which must have fallen into the water. As I watched, he snatched something from the water that fell from the coat and stuffed it back into his pocket.

I felt colder than the water I was standing in as I stared at him. He glanced at me and then looked away. "Ready?"

"Is that *somnaya*?" I don't know why I phrased it as a question; as though I of all people wouldn't recognise a bottle of the iridescent tincture.

"What?" He tried to brazen it out, splashing to the door. "Come on, we've got to go."

I didn't move. "Why are you carrying a bottle of *somnaya* tincture, Cal?"

He shrugged, like it didn't matter. "We've got to go, Deena."

"Throw it away."

He yanked open the door.

"Throw it away, Cal." His hand froze on the door handle. Dismay swelled in my chest, choking me. "I'm not going a step further with you while you've got that."

"We might need it, Deena."

I swallowed so I could answer him. "When might we need it? When you need me to foresee something for you? When you decide to force me to have a vision? So much for respecting my abilities." Helplessness robbed my breath again and I fell silent, blinking hard against the moisture pricking at my eyes. If you wept you were weak; anger was better. I pitched my voice lower and spoke through my teeth. "Throw it away."

"No. We might need it."

"I won't take it. We don't need it."

"I'm not going to force it on you. I'm not Saldamia."

"No? So prove it. Throw that bottle away."

"No. Come on." His own boots slung over a shoulder, Cal held the door wide.

I stayed where I was while the water swelled around my feet. His expression was as implacable as mine.

We must have stayed like that for a minute. I was the one who gave in. Of course I was; I was weaker than Cal, and now we both knew it.

I didn't look at him, ducking from the rain and seething with fury as we crossed to the corner. For a little while, I'd started to think Cal was a friend, that he cared about me. Not the way he cared about Zan. I wasn't stupid enough to think that was possible, but … I'd thought he respected me like any fane should respect another. Stupid me for thinking that was even possible when I was a dreamseer.

I stopped where the roads met and we could look down the main street towards the river. The street might have been a tributary of the river, a steady stream of water flowing along it, surging as high as my knees before dissipating as it spread in different directions at the crossroads.

Most of the townspeople had bounded up onto their roofs, looking at the river and the streets below and talking to each other in tones of distress.

"You know, there's a myth about this on Earth, too," Cal said.

"Do they have a myth for everything?" I snapped.

"Stories are as important to them as they are to us," he replied mildly. He looked up to the clouds massed overhead, closing his eyes as though he was enjoying the water pouring over his skin and soaking his hair. "This particular one says that their god was angry and sent a flood as punishment. It rained for forty days and forty nights, if I've remembered the story right."

"So another thirty-nine days and this'll all be over? That's something to look forward to."

"Yeah." Cal turned away from the rain to face me. His eyes seemed especially bright against the dull backdrop of a grey sky. "Except that by the end of that time, everything on Earth had been drowned. The only people to survive were the few who'd been warned by the god."

"This wasn't sent by an angry god. There's no such thing."

"I didn't say the story was true, or that it's what's happening here," he scolded me mildly.

"Then why tell me about it?"

"Because I was just wondering what will happen if it

carries on for forty days."

"There's no reason it should."

He shrugged. "And there's no reason for it to stop, not especially."

"I suppose you're going to say we have to start back for the palace, aren't you?" I asked.

"We'll make short bounds so we can see where we're going."

I gritted my teeth and nodded. We launched into our bounds pretty much in unison.

*

"You're bounding further," Cal told me when we touched down a couple of hours later, once dawn had brought enough light for us to bound longer distances. "That was easily twice the distance you could manage on the way here."

I ignored him. He was trying to make me forget what he'd done and I'd never do that. Despite myself, I glanced back. I hadn't noticed while I was in motion, but he was right. I decided to speak to him after all. "So I'm not weak and useless. You're going to have to find someone else to look down on."

"I don't look down on you," he snapped back. "I was trying to give you a compliment."

"I don't need your compliments."

"Fine." Cal's shoulders lifted with a deep breath. I watched him tamp down his annoyance. "Shall we?" He held his hand out to me, ready for another bound. I ignored it and pushed off on my own, wondering if I'd go as far this time, or if that bound had simply been a fluke.

When the palace came into sight within an hour, I knew it hadn't been a fluke.

"That was five leagues," Cal told me when he landed beside me, confirming what I'd already guessed myself. "Is there something about the rest of Fane losing its strength that means you gain yours?"

I shook my head. I was sure I knew what was behind it. "It's the *somnaya*. You must have heard that the fanes who take it voluntarily find that it diminishes their elemental abilities. I think I'm finally free of the stuff."

"Have you found this before, when you haven't taken it?"

"I've never gone this long." Druggie dreamseer, he shouldn't be surprised by that.

"But it's only been a week," he pointed out.

"I've had a dose of *somnaya* almost every day since I was six."

That big old frown was bigger than ever. "But why would you do that? Six?"

"I didn't have a choice. My mother gave it to me." I smiled, sadly, to see his puzzlement. He'd lived through brutality, he'd fought in the war, he'd been Issaenaptra's prisoner. Did he really think those were the only circumstances in which fanes were unpleasant to each other? "My mother had a child because she was desperate to die. Dreamseers always get like that in the end, driven half-mad by visions they can't control. She just reached that point earlier than most. And she didn't want to have to wait until I was sixteen to be free of her visions. I had my first vision when I was six. The next day she gave me *somnaya* to bring on another one. I've drunk *somnaya* tincture almost every day of my life. This is the longest break I've ever had, and look what I'm starting to be capable of. Without

173

it, I could pass for a normal fane."

"Oh, Deena. I'm sorry."

I met his sparkling eyes. "Then throw away the bottle you're carrying."

He opened his mouth. Then shut it. Then shook his head. "I can't. Just in case. I swear I won't make you take it if you don't want to."

"Don't make promises you don't mean to keep."

"I'll keep it," he told me, his voice husky.

"Only while it's convenient," I told him and turned away. For a second, I was glad for what Issaenaptra had done to him. He deserved it. Then I went hot with guilt. No one deserved that. It was just a shame we didn't often get what we deserved.

I turned to look at the palace, a grey block in the rain. It was impossible to tell what was happening inside the building. Perhaps the council members hadn't survived whatever Algamel had done to them. I shivered and felt another moment of guilt at the relief that filled me at that possibility. It was more likely they'd be as wide awake as the people of Valderia. "We'll have to sneak in, if we can." I said it aloud in case Cal had any mad ideas about declaring our arrival. The weather would make it easy to be stealthy, at least. We'd be able to bound right up to the walls concealed by the drenching grey rain.

"I know where to go. There are places only insiders know."

Of course, Cal had been one of Issaenaptra's guards before he'd joined the rebels.

"Okay. You lead."

He took a pace forward, reached a hand out, then remembered I wouldn't take it and let it drop. "Stick

174

close." He pushed away and I followed.

We landed at the far corner of the building. So far, all the rain drumming the ground around us had drained into the sandy soil beneath our feet, although if it continued for forty days surely even here would flood.

Cal had already walked to a wooden, ordinary-looking door in the wall and I hurried to catch him up. It was locked, of course, but for a fane in full possession of his powers, a lock didn't represent much of a challenge. As I reached his shoulder, the lock clicked and he wrenched the handle. It led into a narrow passageway that Cal illuminated. Cobwebs and dust. "This way. We can get close to the gateroom."

The passageway was carved into the inside the walls of the palace. After five minutes of walking, another narrow door came into sight. Cal motioned me to be quiet and reached for the handle.

The door swung wide and we were nearly swept off our feet by the fane waiting for us inside.

Chapter Eighteen

Cal and I jumped back as a blast of air from inside slammed the door wide open, nearly catching us as it smacked against the other wall of the passageway.

Cal was first to stick his head back through the doorway. "Keba, it's us."

He'd taken in the scene at a glance. I took a bit longer to understand what was going on. Keba stood with the door to the gateroom at her back, one arm extended to control the shield of air she'd nearly caught us with. The floor of the corridor was scattered with the bodies of more guards. I counted eight.

"About time." Keba dropped her shield so we could step over the body of a guard to reach her side, but she kept her attention on the end of the corridor. "They keep coming and I have to stop them," she explained.

"Are they dead?"

She spared a moment to give Cal a withering look. "Turns out I'm out of practice at killing fanes. They're knocked out."

"What about Algamel?" I asked.

"He's back on Talvar," Keba told me. "At least, he went through the gate."

"Didn't you try to stop him?"

That earned Cal another crushing look. "I was unconscious until he went. And Thanriel's been busy with Zan."

"Algamel's taken the Light of Fane with him. That's why this storm started."

Keba nodded understanding. "I think everyone in the palace woke up when I did, but they all seem to be powerless. Which has been good for me, of course." A clatter of footsteps heralded the arrival of another guard. She had barely stepped around the corner before Keba used the elements to sweep her off her feet, her head thunking against the stone floor with a sharp sound that made me wince.

"So far, I think it's just guards following up on their absent colleagues," Keba explained. "They're still coming singly. Standards really have slipped in this place since you were here. I don't think anyone realises Saldamia's prisoners have escaped, nor that a new gate's been made. Not yet, anyway." She glanced at Cal again. "I can keep on doing this, but do we have a better plan?"

"We have to get to Talvar and get the Light of Fane back. Then the rain should stop."

I held up the knapsack I was still carrying. "The stolen anima crystals are here. We can return them once it's safe."

Cal and Keba exchanged a look. "That'll be when we're happy everything's back to normal," Cal stated.

Keba nodded. "Do you want me to stay here?"

Cal shook his head. "We should all go. Algamel isn't just going to hand over the Light. It'll need all of us."

Keba nodded again and reached behind her to open the gateroom door. She gestured us inside. "We can

177

bolt this from the inside. That'll keep everyone out for a while."

Inside, Tullan and Zan were lying on the floor, still unconscious. Thanriel knelt by Zan's side, tending to her.

I crossed to my father's side, crouching down beside him, shrugging off the knapsack Algamel had given me. He was still breathing, slowly and evenly, but there was no sign that he was ready to wake up.

"How is Zan?" Cal asked, striding immediately to her side.

Thanriel shook his head. "I do not dare try to rouse her." He looked up at us, his luminous face downcast. "I am sorry, Algamel took me by surprise. He slipped through before I could stop him." Thanriel wouldn't look at us. I could see how much that failure cost him to admit.

Keba said, "We'll go to Talvar after him."

Thanriel took a breath and I wondered if he was going to repeat his statement that it wasn't safe.

Cal continued. "We have to get the Light of Fane back. And before it can be damaged." He regarded Zan's unconscious form. "Will you stay here?"

"No," Thanriel replied. "I must deal with Algamel – and the guardian. I have to make things right on Talvar."

"So—"

Thanriel interrupted whatever Cal planned to say. "Zan stays with me. I will keep her safe. She will not be harmed." His tone was so fierce even Cal accepted the assurance.

"Will she be able to close the gate?" I asked. "We shouldn't leave it open behind us. Whatever's

178

happening on Talvar, it won't be improved by Saldamia and a bunch of her councillors joining in."

"I will see what I can do."

I nodded. "Is that it, then? We're going to Talvar? What about Tullan?"

Cal and Keba and I exchanged looks. "Shall I stay with him?" Keba offered.

Cal shook his head. "No. You come with us. We stick together." He looked at me. "I'm sorry, Deena, but we can't do anything for him by staying."

I nodded and touched his face gently, trying to imprint his face on my memory. Then I got to my feet. I didn't want to leave him, but we hadn't created the gate only to stay this side of it.

"Right," Cal drew us together. "Hold hands. We don't want to get split up."

We did so, with the bright gate a step away. I twisted to see Thanriel lifting Zan easily into his arms. "I will follow and do what I can to close the gate."

We stepped forward. I was closest to the gate. I took a single step and walked through the dazzling brightness into another world.

*

"Are we here? Did we all arrive?" I blinked, unsure if the lack of anything to see was something the matter with my eyes, or if this was how Talvar was supposed to be. Maybe it was the middle of the night and this was Talvar's moonsfall night with nothing to light the sky.

"I'm here." Keba's voice called clear and calm through the darkness.

"I think..." Cal dropped my hand and conjured light to reveal bare rock walls on all sides. "I think this is

179

Talvar."

We all looked around. It was similar to the gate room, but there was no doubt we weren't at the basement of the palace in Fane. The air smelt damp and old, as though it hadn't been disturbed for a long time, and still and cold as though we were far underground.

"Where's Thanriel?"

Cal frowned, leaning back to touch the rock behind us. The gate had turned to stone again.

"He must have arrived somewhere else," Keba said. She nudged Cal. "Your blood leads you home, remember."

"But the guardian wouldn't allow him to come back," Cal pointed out. "What if he's stuck between the worlds? With Zan?"

"If that's the case, we'd better deal with this guardian as soon as we can."

"And where's Algamel?" I asked. I stepped forward and trailed a hand along the rock face. The cave we were in was high enough for us to stand comfortably, narrower than it was high, and it lead back – or forward – to a twist in the rocks that bounced Cal's light back towards us.

"He came through hours ago. He'll be a long way ahead of us."

The sound of running water reached us, and something over that, so faint I couldn't decipher it.

"We need to catch up with him," Cal said. "If we can." He walked to the back – or the front – of the cave.

When he reached the back, he turned right. A smooth rock face hid a fissure wide enough for us to walk down single-file.

I followed. Keba crouched down. I looked back to see her scrape a pile of small pebbles together at the edge of the fissure. She caught my eye and winked. "Always know your exit."

The fissure opened up to another, larger, cave. Cal strengthened the light he was casting. I rubbed my finger, realising a moment later that my anima ring was vibrating, like it had when we'd got close to the Isle of Fire. "The Light of Fane must be close by."

"You're sure?" Keba asked.

I nodded. "My anima crystal is reacting to it. It did that on the Isle of Fire."

She nodded, touching her own anima in reaction. "So Algamel's close by, too?"

"I'd guess so." I looked around at the rock formations, water running over flowstone and carved-out softstone before dripping onto the ground, the noise of it thrown around the cave so that it seemed to be coming from all directions. Cal was inspecting the ground. I thought it odd until I realised he was looking for traces of Algamel. I had my talents, Cal had his. The cave was full of hollows and shadows and it was hard to see any distance clearly, but I didn't think Algamel would be close by – he hadn't returned to Talvar just to sit and wait for us, after all. He would be seeking the talvarrine guardian.

"This way." If I followed the vibrations then we'd find the Light of Fane – and Algamel, and the guardian. And possibly another war, but I tried not to think about that.

The walls and the ground shone with slick moisture, the constant drip of water a companion to the buzzing of the crystal. There was a lip of rock at the side that was a little higher and mostly dry. I followed that around the side of the cave, placing my feet carefully while the constant buzzing told me I was moving in the right direction. Stalactites speared down from a roof that vanished into darkness above our heads, and wide mounds of stalagmites blistered the ground, eerie white against the shadows thrown by the rocks.

"Is the whole of Talvar like this, do you think?" It was a long way around the cave. My thoughts wandered as my feet splashed in shallow puddles and the uneven surface of the flowstone walls grabbed at the shoulder of my tunic.

"I doubt it. We're underground. We should get to an outside, eventually." Cal's low voice sounded at my other shoulder. "Are we getting close?"

"Hard to tell," I replied, because it was. The buzzing was still there, but my senses weren't sophisticated enough to tell whether we were getting significantly closer, or not yet. "Can anyone else hear something?" That other noise continued.

"It sounds like fanes," Keba said, then corrected herself. "It'll be talvarrines, I guess. Movement – and voices."

"That's right," I said.

"Are we ready to meet the locals?" Cal asked.

"I'm ready for anything," Keba promised.

I stayed silent, hoping I was ready for whatever lay ahead. A sliver of darkness on the far side of the cave that resisted Cal's light brought us to another fissure. We slithered along the narrow gap, my tunic and leggings clinging cold and damp where the dripping water landed on me while Cal's light flickered and jumped against the rough texture of the rock. I thought the buzzing was getting louder, but so was the other noise. My heart also felt like it was knocking against my ribs but that couldn't be true.

Another twist in the rock. The buzzing grew louder, more intense. My heart banged harder. I glanced back to Cal and Keba. If we were to overpower Algamel, we'd need all of us. And they were the soldiers, after all. The buzzing was so intense now it pressed against my skin as well as against my eardrums.

When the narrow passageway opened we paused, eyes straining to understand where we'd arrived. I looked for Algamel, but I couldn't see him.

Keba stepped forward. Cal stood between us, casting his light as wide as he could. I blinked in awe as the glow chased the dark to the edges of the cave. This cave was bigger than the others we'd come through, dotted about with stalagmites and stalactites that joined together in places to create pale columns giving the illusion of holding up the rock roof high above. The ground was littered in places with the dull mounds of stalagmites, and also with lumps of another rock that cast a faint but definite light.

My breath caught when I understood what I was seeing. I'd thought we were following a single crystal, the one Algamel had taken, but there wasn't just one. Here on Talvar, there were half a dozen of them in this space alone, all joining together to make the noise vibrating in my ears. Algamel's claim that the crystal had come from Talvar was instantly believable. It must have been harvested here and taken through the gate to Fane. But if Algamel needed a crystal to defeat the Talvar guardian, why hadn't he simply taken one from here?

I stepped further into the cavern, attracted by the sight, the sound. Then I saw something else and halted. It wasn't just crystals here. I didn't see Algamel, but a figure sat beside the crystal I was approaching. I looked further. There was a figure beside every crystal. And each one was dark-skinned, like me, and like every other dreamseer who'd ever lived on Fane. The sound of the crystals' buzz was joined by the rush of my blood.

"What is this?" Cal's whispered question barely rose above the vibration of the crystals.

"This must be where the Light of Fane came from." I answered in a similar tone, as though I feared to disturb the dreamseers in the cavern.

Cal took in the sight before us, seeing but not understanding. "So, can we just take one?"

I shook my head. I understood his reasoning – how much easier to take a crystal from here and return to Fane without ever having to face Algamel. But the crystals here were guarded by the figures beside them. That must be why Algamel hadn't taken one from here. "No, these aren't ours to take."

I stepped down so I was level with the crystals and the women beside them. For the first time in my life, I was with other dreamseers. I had no doubt they *were* dreamseers: the barest glance at their dark skin and the dark hair that curled around the faces of each one told me that here were the sisters and cousins that should have been an impossibility. On Fane there were only ever two dreamseers: mother and daughter, but that was perhaps due to the fane blood mixed into our heritage that kept our population small. Here, things

184

were different.

How could I know nothing about this place? There were no stories about Talvar. I had never heard even a suggestion that the Isle of Fire's crystal had not come from Fane. I didn't doubt Algamel's story now. There couldn't be any other explanation but that the crystal had grown here and been taken to Fane. Like the crystal, we must have originated here and been transplanted to Fane – one dreamseer making the journey with a single crystal that had become the Light of Fane.

There it must have been broken into pieces to give the fane people command of the elements, with the rest of it hidden away. To judge from Cal's reaction, it had been hidden away because it was dangerous to ordinary fanes. Perhaps it was so dangerous the dreamseers had deliberately hidden the Light's origins.

"We have to find Algamel before he destroys the Light of Fane," Cal said behind me.

I knew we had to find Algamel, but I couldn't resist the sight in front of me. "Go on without me," I called. "I'll catch up." Then I stepped into the dim, damp cave towards the dreamseers.

Chapter Nineteen

My feet splashed on the damp surface of the rocky floor. It was so wet trickles of moisture ran across it, the rivulets of mineral-filled water cold even through my boots. My breath puffed in tiny clouds as I moved, and the tips of my ears tingled with the chill.

Eyes fixed on the dark-skinned dreamseer guarding it, I stepped closer to the nearest crystal. It had been dark in the cave before we'd used our elemental abilities to cast our lights. It must always be dark there, except for the low glow of the crystals. The figure beside the crystal seemed to be sleeping, eyes closed, head nodded forward to her chest. They all seemed to be sleeping and I wondered if we *had* arrived in the night, mildly surprised that they hadn't woken at the noise we'd made reaching them.

I tried to be as quiet as possible, aware I was intruding, and yet burning with the justification that I had a right to intrude. Coming to Talvar was like opening a door in my house and finding there was a whole room I'd never known about filled with people like me. Here was a chance to discover that perhaps I had never felt I belonged on Fane because I *didn't* belong there – because my true home was on Talvar.

"Deena, we don't have time for this."

I looked around to see that Cal hadn't moved. "I told you to go without me."

"Keba's gone ahead. I'm not leaving you here."

"They aren't dangerous."

"Thanriel said the crystals were damaged. Maybe dangerous is exactly what they are."

And maybe I didn't care. "I'll only be a minute."

I walked up to the dreamseer. She sat cross-legged beside the crystal, head bowed. I crouched to match her level. I put one hand out for balance, as though I would touch the crystal to anchor me in place, and yet my fingers never touched the surface. Somehow, without anyone telling me, I was aware that the crystal and the dreamseer were united – that it would be a familiarity like touching her to touch the crystal. I dropped my hand to my side.

The buzzing noise grew as I neared the crystal. This close I could hear a subtle difference between the sounds of the crystals, which all made slightly different noises, as individual as the dreamseers themselves. They combined to an overall, slightly discordant hum in the cavern.

I cleared my throat, and spoke, my voice soft enough that it wouldn't create echoes. "Hello? Can you hear me?" Tilting my head to one side, I tried to see through the tangle of unruly curls to the dreamseer's face. Her eyes were closed, eyelashes resting on her cheeks. "I'm sorry to disturb you." She remained silent and still, but the sound from the crystal beside me – her crystal – intensified, as though it knew I was there.

"I have come from Fane, although I think my ancestors must have come from Talvar. I need your help. Algamel has stolen the Light of Fane and brought it here. The crystal's loss has brought chaos to Fane. I need to get the Light back." I swallowed at her continued silence as the crystal continued to hum. Did I have the temerity to shake her awake? I should wait for her to waken, and yet Fane was suffering, flooded and drowning with every minute the crystal was absent. And I wanted to ask her about the crystals, and the dreamseers.

"Will you help me?" I asked again, peering closer to see if there were any signs of wakefulness in the dreamseer's face.

There was nothing. I shifted my weight as the muscles in my legs protested my cramped position, and the dreamseer's hand shot out and gripped my arm, her eyes flashing open. "Help us!" she cried, her shrill voice high with desperation that lifted to the roof of the cavern above us.

I tried to pull away, shocked by the suddenness of her movement, and also shocked by her – the eyes opened to me were white with age or perhaps disease. I doubted she could see me. But her grip was sure.

I pulled away but couldn't free myself, sliding to the side instead so I landed in a pool of the chill water that flowed through the cavern. Her second hand joined her first, circling my arm. I thought the problem with her eyes must be disease, because there was nothing infirm about the way she clung to me.

"You must help us." Her voice was low, quiet with despair.

"Have you been enslaved by the guardian?"

"We dreamseers are ruined. Our crystals are corrupted. The guardian keeps us from the light."

"What light do you mean? Do you want me to take you outside?" Had they been forced down here against their will? I glanced at Cal, wondering if he could hear our conversation. I didn't think he'd be thrilled if I told him we needed to guide a bunch of blind dreamseers to the surface of Talvar before we dealt with Algamel and got the Light of Fane back.

"All of Talvar lies in darkness. Can you return us to light?"

"What do you mean it lies in darkness? Is everyone down in these caves?" I felt like an idiot asking, but for the first time I understood Cal's comments about dreamseers spouting nonsense. "Can you be clearer?"

She gripped my arm with renewed pressure. "The guardian has used the crystals to enslave the talvarrines. You must stop him."

Another glance at Cal, arms folded while he waited for me to return so we could get on with what we'd come for. "Algamel brought the Light of Fane here to destroy the guardian."

"Algamel will destroy himself if he attempts it. He does not have the ability. The guardian's crystals must be opened to let the energy within fly free to those it was stolen from. You are a dreamseer – will you do it?"

"How?"

"Use your crystal. See how the guardian trapped energy within the crystals. If you reverse the process we shall all be freed."

"How can I see that? What is the process?"

Her hands tightened even more on my wrist. I sensed impatience. "If you are not old enough to remember then *see* what happened."

189

"How? What should I do?" I thought of the *somnaya* Cal was almost certainly still carrying. If it would free the talvarrines and set everything to rights, would I take a dose?

"All you need to do is *see*. Use the talents you were born with."

"I can't foresee something just because I want to." She was a dreamseer, she should have known that.

"Why ever not? Are you ill?"

"No." Faced with her calm certainty, my knowledge of my shortcomings wavered. "How do you do it?"

"Think of what you wish to see and connect with your crystal."

She was gripping the wrist of the hand that carried my anima. I reached across and touched the crystal on my ring. "And then what?"

The dreamseer slid a hand down my wrist, pushing my fingers out of the way until she reached my anima. She gave an odd, coughing cry that was half-concern, half-derision. "What is the meaning of this useless chip? Where is your crystal?"

"That is my crystal." I looked at the one beside the dreamseer. It was roughly the same size as the Light of Fane, a ball slightly smaller than my head. I wanted to touch it, to feel those glorious colours shift beneath my fingers.

The dreamseer ran her thumb over my anima crystal, back and forth, as though it might change under her attentions. She shook her head wonderingly. "However do you achieve anything?" she murmured.

I didn't know whether she wanted an answer. I murmured back, "*Somnaya*." I wondered if she even knew what it was. If she could have visions just for wanting them, maybe she'd never had cause to taste the foul stuff.

"You need a crystal." She gripped my hand while her sightless eyes peered upwards.

Mine slid down, back to her crystal. I kept returning to it, as though I was trapped by the pale glow of it, and the odd, hair-raising sound it emitted. I wanted to touch it. I wanted to know what I could do with it.

The dreamseer sighed and held my hand between both of hers as though she felt my urge to move and wanted to prevent it. "The crystals here... they are damaged. They need the sun and yet they have had no sun for centuries."

I looked at Cal. I wondered how much he could hear. I raised my voice. "Can you brighten the light?"

For answer, the cave grew brighter. He didn't urge me to hurry up, so maybe he'd heard how important this was.

The dreamseer gave a short cry of pleasure. She let go my hand and reached down, scooping up the crystal beside her and holding it out to me. "Even damaged, it will show you. Use my crystal and see how the guardian has enslaved us all and how his evil can be undone."

Cautiously, I reached out. The crystal's humming vibration cut through the air. The colours swirling beneath the faceted surface were clear. It was beautiful, and yet a little scary.

"Take it," the dreamseer urged and I let her tip the crystal into my cupped hands. The colours swirled more quickly, the hum it emitted changing slightly. It was cold, sucking heat from my fingertips as though I'd touched metal. "Now ask for what you wish to know," she prompted.

I looked down, my vision slipping out of focus as the swirling colours seemed to draw me into the inside of the crystal. I wanted to know how to defeat the guardian and get the Light of Fane back from Algamel, but that desire was mixed up with my desire to discover my past. I wasn't sure what I'd asked for until the crystal showed me.

It was nothing like a vision. I didn't lose control. I didn't lose my awareness of myself and where I was, crouched beside the dreamseer in the dim cave on Talvar. Inside my head, though, I stepped into the skin of someone else.

My name was Esta. I lived in a village of two hundred talvarrines, in a round house with a garden where I grew trees for fruit and vegetables for the cooking pot. The village lay on the edge of a forest and we all worked together gathering fruit and nuts from the forest as well as growing grains and beans in fields we'd cleared between the edge of the village and a steep cliff that provided shelter and safety on the other side. I saw Talvar for the first time through Esta's eyes, the scene oddly familiar even though I knew that I – as Deena – was seeing it for the first time.

Away from the cultivated area, it was hard to see the contours of the land because it was clothed in ever-thicker layers of greenery, trees bursting out from a dense, low canopy of shrubs and grasses. The air smelled fresh and clear, tinted now and then with the scent of flowers that sprinkled the green with bright shades. It was how I imagined Fane had appeared a few hundred years earlier... before the destruction and the wars.

In the vision, a group of us, pale and dark together, were out in the fields, plucking out the weeds that competed with the ripening grains we'd planted a season before. It was our least favourite task and we sang as we worked to ease the repetitive boredom and the aches in our arms and backs. We didn't even notice when the sun overhead became obscured by clouds. There was a crash of thunder that made us jump and cold rain began to fall, a sprinkle then a deluge. I and two friends were close to the village and we ran back to our homes. Others in the field ran into the forest for shelter, or ducked beneath the overhanging shelter of the cliff.

When the rain finished, we returned to the field. Rogun, who had sheltered beneath the cliff, walked over to us with something in his hands. We all stopped work to cluster around him and see. I – Deena – recognised it as an anima crystal, a large one like the one I held now, although Esta saw nothing but a pretty rock. Rogun took it home and placed it on a shelf to be looked at and admired.

I blinked and days passed. I as Esta went to Rogun's house. My mind was on the burgeoning harvest and how harsh the coming winter might be. To distract me from my thoughts, I picked up the rock to get a closer look, and nearly dropped it as pictures flew into my mind. Rogun grabbed the stone. "Be careful!"

I gripped his hand. "A storm is coming. I saw it. We have two days to bring in the harvest or we'll lose it all."

Rogun scoffed. "The grain needs a few more days to be fully ripe. We'll pick it then."

I shook my head, sure of what I'd seen. "There isn't time. I swear. I saw it in the stone."

"In the stone?" Rogun leaned forward, peering into the crystal. "There's nothing to see."

"Will you help me harvest?"

"Not yet. There's no hurry. Summer showers will do no harm."

"This isn't a shower," I insisted. I left Rogun and walked around the village, recruiting others to help. Those who didn't scoff at the idea that I had seen the weather before it was here helped me and we had cleared two fields before night fell on the second day.

At dawn the third day, the storm arrived. It wasn't rain. Heavy hailstones dropped ceaselessly from the sky for two solid days. At the end of it there was nothing worth harvesting in the fields. All the grain the village had for the winter and for next year's planting was what we had already cut and brought into the drying house.

I became a celebrity. I was asked to touch the stone every day and see what weather lay ahead so we could better plan our farming, and better protect the village.

Rogun returned to the cave where he'd found the stone and found others, bringing back a dozen in a cart one bright winter's day.

Everyone wanted to see in the stones, but we found that it was only dark-skinned talvarrines who could see the weather in the crystals. We worked together, excused the usual labour of growing and gathering food to focus on what we saw in the crystals.

With time, our abilities grew stronger. We could see more than the dangers of the weather. One harsh winter one of us, a young man named Garda, saw an attack from another village, starving because their harvest had failed and desperate enough to attempt to steal from us. Prepared by what Garda had seen, we defeated them.

I blinked and it was a few hundred years later. Our village had grown in that span of time, rising on a tide of success to become a city, thronged by those who wanted to share in our success.

The title 'dreamseer' began to be used. I and my fellow dreamseers worked together, testing the full extent of the crystals' powers. We discovered that we could see more than a storm, or a week of sunshine, or a group of bandits creeping down the cliffside with theft in their hearts. Garda in particular spent his days exploring what we could do with the crystals. With peace and space to give his visions free rein, he learned that we could not only read the elements. We could control them. Spring came early and summer stayed long in our fertile valley. The cruellest bite of winter sank its teeth elsewhere.

Our city grew more successful still, our overflowing harvests supporting yet more citizens. We thought ourselves invincible.

The dreamseers studied the crystals further. We discovered the fine degree of control to enable us to harness the elements to protect us: a shield of air, a ring of fire, a rush of air, to keep away those who would harm our city and our people.

Another blink and years passed again. Garda discovered something more remarkable still; although the crystals would only work for the dark-skinned dreamseers, they unlocked astonishing abilities in the pale talvarrines. The crystals could be used to split the

195

talvarrines into separate flesh and life energy. Their energy forms could fly around the world in the space of seconds while their flesh bodies remained behind. Their energy could even pass between the worlds, taking them to other planets. They travelled to other worlds and returned with amazing stories.

The dreamseers were praised even more than they had been before. And yet, many pale talvarrines grew resentful that the dreamseers and their crystals were needed to unleash their abilities. The dreamseers were elevated, esteemed – and envied.

Some stole our crystals, snatched them away, determined to find a way to control them. They failed, and the crystals were returned to their rightful place with the dreamseers. But the anger and resentment we faced grew. We were attacked – verbally at first, and then physically.

The dreamseers banded together to protect each other. The pale talvarrines, fearing to lose us and all the benefits we brought, tightened their control. They hemmed us about, strangling that which was most precious to them. The dozen of us retreated into the caves where Rogun had first discovered the crystals. We felt at home there. We felt safe, using the elements to repel those talvarrines who came after us.

Then Garda discovered that talvarrines could be split into flesh and energy without their consent. As I watched the scene unfold, the dark dreamseer held a crystal in his arms, examining the visions he found within it. A talvarrine leaned into the caves, seeking out the dreamseers. I couldn't see whether they came with good or evil intent but Garda didn't care. He closed his eyes, a high-pitched hum sounded and the talvarrine collapsed. The colours inside the crystal Garda was holding swirled faster. I saw more colours inside – as though the talvarrine's life energy had physically been trapped inside. Garda laughed in triumph and set the crystal aside.

Esta and her friends protested. While they argued, one dreamseer fled to Fane with her crystal. Esta saw that as capitulation, surrender to fear. Feeling her emotions through the crystal I understood why she determined to stay and help peace return. But peace fled ever faster out of reach. Garda grew stronger and stronger, determined to overpower the talvarrines who threatened the dreamseers. A confrontation was inevitable.

Chapter Twenty

Fear prickled over my skin in the cave while I watched myself as Esta confront Garda in the memories trapped within the crystal. I told him to stop abusing the talvarrines. He laughed. "You are afraid. There is no call for fear. I will bring the talvarrines beneath my heel. And you shall not stop me."

I saw nothing unusual in his face. No madness. Nothing to warn me. It was quick. So quick I struggled to understand. My vision blurred. I touched my crystal but instead of the clear connection I was used to, there was only mist. Garda had destroyed my ability to see. Mine and that of every other dreamseer who had opposed him.

Another blink. My vision drifted away from blind Esta, following the path of the caves to the surface of Talvar. The peace and plenty of earlier centuries had faded. The fields were overgrown, the city deserted, houses tumbled down from neglect.

My vision took me further. I found the talvarrines in a clearing in the forest, strange, unfamiliar and beautiful trees arcing high above them. I could almost imagine fanes in the same situation, except that these people were clearly not the same as fanes.

It wasn't their appearance. What made me shiver

was their silence and stillness. A group of fanes in a similar situation would be talking, maybe making music and dancing if they were relaxing, or working together to gather wood or harvest food. These talvarrines were doing... nothing.

Each sat with his or her legs crossed, arms folded, eyes staring into the distance. The talvarrines faced each other in what was roughly a circle, but no one spoke. The only sounds came from the birds in the branches overhead and the chirrup of unseen insects.

I stared into the blank eyes of the talvarrine. There was no sign of animation. No sign of life. I drew back, horrified. The talvarrines weren't dead. They breathed, they were perfectly healthy, but there wasn't a thought or an emotion shared between any of them, they were... empty.

I was looking at the other side of what Garda had done. These talvarrines had been split from their energy, from whatever it was that animated them. These were the flesh shells left behind when Garda ripped their life energy from them.

For a moment, all seemed lost. Then, in the stillness, something stirred. A figure came into sight. Algamel, stumbling through the undergrowth. He paused, shaking the shoulders of the talvarrines as he passed by, crouching down to look into a face, urging them to respond. Whatever Garda had done to the talvarrines it didn't affect Algamel. Or he had grown immune. Somehow, he had re-joined his energy and physical forms. He walked like a man drunk, like someone throwing off the effects of drugs. He looked at the cliffside where the entrance to the cave lay and set out towards it.

My vision switched to the inside of the caves, where Garda sat surrounded by the crystals he'd used to keep everyone at bay. He observed Algamel's approach with thin-lipped anger, listening to him draw closer through the echoing outer caves.

As Algamel staggered into sight, Garda selected a crystal from those around him and cradled it in his arms as he had done earlier. His eyes closed and a hair-raising sucking sound echoed through the cave as he ripped Algamel's energy from his body. The talvarrine collapsed like a discarded doll and for a moment, the brilliant white of his life energy lit the darkness until it was drawn, swirling, into the crystal Garda held. Smiling, he set the crystal back down.

But Algamel got up. He staggered, but forced himself to continue towards Garda. Still thin-lipped, Garda picked up the crystal. Once more came the slurping, sucking noise, once more Algamel collapsed, and the shine of his energy glowed for a moment before vanishing into the crystal. He lay immobile for a long time, but neither I nor Garda took our eyes from him. I already knew this wasn't the end of it.

At last, the figure stirred. He pushed up to hands and knees, then sat back on his heels, glaring at Garda and the crystal he held. I guessed Algamel was summoning the strength to move again, knowing that each step would provoke a similar collapse.

Garda watched him, pale with fury.

Algamel staggered, wavering, to his feet.

"This ends now," said Garda.

Algamel bared his teeth. "This ends when you free us. This ends when I end you."

Another flash, suck and drop as his flesh was

separated from his energy. Another wait.

Watching, nausea rose in me, the sensation amplified by the expression on Garda's face. In his cold fury, he was enjoying playing with Algamel.

At last, the talvarrine rose, slowly, feebly, like someone far older than he appeared. His eyes gleamed hatred. "You will not stop me. I will keep on coming."

"Then I will send you further this time." Garda gripped his crystal, rising to his feet.

The process was slower this time. The sound of ripping rang through the cave and Algamel hung in two parts for a longer time before his flesh body slid to the ground. His shining energy form hung in the air. It fluttered, like a pennant in the wind and I realised he was struggling against whatever Garda was doing to keep him there. His energy form had wings which flapped urgently behind him, pulling away but not strong enough to break Garda's grip.

Another tearing sound made my skin crawl. Algamel's brilliant wings fell, one after the other, to the ground. The shining form sagged, as though the loss were a physical wound.

"I banish you," Garda hissed, picking up another crystal. "You will not come back from another world." The bright light slithered into the crystal and Garda used his elemental powers to send it flying through the air, out of the caves and through the forest Algamel had earlier staggered through.

My vision didn't follow the crystal, but it didn't need to. I knew Algamel's past. Banished from Talvar, he had gone from here to Earth, where he would work with Issaenaptra to destroy the people of Earth.

Another blink and alone in the caves, Garda

frowned at what he saw in his visions. Again I could guess – Algamel's plans to help Issaenaptra and lead an army to Talvar. Elemental power flew through the caves, fuelled by his fury. Then he calmed, and found a solution. A talvarrine's energy was released from its crystal. More compliant, this one, who must be Thanriel, was given instructions and sent to follow Algamel.

I blinked and returned to myself, Deena, in the cave. The crystal couldn't show me what happened away from Talvar, but I didn't need to see that. I already knew. Algamel had gone to Earth. Thanriel had followed to stop Issaenaptra destroying the people of Earth. Thanks to Zan, Issaenaptra and Algamel were defeated. Peace returned to Fane. But nothing had changed here.

The sightless dreamseer in front of me came into focus. "You are Esta," I said, understanding. "This is your story."

She inclined her head. "The crystals become one with us. Our history becomes a part of them."

My breath hitched. The Light of Fane was the crystal taken from here to Fane. That would tell my ancestor's story. There would be gaps between her life and mine, a span of many years to be jumped, but it would tell the story of how the crystal had arrived on Fane, how the dreamseers had shared their power with fanes. It should even show why the Light of Fane had been enclosed so securely on the Isle of Fire. I'd just found another reason to get the Light of Fane back before Algamel could damage it.

"So if I destroy the crystals, the talvarrines will recover?"

"No! If you destroy them you destroy their contents. You must simply make them release the energy they hold. A dreamseer can do it."

I nodded. I wondered if Algamel would understand the difference. The Algamel I knew was ruthless enough not to care. "That will solve it?"

"Yes." Esta sighed, a breath of air full of hope despite everything she'd seen and endured. "And finally our world will find peace again. We can live together once more."

I thought back through the history I'd seen. "What if the talvarrines try to force you again? What if someone else hoards all the crystals' power for themselves?"

"Now we know where greed and envy lead, we will guard against it."

I paused. That seemed a precarious plan. And yet, these weren't children. "I will help you," I promised. "How do I stop Garda?"

"Use my crystal. It will lend you its strength. You must break Garda's connection with his crystals and make them open to release the energy they hold."

I nodded. "I will do it. I'll stop him and then I'll return for you."

Esta smiled, her blind eyes turned up to me. "I have longed to feel the sun on my face for many years. I wish you strength and clear sight in what lies ahead."

"Thank you." I turned away from her and returned to Cal, carrying Esta's crystal.

"What did you learn?" Cal asked.

"We need to stop Garda without damaging the crystals."

We were already walking in the direction Keba had gone. "Is that possible?"

"The dreamseer thinks I can do it. Otherwise, Algamel's going to kill all the talvarrines he's trying to help."

"We'd better catch up with Keba, then."

"I'm sorry it took so long."

Cal shook his head. "A couple of minutes won't matter. And you discovered useful information. But we should get on." He hurried around the edge of the cave. I frowned as the noise of people ahead became apparent. I hadn't noticed it while I was in my vision. I wondered if it was wise for Keba and Cal to have split up. I hurried to keep pace with him.

The crystal I'd borrowed from Esta continued to vibrate. It was hard to concentrate through the agitation it sent running through my veins. With its power, I was going to be capable of remarkable things and I was eager to try them.

The sound of people grew louder. They seemed to be gathered in the next cave, hidden from our sight but close by. We sloshed through an ankle-deep puddle. I splashed water up my leggings to my knees. I barely noticed the discomfort, stepping carefully forward, ensuring the crystal stayed safe. It held the power I would need to defeat the guardian, this Garda, and set the people of Talvar free. I couldn't let any harm come to it.

Instead of another fissure leading from one cave to the next, we ended at a narrow opening that lead roughly upwards. It was too small to bound through, nor could we simply walk through the tiny gap.

Cal inspected the gap between the rough rock and uneven flowstone, slick with water that greased over the stones to form the pools that littered the floor of the cave. "I'll go first. I'll help you if you need it."

"I won't need it." Coming out of *somnaya* addiction had returned my strength, and in possession Esta's crystal, I was stronger still. I followed Cal up the narrow route.

The water that slid over the rocks wasn't deep, but it was cold, chilling the hand I spared from holding the crystal so that my fingertips were numb before I'd pulled myself up half my own height. Cal slipped above me, his feet dislodging a scatter of tiny pebbles which cascaded past me. My feet slipped on the greasy rocks and I paused, checking my footing before I pressed on. The sound of water filled my ears, along with my own breathing. Beyond that came the murmuring noise of the talvarrines and whatever they were doing.

The crystal cradled in the crook of my arm hummed. My sense of excitement rose to match it. I was in a place I belonged, I had a role to fulfil and for maybe the first time ever, I wanted to be involved. I wasn't being dragged into this by a mad queen or her guards, I'd made my choice. I was about to come face-to-face with the guardian, defeat him, and free the talvarrines.

I wondered if this was how Cal had felt when he'd decided to rebel against Issaenaptra – a nervous sense of excitement for the fight ahead tempered by the certainty that he was doing the right thing.

The narrow rock passageway levelled out abruptly and we were met by a blast of noise, voices and energy clashing violently.

"*Ernith!*" Cal sent a blast of elemental energy into the cavern while I was still trying to understand what I was seeing. We were on a shelf of rock looking down into a huge cavern so crowded it was hard to see what was happening.

It was a battle. Talvarrines filled the cavern, fighting against something trying to gain entry at one side of the cave. From our high-up vantage point I could see that it was Algamel they were ranged against. He stood on my far right, the Light of Fane cradled in his arms like Esta's crystal was cradled in mine, using the powers the Light lent him to push back the talvarrines. They were outmatched by the elemental energy he was directing at them. As we watched another two were swept to the ground and didn't attempt to get up. Dozens already lay, motionless. Dread rose in me. Algamel was ruthless enough not to care if he killed them.

Keba stood in the middle, battling to hold her shield steady and protect the talvarrines who seemed to be fighting with their bare hands. Keba was doing her best to protect them, but they were trying to clamber past her and reach Algamel, uncaring of their safety. Elemental power coursed through the cavern, creating a tide of movement back and forth as Keba on one side and Algamel on the other pushed forward, gaining and losing the upper hand.

Cal bounded into the cavern, close to Keba. With his strength added to hers, Keba stood more steadily, their shields forcing a temporary ceasefire. It couldn't last for long, though. Algamel buffeted their shields and the talvarrines seemed just as eager to fight, pushing against Cal and Keba's shields to reach Algamel rather than using the opportunity to regroup and plan how to combat his elemental powers.

I looked past Cal and Keba to see what the

talvarrines were so desperate to protect. At the back of the cave were hundreds of crystals, perhaps thousands, tucked into crannies in the rocks to keep them safe. I'd recognised them from my visions – they were the crystals used to trap the talvarrines' life energy. I frowned, trying to understand. If the talvarrines were trapped, why were they fighting? I looked more closely at them. Their eyes were strangely unfocused, they way I'd sometimes seen my mother's when she was in the grip of a vision. And I realised. The crystals didn't only trap the talvarrines' energy – they enabled them to be controlled by the guardian. The talvarrines were under his power and he didn't care if they died, only that they prevented Algamel from reaching the crystals.

But with this fighting going on around them the crystals weren't safe. As I watched, one was swept from its cubbyhole by a blast of air. It fell to shatter on the ground. "Stop this!" No one heard. Cal was side-by-side with Keba, keeping the battling factions apart.

I peered into the thickest of the fighting, searching until I found the distinctive sign of an elemental shield pushing out from the one casting it. Algamel was so eager to defeat the guardian, he didn't understand that he would kill talvarrines if he destroyed the crystals.

I bounded down to the bottom of the cavern, as close as I could safely get to Cal and Keba. "Try to keep them apart. I need to stop Algamel."

Cal and Keba nodded, their focus on their shields. Air swirled through the cavern, dragging heat with it, sand and pebbles forming a cloud that forced its way between the talvarrine fighters and the furious Algamel, driving back each side.

I cradled my crystal and drew a shield around myself while I faced Algamel. "Stop this. If you destroy the crystals it destroys the energy inside them."

His lip curled. "I will stop the guardian."

"Yes. And I'll help you."

He barely paused in his assault. More crystals slipped from their ledges and fell to the ground. "This is not your concern, dreamseer."

"You're killing talvarrines. If their energy is destroyed, they die." Algamel hesitated. That was all I needed. I used my shield to pin him back, knocking the Light of Fane from his hands. "Stop and think. I understand your anger but you're killing the people you said you wanted to help."

He pushed back against my shield and I struggled to hold him. "I will work with you to free the talvarrines." I met his furious, dark eyes. "Agreed?" For answer, he simply struggled. "I gave you the Light of Fane," I reminded him. "I *want* you to defeat the guardian. But not at the cost of talvarrine lives."

Abruptly, he stopped struggling. "If you help the guardian, I will kill you," he snarled.

"I'm here to help the talvarrines." I shifted the crystal from the crook of my arm to balance between my hands. "I'll show you."

The cold pull I'd felt when I first used it intensified. The swirling colours beneath my fingers changed, brightening, sending out a glitter of golden dust that bounced against the facets of the crystal as though attracted to my fingertips. The sensation of power rose, hot and unstoppable through my chest.

Without thought, I let my awareness relax, becoming one with Esta's crystal. It was a little like falling into a vision, but nothing like it, too. Unlike when I took *somnaya* tincture, I was fully aware of everything around me, hyper-aware, seeing and understanding everything. Algamel reached for the Light of Fane once more, but this time he helped me move through the cavern. With his help, and Cal and Keba holding back the talvarrines, I reached the back of the cave and touched a hand against the first crystal I found. Through my fingertips, I felt the energy within the crystal. Two talvarrine energy forms were trapped inside. I could picture them as they had been, bright and glowing. The cold at my fingertips tingled up my arm and the crystal was abruptly emptied. The energy was released, returning – I hoped – to its flesh bodies.

"Hurry." Algamel grunted the word at me and I reached out for the next crystal. I heard sounds behind me as Cal and Keba and Algamel all fought to keep the talvarrines in the cavern away from me while I worked.

Minutes passed as I touched crystal after crystal and released the talvarrine energy forms inside. My arm grew numb from the chill of it.

Then I reached for another crystal and a talvarrine flung himself over Keba's shield, grabbing me and hurling me backwards. I slammed against rock and slid to the floor.

"Are you all right?" Once more Cal was leaning over me.

"Yes." I looked past him, to where Algamel and Keba were now working side-by-side, helped by those talvarrines who had already returned to their natural selves. The talvarrines who were still controlled by the guardian were standing in front of the crystals so

Algamel couldn't get close.

Cal helped me up. "I think that crystal is their guardian."

He nodded towards a niche behind the talvarrines. What I'd thought were more crystals was something subtly different. It looked like a crystal, but far too large. Like a hundred of the dreamseers' crystals stacked on top of each other. The result was oddly person-shaped, like an overlarge figure seated in the rocky shelter, carved from crystal. I shifted forward to see better – and understanding dawned.

This was the guardian, Garda the dreamseer. He had grown so close to the crystals he used to control everyone on Talvar that he had become one with them, his flesh and blood replaced by the solidity of the crystals.

I strode forward. "The guardian is there, shielded by the last of his talvarrines." I stopped beside Algamel. "Both of us together should be able to destroy him."

He nodded and rose, holding the Light of Fane securely in front of him. "Now."

Chapter Twenty-One

We faced the guardian. Algamel used the Light of Fane and I held Esta's crystal between my fingertips. Wind whipped around us, building up speed. Cal and Keba dropped their shields and we sent destruction flying over the heads of the remaining enslaved talvarrines to the niche in the cavern. Our elemental energy bombarded the crystal shape. I flinched at a series of sharp cracks. The crystal split in the face of our onslaught, shards the size of my fist flying towards us. Keba and Cal worked smoothly together, using their shields so none of the debris reached us.

Energy screamed around us. The controlled talvarrines pushed forward to stop us, throwing themselves into the storm of energy to protect the guardian. Heedless of their safety, one of them was ripped apart, his body torn into its component atoms that exploded around us like silver raindrops before fading to nothing.

"Stop." I drew back and the power of the storm dimmed. Algamel didn't pause, his face savage as he threw destruction at the guardian who had subdued and then exiled him. But his destruction didn't reach the guardian, it reached his protectors. Another of the talvarrines broke apart. I grabbed Algamel's wrist, pulling his hand away from the Light of Fane. Our storm lessened while Cal and Keba maintained their shields to keep the talvarrines away from us. They battered against the other side of the shields, eager to reach me and Algamel.

"You're killing them," I told Algamel.

"If they are in my way, I am not afraid to kill them."

"Give me a chance first. I think some of their energy is trapped in the crystals that have become a part of the guardian." I turned to Cal and Keba. "I need to reach the guardian. Can you give me a space through your shields?"

Their faces were tense with the effort they were using, but both nodded. I stepped forward and the energy in front of me moved, becoming a tunnel that I could walk through with the talvarrines on either side helpless to reach me.

With Esta's crystal cool against my fingers in one hand, I reached out to the crystalline figure in front of me. I couldn't make out the separate crystals, they seemed to have grown into a single, solid mass. I touched it and a shock of cold flared up my arm, a thousand times stronger than I had felt with Esta's crystal. I took a deep breath and told the crystal to release its cargo of talvarrine energy.

"It's working."

I nodded, then refocused on the crystal of the guardian and tried again.

Join me. It took a moment for me to realise that the voice I was hearing wasn't Cal or Algamel or Keba behind me. It was coming from the guardian.

Join me. You could be the most powerful dreamseer in this world.

212

I shook my head, ignoring the cold climbing through me as I told the crystals to release the talvarrines. A lessening of the noise behind let me know it was working. I glanced around. Only three talvarrines were left, throwing themselves against the shields, desperate to protect the guardian.

Come. You know what it is to be a tool of others, I know you do. I've read it in you. Join me and you will be free.

"This is not freedom," I muttered, trying to ignore the voice so I could do what was needed. Another talvarrine vanished from sight, reunited with its energy and slipping from the guardian's control. The cold had reached my shoulder, but I didn't waver. I had to finish my task.

On your own, you will always be in danger. Others will envy you. They will force you to do their will. Join me, and Saldamia will never be able to control you as Issaenaptra did.

The guardian had read my past, but he hadn't read my future. "You're right," I told him softly. "Saldamia will never control me. But that's because I was weak and now I'm strong. I know how to control my abilities. I know what I'm capable of." I took a breath. "And I'm capable of defeating you." A final command through Esta's crystal and the last two talvarrines were free. The guardian screamed, half-noise, half-energy that shook my bones. Then came silence.

The energy around me calmed as Cal and Keba lowered their shields.

"Is that it?" Keba asked, poised to act if needed.

As though for answer, Algamel dropped the Light of Fane and sprinted to the narrow exit at the right hand side of the cavern.

"If Algamel doesn't need the crystal he stole, it must

213

be over," Cal said.

"All the talvarrines are free," I agreed. Those left alive in the cavern were already flooding after Algamel to reach the outside. I shifted the crystal in my hands and remembered the ones who weren't. "Except the dreamseers. We need to get them out to the sunlight."

Cal and Keba exchanged a look.

"I know it won't be easy," I continued, "but we can't leave them down there."

"I'll clear the way," Keba said. She crossed to where we'd entered the cavern.

"Don't bring the whole place crashing around our heads, will you?" Cal asked mildly. He looked almost relaxed now it was over.

"I do know what I'm doing," Keba replied. She inspected the stone in front of her, then focused a spray of water down a particular part of the stone, boosting it with air to drive it into a crack I didn't think I'd even have noticed. Keba glared at the wall as though she held a particular grudge against it, forcing the water faster and faster. There was a creak, then a split, and a triangular crack appeared in the rock. Keba changed focus, using the element of air instead of water. The stone inside the triangle desiccated into dust and swirled out of the gap to drop to the ground in a pile to one side of us. When the gap was big enough for someone to walk down, Keba nodded with satisfaction, wiped the sweat from her forehead and stepped back. She turned to Cal.

He smiled. "I never doubted you."

We cut through the shortcut Keba had made into the cave where the dreamseers were exactly where we'd left them. I hurried to Esta's side.

"It's over," I told her, crouching down and setting her hand on the crystal I'd carried back to her. If I understood correctly, it would tell her the story of what had just happened.

Esta set her hand on the crystal, her fingertips nearly touching mine. She didn't move except that a smile slowly spread over her face. Her hand shifted deliberately so her fingers covered mine. They were cold from the crystal. "Thank you."

"It's over. You can return to the surface of Talvar now. I'll show you the way."

Esta gathered the crystal under her arm and gripped my hand while I helped her to her feet. I'd expected her to be slow, but again there was no sign of infirmity. "Come, Hinna; time for us to go home," she called to another dreamseer. Hinna had seemed asleep, but when Esta spoke, she lifted her head and stood up, taking my other arm. They matched my pace as we walked into the cavern and then followed the path Algamel had taken to leave the caves. Behind me, I heard the sounds as Keba and Cal guided the other dreamseers out.

On the far side of the cavern was another short passageway, and then the caves opened to the light and we got our first real view of Talvar.

What I saw seemed wrong, and I knew I was jarred by the changes from when I'd seen it in Esta's memories.

There was almost no sign of the city and I wondered how long the talvarrines had been enslaved. The buildings had been swallowed up by nature. Where houses and streets had once been was now indistinguishable beneath spreading trees, bushy

215

shrubs and enveloping greenery.

But nature wasn't all we could see. Out of the trees came figures, the talvarrines, reunited energy and flesh for perhaps the first time in years, walking in pairs and groups, many with hands held. My heart lifted. "Can you see this, Esta?" I murmured.

Her hand was still spread over her crystal, translating the scene for her. "I see it," she said. Her smile lit up her face and she seemed taller than she had been a minute before. "Thank you."

Hinna and Esta stepped away, guided by their crystals as they walked towards their friends. The other dreamseers passed by me, and then Cal stood beside me, shading his eyes as he looked at the talvarrines advancing towards us.

"There's Zan." Keba was the first to spot her, pointing her out to me and Cal.

She seemed recovered from whatever had happened when we had created the gate, walking strongly beside Thanriel. He must have found his body because he looked like a flesh and blood talvarrine instead of the shining being of pure energy he'd been on Fane. There was something strange, though, a shine between them as though some of Thanriel's energy had fallen out of him, or couldn't quite be contained.

Cal set off down the hillside towards them. Keba and I followed. He reached them before we did, embracing Zan but careful to avoid the shine beside her.

"I missed all the excitement," Zan grumbled when we reached her, although she was smiling.

"Do you care?" Cal challenged.

"Actually, no." Zan smiled and rested a hand on his

shoulder, as though she couldn't quite believe he was really there. "I'm happy to have left it to you this time. Although I'm glad I have the chance to introduce you to my daughter."

"What?" There was no sign of a baby.

Zan smiled at all of us. "Things appear to work differently on Talvar." She patted her stomach. "The flesh will still take a while to develop, but her life energy was here from the moment we crossed through." She indicated the shine between her and Thanriel and when I looked closely enough, I saw the figure inside it, a tiny child, curled up sleeping, thumb in her mouth.

"That's your baby?" Cal asked.

"That's her. We'll have the chance to get to know her properly before we meet her in the flesh." She smiled at her cousin. "I like that idea."

"She's beautiful," Cal said.

Zan nodded, her attention on the baby.

Thanriel looked up. "What happened? I barely had time to act before the talvarrines began to wake of their own accord."

"That was down to Deena," Cal said. "She figured out how to set the talvarrines free without harming them or the crystals."

Thanriel's grey eyes met mine. He inclined his head in respect. "You have my sincere thanks."

"It was a pleasure," I said, smiling when I realised how true that was. Freeing the talvarrines had been my choice and my decision. I had used my abilities strengthened by another, not compelled, forced or drugged. For the first time, I was proud to be a dreamseer with skills no one else on Fane had.

Cal nudged me. "You keep on like this and I might have to revise my view of your competence."

My stomach lurched. What did he think I'd done wrong now?

His expression relaxed into a smile. "Another show like this and I might have to concede excellence."

I smiled, and wished I were confident enough to nudge him back.

Keba shoved him. "Only you would demand more proof after that."

He held up his hands. "Okay, okay, you were excellent, I'll admit it. We all were. We made a great team." His gaze met mine and held. Warmth slid through me. He didn't look away. Nor did I. The heat in my face grew uncomfortable and I looked down. When I looked up, Cal had turned to Zan and the moment had passed.

"You're staying, then?" His tone said that he already knew Zan's answer.

Zan nodded. Thanriel's arm went around her. "We're staying," she confirmed. "I've found where I really belong."

"We should get back," Keba said. "Fane needs us." She stepped forward to embrace Zan goodbye.

"What about you?" Cal turned to me. "Are you staying?" There was nothing in his tone to indicate whether he wanted me to return to Fane or would be glad to leave me behind. But it wasn't his decision, it was mine.

I looked past our group, past the talvarrines reuniting with friends and families. I looked at the lush world Zan and I had made the gate to. A place where I wouldn't be hounded for what I could do. Where I wouldn't have others trying to control me because of the powers I wielded. I had found my escape.

And I didn't want it.

This wasn't my home. My ancestors had come from here, but I was equally a part of Fane with the blood from my father and all *his* ancestors. A part of my past was here, but I wanted my future to be spent on Fane. I had the confidence now to control my abilities. I wouldn't be exploited by Saldamia. And I hoped Keba and Cal would help me if I needed help.

"No." I met Cal's gaze. "I'm going back to Fane."

He nodded. I faced Zan. "Thank you for everything. You would have made a good queen, you know."

She shook her head. "I've had my moment of glory. I just want a quiet life now." She reached out and put an arm around my shoulders, pulling me against her for a moment so brief I only felt warmth and caught the smell of flowers in her hair before she had let me go. "I'm sorry, I know you don't like being touched, but I want you to know how grateful I am. I wouldn't be here without you."

"That's okay." I smiled. "I don't mind a hug from a friend. It's being handled like something inanimate I don't like. But that's not going to happen again."

Zan smiled. Happiness shone from her brown eyes. "Good. You're going to be an amazing dreamseer, I just know it. It's been a privilege to work with you, Deena."

I inclined my head. "Likewise, Honourable Gatekeeper."

Cal stepped forward, taking my place to pull Zan into a suffocating hug. I looked down so I wouldn't intrude on their goodbyes, staring down at my hand

and the anima ring blinking at me in Talvar's evening light.

Something was wrong. It took me a stupidly long time to realise what it was. My hands were empty. They used to be full of crystal, but I'd given Esta's crystal back to her. Slowly, I realised what I should be holding. "The Light of Fane. It's still in the cavern."

Keba and I stared at each other stupidly. Cal turned. "Algamel dropped it in the cavern. It must still be there."

I started towards the cliffside, unease making me shiver. "I have to get it back." It held everything that had ever been forgotten about the dreamseers on Fane. It held my history. How could I have been so stupid as to forget about it?

"Don't worry." I'd got three steps before Cal caught me up, Keba hurrying behind him. "Algamel doesn't want it and the dreamseers have all got their own crystals. No one else is going to steal it, are they?"

My heart was thumping, and not just from the pace of my walk. "It's what we came here for. I can't believe I just forgot."

Cal was silent for a moment before saying, "You're very hard on yourself, you know, Deena. You don't have to be perfect."

I kept walking. How could he not understand how important it was? It was the entire reason he'd come to Talvar.

"We'll get it and head straight back to Fane." Keba's calm tone made me feel better. I glanced around. Zan and Thanriel were tiny figures already.

"We need Zan. The gate closed."

"No we don't," Cal said. I looked at him but he just

smiled at me. "Haven't you realised, Deena?"

My mind was full of the Light of Fane and what might have befallen it in the half hour it had been out of sight. "Realise what?"

"You're a gatekeeper."

"No, I'm not," I countered automatically. Then I fell silent, stumbling over a rock as the truth filled my mind.

"Your maternal ancestors are from Talvar, your paternal ones from Fane. You combine the blood of two worlds. You're definitely a gatekeeper, Dee."

I stopped. "I don't want to be a gatekeeper." I gulped a breath. "You know what Issaenaptra did to them." I'd only just gained the courage to be dreamseer. I couldn't cope with more.

"It doesn't have to be a curse," Cal promised. "And we're the only ones who know. I swear your secret's safe with me."

Keba nodded. "Likewise. I won't tell anyone. You can trust us, Deena. Everyone will think this is down to Zan. We don't need to correct that assumption."

I looked from one to the other then nodded and resumed walking. I could trust them. They were my friends. They'd be as loyal to me as they had been to Zan.

The distance to the mouth of the caves was eaten away as I strode towards it. Together we would get the Light of Fane, return home and set nature back in balance. Then I could use the Light to show the truth about the next queen.

Cal conjured illumination when we walked into the cool interior of the caves. The cavern was just as we'd left it. Cal's light didn't quite reach the edges and eerie shadows climbed around the walls as I strode towards the pile of crystals that had once been the guardian. There were enough still in place to look like a figure and I had to remind myself that the guardian was no longer there, no longer any kind of danger to us.

On the floor was a scatter of broken shards of crystal, but there, too, was the Light of Fane, its soft glow a beacon to my worried heart. I reached down and scooped it up, then gasped in alarm.

"What's the matter?"

"There's something wrong with the Light of Fane." I walked towards Cal so I could see better. The crystal was still in one piece, but inside it looked as though it had been split into two. Only one side had colours swirling inside it. The other was filled with a dull grey cloud, as though the energy inside it had gone bad.

I met Cal's dismayed look. "Thanriel said the Light of Fane could be damaged. This must be what he meant."

"What are we supposed to do?"

Keba reached us, frowning as she looked at the Light, but she didn't say anything.

"The Light's your area of expertise," Cal said. "What do you think we should do?"

I wanted to snap that I didn't know, fear gnawing at me as the chance to discover my history slipped away. But Cal was right. This was dreamseer business. If I didn't know what to do, I had to make a guess – and a good one.

"We take it back to Fane." I nodded, gaining strength in my convictions. "It was kept in the light, maybe coming into the dark has caused this. We'll return it to the Isle of Fire." And we'd hope, but I didn't add that.

"Right." Keba started towards the passageway she'd made earlier that would lead us back to the gate we'd crossed through.

Cal smiled. "Look at it this way – Fane can't be any worse off than we left it, can it?"

"I guess not."

He turned towards the passageway. I followed, sending a brief look back towards what remained of the guardian.

A prickle of unease made me pause. The energy in the cavern felt different, changed by the battle that had taken place there, perhaps. There was a sense of... expectancy. I frowned and took a step towards the remaining, broken, crystals. We *had* defeated the guardian, hadn't we?

The cavern's energy hung heavy around me. There was a moment of peace like an indrawn breath and then a crash exploded out from the remaining crystals as what was left of the guardian shattered into a thousand pieces, filling the air of the cavern.

I flinched away, but not quickly enough. A dagger of cold agony sliced through my eye and everything went black.

Chapter Twenty-Two

When I awoke, my ears were ringing with the echo of the explosion, and my head ached as though it had been crushed. My eyes were sore as though my eye sockets were filled with sand. I struggled to sit up.

"Take your time. Are you all right?" It was Cal's voice, an edge of comfort that softened the pain. His hand was on my shoulder, warm and solid. I opened my eyes, finding that only one obeyed the command. The other was hard and sore. I sat on the ground, in amongst the crystal pieces scattered around me. The sparkle of Cal's face stood out above them.

"Don't scare me like that. I thought you were dead." His hand tightened on my shoulder.

"No, not dead. Not yet. The guardian wasn't quite done."

"And is he finished now?"

I wasn't sure. He'd half-blinded me. I moved to rub the gritty blurriness away, supported by Cal who shifted behind me so I had someone to lean against. I gasped as I touched the skin over my eyes. My right eye was the same as ever, but my left felt strange – hard in a way an eyeball never should be.

"Are you still alive in here?" Keba's voice called from the other cave. "That was quite a crash."

"Just." Cal called back a reply. I was too busy trying to work out what was wrong with my eye.

I wiped my damp face. Both eyes were watering. When I blinked, my vision was a little better. I squinted. The view from my right eye was the same as ever, but when I closed that to look through my left, the cavern took on a strange sheen, a glittering glow as though everything was made of crystals. That eye started watering furiously and I wiped it once more. I turned to Cal.

"Hell!" His pale face grew paler still.

"What is it?" He looked strange, as though he was shining, an odd effect that grew stronger if I closed my right eye, and weaker with both open. He swallowed. Fear clawed at my throat. "What?"

The watering didn't seem to want to stop and my eye was throbbing worse than before. I wiped at my cheek again. "What's happened?"

"Your eye — the crystal..." He shook his head, the expression on his face sending waves of panic crashing through me. My head ached, my eye throbbed. "Your eye has turned into crystal," he said.

"You mean a shard of crystal has got into her eye." That was Keba's voice, growing louder as she drew closer. "Let me see."

Cal didn't move away from me, warm at my back. "No, that's not what I mean," he snapped.

I leaned forward, braced against my arms as I craned over one of the many puddles on the cavern's floor. With the dark rock behind it, it became a poor mirror. A whimper keened out of me.

My eye throbbed as though it were pushing against its socket and I had to blink several times to clear my sight enough to see my reflection. "Moons, no." I gasped for air. This was a vision. It was a dream. It couldn't be real. I blinked again and touched my fingers to my cheek, the dint of my eye socket below my left eye. Above my fingers where my dark eye should have been reflected back to me there was instead the dull white of crystal. "This isn't real." I opened my eye wide and touched the tip of my finger to the very corner. Instead of giving flesh, my touch met hard, cold stone.

You will join me. I flinched, unsure if the guardian's voice had really spoken in my head, or if fear was making me hallucinate.

"No." I pushed away from the puddle, my hands shaking. I dug my fingers into my palms. "How do I get rid of it?" Water flowed down my face.

When I looked up, Cal and Keba were staring at each other as though each expected the other to come up with a solution. My panicked heart bounded to life. "This is part of the guardian. He wants to control me. I have to get rid of it."

Cal nodded. "We'll get you back to Fane and find a healer."

You belong to me now.

"Come on, I'll help you." Cal grabbed my arm.

My head spun. "Wait."

But he was already heaving me to my feet. Dizzy, I leaned over and vomited, heat climbing my spine while my stomach wrung itself out and its contents splattered the ground close to my feet.

"Sorry, sorry. I didn't mean to hurt you." He let me go, stepping a pace away. He probably wanted to turn and run.

I heaved again, dragging out what was left in my stomach to splatter again dully at my feet, mingling with the puddles of water and the shards of crystal. I wiped my mouth and looked away. "I can't take this to Fane. I can't risk it."

"We'll carry you."

I shook my head. "That's not what I mean. The guardian's inside me now. I can't risk him enslaving fanes like he did talvarrines."

"So what do we do?"

"You take it out."

He took a pace back. "*Ernith*! I don't think so!"

"You're just moving a stone from one place to another. You could do that in your sleep, Cal."

"That's not what I'd be doing, Deena." He motioned to Keba. "Go and see if there's a healer here who can help."

"No." I twisted my fingers in his sleeve, forcing him to face me. "There isn't time."

"It won't take long." He motioned Keba impatiently and she started towards the exit.

My grip tightened. "And I wouldn't trust them like I trust you, Cal. Please."

His face hardened. "I don't want to hurt you."

"It's already agony. You must have done worse things than this when you were fighting Issaenaptra."

"Not through choice," he muttered.

Pain throbbed through me. "Please, Cal."

"If it hurts too much, tell me and I'll stop. Okay?" He waited for my nod of agreement. I wouldn't stop him. I couldn't risk it.

"Hell's bells," he muttered. Then he took a deep breath and got on with the job in hand. "Lean against me." We shifted so I lay across Cal's lap, my head against his chest. I stared up at the roof of the cavern high over head and pulled my eyelids wide apart. It hurt, but my nerves were already buzzing with pain so it barely made a difference. Cal's breath warmed my cheek, his face so close it was out of focus. Then I felt a sucking tug as Cal used his elemental powers to pull the crystal from its new home in my eye socket. I gritted my teeth, huffing short breaths as the pain filled my skull and flowed through the rest of my body. It wasn't true that the new pain made no difference. The agony had become dulled, but Cal's actions sharpened it right up.

"Keep going," I forced through my teeth when he paused.

Then I was beyond speech.

*

"Deena? Can you hear me?" Cal's tone swam in and out of my hearing. "Don't be dead. I said I wasn't a healer."

"Don't panic. Does she still have a pulse?" Keba's calm voice also rang out overhead.

"I'm not dead." I spoke to assure myself as much as them. I realised I was on the floor when my elbows connected with the ground. I struggled and sat up. My vision was oddly lopsided. I closed my right eye and everything went dark. My hand quested to my left eyelid, finding it free of that horrible hard sensation, but soft and sunken in exchange.

"I'm so sorry, there didn't seem to be anything left once I took out the crystal."

I took my fingers away. "It's okay. At least the crystal's gone." I swallowed. "It can't hurt me now, not any more. And it can't hurt anyone else." I stood up, surprised to find the pain gone but for a sense of numbness. No eye, no problem. "Where's the crystal?" I hardly dared to ask.

Cal pointed. "I didn't touch it. Just in case."

I followed his hand to the small lump of pale crystal on the ground. It was bigger than I'd have thought possible to fit in my eye, but far smaller than the Light of Fane. Otherwise it was a perfect replica, streaks of white and grey swirling with calm beauty beneath the faceted surface. It gave no clue as to how dangerous it was.

"We can't let anyone in here," I said. "Not with all these pieces of crystal lying around."

"At last, something I'm happy to do." Cal turned to the entrance and sent a blast of energy coursing towards the rock there. There was a rumble and crash and the route to the surface of Talvar was obliterated by a rock fall. No one could reach this cavern from Talvar's surface now.

I got to my feet and picked up the Light of Fane.

"Are you sure you're all right?" Keba asked.

I nodded. "Let's go."

"Agreed." Cal ushered us towards the passageway back to the gate.

Keba lead the way, I walked in the middle, and Cal followed behind. I expected something awful to happen every single step, but we reached the gate without incident.

"Ready?" Cal asked.

I nodded.

He took Keba's hand, then reached for mine. He wrapped his warm fingers delicately around my wrist so I could still hold the Light of Fane. I opened my mouth, and he read my mind. "Just expect it to open."

I put my hand against the stone, unsure what would happen, and a moment later, we were back in the gateroom.

Chapter Twenty-Three

I staggered, as we stepped into sudden darkness. Something solid pushed against us and the Light of Fane slipped from my arms. I bent to try and find it in the gloom, then stopped as a voice rang out.

"You're surrounded. We have Tullan Fabler as hostage. Do as you're told or we'll kill him."

Light filled the room, brighter than we'd grown used to and my eye watered. I identified the speaker, the captain of more than a dozen guards holding a shield steady. We either had to obey or step back to Talvar.

"Very well. Take us to the queen." Cal was used to being in tight situations. He didn't lose his cool for even a moment. "We'll cooperate."

The captain smiled unpleasantly. "Oh, the queen will be very pleased to see you. You might not be so pleased to see her."

The shields were lowered cautiously. I tried to reach down for the Light of Fane but I was jerked back with an abrupt command to stand still. I reached behind me with a silent command for the gate to close and the light behind us vanished. Keba and I were relieved of our anima crystals. Cal's word was accepted since the guards could do little else.

I could have told them what was on the floor, disregarded, but if I did, I knew it would be taken from me. It would be safe enough where it was. A guard walked either side of me, gripping my elbows to make me walk quickly. I half-tripped on something soft near the door. It was the knapsack Algamel had kept the anima crystals in. It was empty now, so everyone here should be back to normal. Normal and furious, to judge from our greeting.

One guard sneered as she dragged me through the door. "You should have stayed where you were. The queen will kill you for what you've done."

"The queen should be thanking us," I muttered, but low enough so the guards wouldn't hear. I knew already how unlikely it was that Saldamia would appreciate what we'd done for Fane.

*

Saldamia paused pacing the throne room long enough to throw a glare of loathing at us as we were dragged to stand before her. The windows down one, long side of the room drummed with the constant fall of rain and all the lamps were lit to drive away the gloom. It was hard to tell through the weather, but I thought it was approaching nightfall; we'd been on Talvar hours. Tonight was moonsfall. Tomorrow would be the confirmation ceremony. No wonder Saldamia was so angry. She must be terrified the storm would disrupt her elevation to queen.

Between the windows, another two guards flanked Tullan, who stood with his head bowed, arms bound behind him and anima gone from his arm. I wanted to go to him, but the guards were still gripping my arm.

I focused instead on the windows. With nothing to

stop it, the storm was at full strength.

The guard pressed the two anima crystals they'd taken from Keba and me into the queen's hand. Saldamia regarded them with a sneer before turning and flinging them into the corner, the clatter of their landing drowned out by the patter of rain.

She advanced, and yet stayed far enough away that her guards would be able to cast a shield if any of us moved a step. "You!" She addressed Cal first. "If you disobey me or my guards, I will have you killed. You're no use to me." Her glare moved to Keba. "The same applies to you."

She turned to me. "Dreamseer. I told you to stay where your queen could find you if she needed. You did not ask permission to create a gate and look what has happened as a result."

"I do not need your permission for—"

Saldamia took another step and slapped me hard across the face. Since the guards wouldn't let go of my arms I rubbed my cheek against my shoulder to rub away the pain. I watched Saldamia silently.

"We are drowning. You have placed us all in mortal danger. I suppose you think yourselves clever to defy me?" She didn't wait for a reply. With my example so recent, none of us would have been unwise enough to give one. "What did you hope to achieve?" Again she swept on before we could reply. "Crops and homes are destroyed and still there is no end to the rain."

"The council has suggested that our only hope is to complete the work Issaenaptra started and defeat the people of Earth so we can make a new home there."

I wondered if I dared to point out the flaw in that plan, but I didn't need to.

Saldamia sent a loathing glance towards Tullan. "But we no longer have a gatekeeper. Tullan Fabler has pointed out the impossibility of creating one without her."

"So what punishment should I devise for the fanes who have brought us to this pass? What punishment could possibly match such a crime?"

"The storm can be stopped."

Saldamia looked as though she wanted to hit me again, but if there was a solution she wanted that more. "How? No one has been able to control it."

"We have the Light of Fane."

"The Light of Fane?" Her eyes glittered. I could almost see her mind working. She wanted to dismiss the story as a myth and condemn us for trying to deflect her fury with a child's story – but she didn't want to lose a chance at salvation if it were true.

"Algamel stole the Light of Fane. We went to Talvar to get it back."

I saw the questions she wanted to ask reflected in her expression, but she started with the most important thing. "Where is the Light of Fane?" She looked from one of us to the other. "Who has it?"

"It's in the gateroom."

"You left it in the gateroom?"

I looked at her. "I dropped it. Your guards should have been more careful."

She raised her voice. "My guards should have been more observant." She singled out the captain. "Go and fetch it. Bring it here."

The captain's steps were loud on the wooden floor, then silence fell. Saldamia retreated to the throne with a swish of skirts.

The rest of us simply stood. I wanted to go to Tullan, but I didn't dare risk calling Saldamia's wrath down on my head. Or on his.

Cal cleared his throat. I glanced aside. He raised a brow and looked deliberately at the windows, where water was still cascading down outside. I suspected he was thinking the same thing I was: if Algamel taking the Light of Fane to another world had started the storm, why hadn't us bringing it back made the deluge stop? I lifted my shoulders fractionally. I was trying not to think about the strange split in the Light, the half filled with grey where colours should have spun around each other. I was trying not to think that it was broken and useless, as Thanriel had warned.

We stood in silence. Outside, the sound of the rain continued, oddly comforting since it reflected our doom. But over that came another noise. One that I now recognised, because it was unpleasantly similar to the noise we'd heard in the caves on Talvar – the sounds of a crowd fighting someone, or something.

"Where is everyone else?" I asked. "The rest of the palace guards – and the council, where are they?"

Saldamia frowned as though irritated that I'd pointed out the fact. Adrenaline coursed through me at the thought that they might not have awakened when Algamel left. Maybe they were still sitting at the council table, unconscious and helpless. Saldamia waved away my concern as though the fate of everyone else in the palace was a mere trifle. "My guards and the council members are keeping the palace secure. The storms and flooding have driven the fanes half-mad. They came here and demanded I fix matters." She sounded mildly affronted, as though everyone was acting unreasonably. "Which I will do just as soon as I am able."

"Have you tried working in unison?" Keba asked. It was the first time she'd spoken.

Saldamia frowned at her. "Yes, we have tried that. Even together we could not stop the storm." She glared at me. "So your Light of Fane had better work."

I wanted to ask, Or what? Would she kill me first and then leave the rest of Fane to drown? We all needed the crystal to work.

We stood straighter when the captain returned. Saldamia stalked down from the throne to snatch the Light from her.

"This is the Light of Fane?" She sounded disappointed, regarding the crystal in her hands as though it should have been gift-wrapped, or covered in gold, perhaps.

"That's the Light of Fane. I will use it to stop the storm." If I could – I thought but didn't add.

"You? No, this is a job I will do myself." Saldamia moved away, turning her back to me. I still heard her murmur, "The queen who restored balance to Fane. I will be worshipped." A pause. "I'll be adored."

I wondered which outcome she valued more. Her hands stroked greedily over the surface. Unease slid through me. "It needs a dreamseer. The crystal is too powerful for an ordinary fane." I couldn't get the talvarrines out of my head, the population of a world turned to slaves, powerless to overcome the guardian, their flesh bodies separated from their life energy and trapped in the crystals so the guardian could do as he wished without opposition.

Saldamia looked up. Disbelief wreathed her face, as

236

though she might have misheard my words. Then she laughed. "But I am not an ordinary fane. When the sun rises tomorrow I will be crowned queen."

Moonsfall was tonight. And not far off to judge from the grey outside. My unease twisted and grew to fear. In the morning the queen should be crowned – but I was still sure that queen wouldn't be Saldamia. "The Light was damaged on Talvar. It's dangerous. You shouldn't try to use it." I told Saldamia the truth, but I already knew she wouldn't listen.

Saldamia's face twisted in contempt. "You believe you can control it but I cannot? Don't be ridiculous! You are young and weak. I am stronger. And I am the queen. I *should* be the most powerful."

She wouldn't have power just for wishing for it. That was what was wrong with her bid to be queen. She was more interested in the glory being queen would give her than in the hard work that would be required to lead the fanes and prevent disagreements becoming wars.

"Let me use the crystal. Please," I begged. "I don't want harm to come to anyone here."

"Neither do I, you stupid *zangtaff*. I was commanding the elements through my anima crystal centuries before you were born." Her eyes blazed. "If you can control this storm, then I will be able to do so more easily."

She walked up the steps of the dais to the throne. I tried to follow her, but the guards stopped me before I had even taken a step. "You must be careful," I called to her.

She inclined her head, but her tone was sharp with anger. "I am not a fool. If you still haven't learned that

237

lesson, you will learn it now." Saldamia set the Light of Fane securely in her lap, her hands spanning the curve of it, fingertips pressing lightly against the faceted surface.

She took a deep breath and then another. A smug smile played around her lips. I watched her but nothing awful happened. The energy in the room didn't change. A minute passed. I'd been too cautious. There wasn't danger in a fane using a whole crystal rather than a tiny anima. I glanced towards the windows. And yet, the storm didn't seem to be letting up.

Then Saldamia screamed, a high, ringing sound of terror and pain. It lasted a count of five then she fell silent, slithering from the throne to lie on the dais steps, the Light of Fane rolling from her hands and bouncing to the floor.

Everyone in the room stared, as though Saldamia's command of the Light had frozen us all in place. It was Cal who broke the silence. "Look to your queen, you fools."

The captain took a faltering step then strode to Saldamia's side. She lifted Saldamia's hand and felt for a pulse. "Fetch a healer," she barked. Two of the guards left the room. In the disarray, they weren't watching us. I could have gone to the Light, but instead I hurried to Tullan.

"Are you all right?"

He nodded. "You?"

"Yes. Zan got to Talvar."

"And you came back."

I looked up into his blue eyes. "Yes. This is my home."

238

He nodded and I knew he understood.

"Here. This is yours." Keba interrupted, handing my anima ring to me as she fastened her own anima around her neck.

"Thank you." I slipped mine onto my finger.

Tullan half-turned to show the metal binding his wrists. "I'd be grateful if you'd oblige..." I concentrated my elemental powers, glad to find they were strong enough to make his shackles fall apart. He put his arms around me in a powerful hug. "I'm glad you came back." He let me go. "And I'm glad Zan stayed away. I'm sure Saldamia would have commanded me to make another gate. I'm glad that's not possible now there's no Earth blood on Fane."

Our eyes met. If he didn't know for sure, I thought he'd worked out what ran in my veins. Like Cal and Keba, he was telling me that secret was safe with him. I nodded. "Fane must sort out its problems alone. I don't think that's a bad thing."

"Nor do I."

The opening door drew our attention. We turned as a healer strode in, flanked by the guards the captain had sent.

"What happened here?" The healer immediately took command, pushing the captain out of the way to check Saldamia's health herself.

"The queen touched a crystal. She screamed and collapsed," the captain explained.

"A crystal? An anima crystal, you mean?" she queried.

"The Light of Fane," I said, because I didn't trust the captain to include that detail. "It was too powerful for her."

239

The healer scoffed, still busy about her checks on Saldamia. "The Light of Fane? Isn't that a myth?"

How many more times was I going to have to say it? "No. It's not a myth."

Cal walked towards me, his back to the healer and the guard captain. I saw he was carrying the Light. I nodded. It was safer with us than it was with them.

"Right, well, I don't think—" the healer broke off when Saldamia stirred. "My queen..." The healer patted Saldamia's hand to rouse her, easing an arm around her shoulders to help her sit up. Saldamia murmured something. Her eyes remained closed, a frown of pain creasing her brow but she sat up, raising a hand as though to halt queries and investigation.

"How do you feel, my queen?" the healer asked, all deference now Saldamia was conscious.

"I am ... powerful," she said in a low tone unlike her usual voice. Then she opened her eyes.

Chapter Twenty-Four

The captain swore. Even the healer looked shocked.

Saldamia's eyes were blind white. The crystal had destroyed her sight, like the dreamseers on Talvar. I shuddered and looked away.

The healer cleared her throat. "How do you feel, my queen?" She checked Saldamia's pulse, then peered to look closely at her eyes.

"The light is too bright. Why am I being dazzled?" She pulled away from the healer's reach as though she had only just realised her arm was being held. "Who is that? Show yourself."

"I am right here, my queen," the healer replied. "In front of you. Can you not see me?"

"It is too bright. I need darkness. Take me into the dark."

The skin on my arms crawled. Her tone was confused, but the intent was clear enough. I remembered the dreamseers on Talvar, blind in the darkness with their abilities robbed from them. Saldamia wasn't a dreamseer, but she had her own powers. "Don't take her anywhere. Keep her in the light," I said, waiting until the healer nodded.

"I shall need light to see what is wrong with her,"

the healer said, leaning forward to look into her eyes again. Saldamia's head moved restlessly, as though if she found the correct angle she would be able to see again. The healer considered her patient. "The queen's mind may have been damaged by what just happened."

The captain shifted uneasily. "And what did just happen?"

The healer shooed her away with a flick of her fingers. "I'm not sure. I need to work. The queen is ill."

At a nudge from Cal, I looked at him. He held the Light of Fane towards me. For a moment I thought he meant me to take it from him, and then I saw it more clearly. The side with the grey cloud had grown darker still, threads of black swirling through it in a dull echo of the swirling colours in the other half.

I looked at him and nodded. I'd got rid of the crystal in my eye, knowing that to be dangerous, but the other crystal we'd brought back from Talvar looked as though it had also been infected by the guardian. The dark side must be damage, a focus for whatever was leftover of the guardian's power. That side wanted to take over and control the population of Fane. Starting with Saldamia.

"How do we fix the Light?" Cal murmured.

"I don't know," I returned, my voice similarly low so the guards wouldn't hear. "If we take it back to the Isle of Fire, perhaps the heat and the light there will repair it. That must be why it was kept surrounded by fire."

The healer sent a scowl in our direction. "I need peace for healing."

But as though the world had heard that request and decided not to comply, a sudden roar of voices echoed outside, and the walls of the palace shook momentarily, as it had when Algamel had been testing his powers.

Cal reached the windows at the same time as the guard, a moment before the glass imploded. Both threw up shields and the fragments flew past them, diverted to scatter on the floor. The healer, bent over Saldamia, cursed and cast a shield over them both without pausing in her work.

"The guards outside have been overwhelmed," the captain said, peering through the now-empty window frames to confirm the situation. She turned to face the room, her gaze gliding over Cal, me and the healer, then halting on Saldamia. "The Council must keep everyone peaceful until the queen is healed."

"We can help the council," Keba said, addressing the guard. "We have to tell them what has happened. They will know what to do in Saldamia's absence."

"Very well." The captain motioned two of the guards to accompany us. "The rest of you will stay with me and keep the queen safe."

Cal strode out of the room, casting a light so he could see his way through the dim corridors. We hurried after him, the guards barely keeping up.

"We can't do much against everyone outside," I pointed out. "There are only three of us."

"Yeah, but two of us are me and Cal. You'd be surprised what we can achieve together," Keba told me.

Cal shook his head. "I'm not planning to fight. The council are the ones in charge. They need to keep the

243

situation contained until we can restore the Light of Fane and stop the storm."

"Cal." I grabbed his arm, pulling him to a stop. Keba halted a few steps away. "We've brought the Light back and it hasn't stopped the storm. I only need to look at it to know it's been damaged. What if it *can't* restore balance to nature?"

Cal folded his arms. "What other ideas do you have?"

I shrugged. "Maybe if we all work together—"

"We will," Cal stated firmly.

"No, I mean *all* of us. There are a lot of fanes outside and they all have their anima crystals now. Saldamia said they couldn't control the storm, but maybe with the Light of Fane added to all that power, we can make it work without overpowering us."

"Right, then that's what the council needs to make happen." He swerved the wrong way around a corner, heading away from the noise.

I hurried after him to stay in the light, too worn out to cast my own. "Where are you going?"

"The council chamber's the other way," Keba pointed out, calm as ever.

"If we're going to persuade the council to do anything, then we need some authority of our own." He threw open a door and strode into one of the palace chambers.

I followed, stumbling against the doorframe. I was discovering that it was hard to judge distance with only one eye.

I'd barely entered before Cal was striding back out. He paused to throw a piece of heavy cloth around my shoulders. I touched the stiff, ornate fabric. One of the councillor's ceremonial robes.

Cal continued, "Like Fane's dreamseer telling them confidently what to do."

"They won't listen to me. Half the council helped Saldamia drug me, they won't pay attention to me now."

Cal grabbed my hand. "Of course they will. They'll listen to you if you look like a dreamseer and act like a dreamseer," he promised. His sparkling eyes met mine. "You're not a helpless child now, Dee. You are Fane's Honourable Dreamseer and you've just been to Talvar and back to rescue the Light of Fane and return balance to our world. They *will* listen to you."

As he looked at me, my confidence returned. "Yes. They'd better."

Cal smiled. "That's right."

Another crashing sound battered the other side of the palace.

I fastened the cloak Cal had found for me securely around my shoulders. And I thought I'd got rid of the trappings of a dreamseer. "Right." A sceptical council and a population of crazed, violent fanes fearful for the end of their world. And I wasn't fond of crowds at the best of times.

"Are you ready?" Keba asked. Cal was already halfway down the corridor.

"Yes." I straightened my shoulders and started after Cal. I was the dreamseer. I could do this. Armed with the damaged, possibly powerless, Light of Fane.

I looked down at it. The swirling in the crystal was agitated, drawing heat from my fingertips. The contrast between the two sides seemed to grow bigger each moment. The colours were brighter, the grey side darker. The Light of Fane might be damaged, but I was sure it wasn't powerless. It had caused Saldamia's blindness, and yet I had to make it end the storm and return peace to my unstable home.

Misgiving gripped me and I stumbled. I'd lost one eye already. I didn't want to lose my sight in the other. Before Keba could offer help, I straightened and raised my chin. I wasn't Saldamia. I combined the blood and the abilities of fane and dreamseer, I would be strong enough to control the Light, to use its beneficial power without falling prey to the negative. I thrust any competing ideas out of my mind and followed Cal into the council chamber.

*

As we strode inside, the noise increased threefold. Guards were dotted around the edges of the room and the eleven remaining members of the council were clustered in the middle, talking.

They looked up when we walked in. Glances paused on me and then passed by to rest on the guard beside us. "Where is the queen?" Gallia, second in command, was first to speak.

I didn't wait for the guard to answer. I was the dreamseer. I held equal authority with the council members here.

"She is not available," I told Gallia, looking straight at her as I spoke. "The queen has been taken ill."

A murmur of distress passed through the council.

Gallia's eyes gleamed with distrust and alarm. "I am sorry to hear that. What ails her?"

"She tried to use the Light of Fane but it overwhelmed her. A healer is with her."

Another councillor stepped forward. I dragged his

name from my memory: Edo. "The Light of Fane?" His tone was disbelieving.

"Yes, the Light of Fane." I lifted it up. They could argue with the crystal itself if they were going to claim it was a myth.

The sight of it prompted more murmurs. Edo wasn't done yet, though. He glared at me. The back of my neck prickled. I could almost feel his hands gripping my hair, forcing my head back so Saldamia could drug me. "Did you kill Saldamia?" he demanded.

"No. She's still alive. The Light of Fane blinded her." I ignored the rumble of alarm that statement provoked. "I should be able to use the crystal to control the storm, but I will need help. The fanes outside must stop using their energy so they don't collide with what I'm doing." I sounded authoritative and in control. I waited to be challenged but the murmuring was no worse than before.

The council exchanged anxious looks. As was, perhaps, fitting, Gallia stepped forward again. "Can you do this, dreamseer? Can you stop the storm?"

It occurred to me that the council would need a scapegoat if the storm couldn't be stopped. I cleared my throat and looked at them all. "I know that if I can't, no one can."

Gallia considered me, ignoring the comments the other councillors muttered behind her. She inclined her head briefly. "Very well, Honourable Dreamseer. The council will support you in your task." She turned and motioned to the guards standing either side of the doors leading to the balcony which overlooked the grand entrance below. The guards tugged the doors wide and the sound burst into the room, the desperate

247

cries of the crowd rising over the susurration of constant rainfall.

The fanes below seemed to have enough deference for their queen and council that they weren't trying to break into the palace. Instead, they were battering the walls until someone came out to speak to them. On top of that, the storm was still throwing water from grey clouds, the rain bouncing and running off the shields they'd cast overhead. The sun hung low on the horizon, dusk's glow nearly extinguished so the only light on the scene was that cast by the fanes themselves. For them all to stand in that with only the barest shelter, they must have been beyond fury. I could only hope they weren't beyond reason.

And I had just said that I could stop the storm. I swallowed and stepped forward, squaring my shoulders against the pull of my borrowed robes. Gallia walked on my right and Cal stayed close to my left.

At the doorway we paused. Gallia glanced in my direction. She smiled and inclined her head. For the first time I thought she was seeing me as a fane and as an equal, instead of as a servant or one of the guards to be commanded. "Are you ready, Honourable Dreamseer?"

I forced a smile in return. "I am ready, Honourable Lady."

She nodded and we stepped forward. Cal had conjured a shield to protect all three of us, but when we stepped into view, the drenched fanes below paused shouting and using elemental energy to rattle the windows and shake the walls.

"Fanes." Gallia's powerful voice reached the crowd

below. "Help is at hand. Our dreamseer will use the Light of Fane to end this storm, but we must all play our part to help her."

Silence. Gallia took that as assent and motioned me forward. The Light of Fane was slippery in my suddenly-sweaty hands. I hated groups, and now I had to stand in front of everyone and save the world.

Murmuring started in the crowd below. I closed my eyes and began. "I just need peace. Do not interfere with the elements. I will be as quick as I'm able."

I didn't wait for anyone to agree or disagree, I got on with my work. The Light of Fane was heavy. I wrapped my hands around it. I had promised to make it return order to Fane. Now I had to make good my vow. I had nothing to help me, no clues from the books I'd spent my life reading, no guidance from another dreamseer. All I had were my own instincts, reawakened by what I'd found on Talvar after years of *somnaya* abuse. I glanced down and saw the bright colours swirling through one side, with grey as dark as the clouds overhead shifting restlessly on the other side. My sweaty hands were immediately cool as it drew warmth out of me.

I spread my fingers over the top of the crystal, *feeling* the swirl of the colours inside. I could hear its hum beneath the drumming of the rain, discordant and eerie. I closed my eye, remembering the Fane of before, the Fane I'd only seen in visions, long before the war when our world had been green and peaceful. This was what Fane should be like. There would be rain, of course there would, but sunshine and rain, storms and calm, would be balanced.

I thought of the flowers in my garden, the *gimfruit*

bushes and *marbay* nut trees. A lump formed in my throat. I missed it, even though I'd once determined never to return. What a fool I'd been. This was my home. Calm, peaceful and beautiful Fane, it was where I belonged.

It wasn't a noise that told me it was working, it was the opposite. There was absolute silence as though the hundreds of fanes below were holding their breath.

I opened my good eye. I'd been focussing so hard on the pictures in my head I hadn't heard the sound of the rain ceasing. Cal and Gallia were staring upwards, like all the fanes below who were staring at the suddenly-clear sky with wonderment.

The clouds dissipated and the last rays of dusk shone on the damp ground, sparkling glints of pink gold off the sand. Fane looked new, beautiful to match my memories. "We did it." My voice was low. I opened my hands to see the crystal nestled in my palms, pinks and golds swirling through what I was starting to think of as the 'good' side like an echo to Fane's setting sun. Black threaded through the grey on the Light's other side.

"*You* did it," Cal corrected.

I looked at him and smiled. Here was what a dreamseer could do when she had full access to her powers. No wonder we had been honoured and revered in centuries past; so we should be.

"The Queen!"

Irritation swept through me – was the crowd assigning my miracle to wretched Saldamia? Then more voices took up the cry, some cheering, others angry. The crowd pushed in a solid mass towards one side of the palace.

"The Queen!"

A figure shuffling across the corner of my vision caught my attention, and my heart dropped to the damp sand below. The cries for the queen weren't appreciation or condemnation for what the crowd supposed she'd done, they were a simple acknowledgement of her presence. Walking around the corner of the palace was Saldamia, the healer at her elbow guiding her forward.

It couldn't have been more perfectly, devastatingly timed if a record keeper had been standing by, directing her to step forward at precisely the worst possible moment. As Saldamia groped blindly around the corner of the palace and stepped into the area in front of the palace, filled with the crowd who seemed equally matched supporters and detractors, the final sliver of sun dipped below Fane's horizon and darkness fell.

The absolute dark of moonsfall night.

Chapter Twenty-Five

The Light of Fane heated as though channelling the fire of the newly-vanished sun, and then it seared ice cold to my skin.

A voice in my head roared, *I will be your queen!* and I fell into a vision so real all I could see was my single, inevitable future burning through the dark.

I sat in the gate room of the palace of the once-great fanes, the darkness a boon, the only warmth in the world coiled in the Light of Fane in my lap. The Light was now filled entirely with black that swirled inside the crystal, concentrating where my fingertips rested.

Energy pulsed into the crystal, robbed from the fanes who could no longer use their elemental abilities to control their world.

This is as it is, the crystal in my head told me. There was no escape. My existence was to end as it started – my abilities under the control of someone else who would exploit me without thought.

My vision clung at me as I tried to focus on the present. This wasn't real. It wasn't true. There was time to avoid it. But if I didn't find my way out of the vision, it would become real. "I need light." I tried to speak aloud but my words weren't strong enough to break through my vision. In darkness, the crystal would win. The grey, destructive side of the Light of Fane would swamp the beneficial colours. It had already overpowered Saldamia and it would overpower me.

I needed light, and heat. I understood why the Isle of Fire had been created now: to drive back the darkness. There was nothing intrinsically dangerous in taking the Light to Talvar – the danger lay in the dark whether that was on Talvar or here on Fane.

You and I will sit in the dark and rule this place.

My vision crowded around me, darkness and stone, chill cold seeping into my bones until the blood ceased to run in my veins. This wasn't ruling: it was a living death. "I need light," I mumbled, before the crystal froze my mouth to silence.

Light burst through the darkness. Welcome warmth flooded into me while the crystal recoiled. Then cold overwhelmed the warmth again. *You belong to me.* Reality slipped and slithered from my grip and I remained locked in my future.

Then light broke through again. But it was weak, light but no heat.

I will have darkness.

"You aren't going to win."

I tried to make sense of the sounds, another voice joining me in my vision. Was the voice speaking to me, or to the Light of Fane grown dark in my arms? The crystal knew. It laughed, the sound echoing around the gateroom. *I have already won. You are powerless.*

"Don't tell me that. It'll only make me more determined."

"Cal." I recognised the fane arguing with a stone

253

that couldn't be argued with.

"Dee. I know you're in there."

Cal was real. My vision wasn't real. I wasn't in the gateroom. I was on the balcony of the palace. I could fight the Light of Fane. Warmth surged through me.

"I'm coming for you."

I tried to open my eyes but I was surrounded by darkness. Moonsfall. It was only moonsfall.

It wasn't moonsfall. Light never came to the gateroom. I would never leave.

"Your name is Deena. You are fane's dreamseer. This isn't real."

This is as it is.

I knew which voice I wanted to be right, but I had no strength to fight. The Light of Fane connected with Saldamia, drawing her energy into itself, consuming her strength so it could crush my feeble attempts to hold it back. I fought, but darkness overwhelmed me, the Light leeching warmth from me until I was frozen in place, tied to the dark by the crystal I had brought to Fane. There was nothing but this. Nothing but eternal darkness.

"You have to fight it, Deena."

You're too late. The dreamseer is mine.

"The dreamseer is her own person."

My vision wavered for long enough for me to know that it wasn't real. This was the future, *a* future. It wasn't true. Not yet.

"I'm coming for you, Deena. You and I can beat this thing."

Laughter filled the air. It vibrated through me, high and triumphant. The crystal controlled me. We were already one. There was no escape. Beneath my chilled fingers the strength of the darkened crystal surged out to the fanes standing outside the palace, reaching greedily for their energy, hungry for more power.

Your only hope is to get away. Far away, I told Cal, dully, struggling to hold back power far stronger than I was. If he could be saved I could bear the cold and the darkness.

"I'm not going anywhere. This isn't real. The darkness is moonsfall, that's all. It will pass. The sun will return, Dee, it's not gone forever."

The Light of Fane reached the first of the fanes, curling around them in a swirl of black only visible to myself. The future was already coming true. *It's too late.*

Cal's brilliant eyes glinted. "I've never accepted that from anyone. I'm proof it's never too late. You're proof of that, Deena."

And I saw him. Cal, the rebel who didn't know when he was beaten. My heart jumped in my chest as he stood before me, his eyes shining brighter than Fane's moons, warmer than the sun. He placed his hands on my shoulders and heat burned through the chill the Light of Fane had placed in me.

"I'm here. How do we stop this, Deena?"

The black swirls grew more agitated, trying to find a way to access the fanes' energy. "The Light of Fane is too powerful. I can't control it."

"Then we'll do it together." One of his hands moved to my face, cradling my cheek. "I'm here, Deena. I'm not going to let you face this alone."

You do not need help. I am all you need.

I reached out to Cal. "I need you." In my vision I could admit it. "Don't leave me."

"I won't leave you until we've won. Together we can

do this."

His eyes were bright. His arms wrapped around my shoulders and his lips touched mine… brief, but eternally warm and safe. He pulled away. "How can I help, Dee?"

My lips tingled. Oddly, that made everything clearer. "We need light and heat, but it's moonsfall. We need the sun but there is no sun."

"We're fanes. We will make our own sun."

I remembered the weak light of earlier: light without heat. "It won't be enough. We need to remake the Isle of Fire, that's the only thing that can control the Light of Fane. We can't do it alone."

"Dee, when are you going to realise? If you're doing the right thing on Fane you're never alone. There must be ten thousand of us here. Everyone will help you."

You do not need him. Together, we will rule this place.

Some sort of together when I was its slave.

"The fanes here will help you," Cal told me. "Show them what to do. Show us all what happens if the crystal wins."

Stronger than *somnaya*, his words made my vision change around me, shifting from the gateroom to the Gillabar Plain. Reality meshed with my vision. The Light of Fane had already connected with the fanes, trying to take their energy as it had done with Saldamia. I used that connection to enable everyone to see what I saw, what would happen if we didn't work together to defeat the crystal. Horror surged back through the connection towards me as the scene came into focus.

It was, as I'd seen it the day of my mother's funeral, a battlefield after the battle, but this time I could identify the location. We were right here, as though the future were only days ahead of us, the sun high over the fane queen's palace, shining down on the scene of destruction. From horizon to horizon, the ground was strewn with bodies, the sand beneath them stained red. The fanes were silent in death, but the scene wasn't quiet. The flapping of wings snapped at the air as carrion birds plunged from the sky to feed. The squabble of birds fighting over a morsel of torn flesh tore at my ears.

The war-like fanes had fought, some controlled by the crystal, others fighting against it. That division resulted in this scene: thousands dead. Bile rose in my throat, my own revulsion echoed and swollen by the responses of the fanes around me, as appalled as I was.

I will bring you peace. The crystal cried out in my mind and my vision changed again, out of my control like I'd taken *somnaya*. We remained on the Gillabar Plain, but now the fanes were whole and well. But not in a way that any fane would accept as natural. Everyone sat cross-legged, blank faces staring unseeing into the air. The Light of Fane, unchallenged, fed off their energy.

I will take your energy and I will give you peace.

The fanes didn't respond to this vision as the crystal expected. It had misjudged them, expecting them to be lulled by its idea of peace. Instead, ripples of unease and protest surged through the air towards me. They swelled to anger and with a sudden sense of terror, I realised showing everyone this future might end by making the first one, where everyone was dead, more likely.

"Find us a better future. Show us what is possible." Cal's voice prompted me and possibilities swung around me. *This.* For the first time in my life, I welcomed a vision.

At first there were only vague images, snapshots of possibility that flowed from the future towards me, snippets of scenes that barely lasted long enough for me to understand what I was seeing. I held still and let my mind fill with the idea of peace and unity; fanes as friends rather than enemies. Slowly, the steady image of a single, beautiful future came into focus.

I held the scene steady in my mind and laid it before the fanes below, ensuring everyone saw what I saw.

The new vision was the opposite of the others. It showed a river, the Paengan, as though we were bounding past high in the air. The river snaked through fertile fields bursting with ripening crops as it flowed towards the coast. Either side of the banks as the vision swooped along the river's length were villages, home to content fanes supported by the bounty of the land. It could have been a scene from a few hundred years before, before the gates to Earth had poisoned the land, before we had fought amongst ourselves about the best way to stop the damage.

My vision made it clear that was within reach again. The gates to Earth were sealed thanks to Zan. We needed to control the Light of Fane, to place it within the Isle of Fire once more so the evil inside it was contained and then this vision could come true.

"If we want peace, we must first make fire," I told everyone. "We must contain the Light of Fane in fire and it will never grow strong enough to harm us."

Barely had I spoken the words when heat flared

258

around me.

No! The voice in my head screamed, hard and furious. The heat burned, strong and steady. The crystal scrabbled at the fanes, darkness swirling around them but unable to get at their energy now they were united against it. Finally, the voice fell silent.

"It's over, Dee."

"I know."

The words triggered my return to reality. It took me a moment to understand where I was. The scene around me was wrong. I had returned to the Isle of Fire instead of the palace. I turned a full circle. It wasn't possible to have travelled so far. My heart soared as I understood the truth. I was still at the palace. My surroundings had changed, but I hadn't moved. The flames formed a perfect circle. The Isle of Fire was remade, subduing the Light of Fane in my arms. I looked down. The crystal was still in two halves, but the colours swirled more brightly while the dark side had faded to a dirty white instead of the black that had filled it only moments before. It was safe. It was over.

But I was alone.

"Cal!" Fear made my voice high and thin. Panic turned somersaults in my stomach. "Cal!" I put down the Light of Fane and drew on my elemental powers to keep the flames from burning me. The elements were slow to do my bidding, my abilities worn out by the visions I'd just seen and shared. But I wasn't scared for myself. Heart hammering against my ribs, I called his name again.

"Here." The croaking word descended to coughing. I turned in the direction of his voice but I couldn't see

259

him through the orange flames that cracked and roared higher than my head.

"Are you all right?" I gripped my anima ring and forced the flames to subside. Tired or not, I would find him. Cal had got me through my vision. I had to know he was all right.

When I concentrated on forcing down the heat the flames dipped, giving me space to move. Leaving the Light of Fane behind, I walked between the columns of flame until I was through the heat. I stepped into cool, fresh air. My hip bumped into the stone wall of the balcony of the palace. Lying in the corner was Cal, his eyes sparkling madly.

"Cal?" I crouched down, the fire at my back, the chill air of Fane on my face.

He lifted a hand. "I'm all right." He struggled to his feet. I rose alongside him. He put a hand on the top of the balcony wall for support. "Okay, I've felt better." He looked up and grinned. "But I've felt much worse on other occasions, too." His smile fell away. "Did we do it?"

"Yes." The fanes on the Gillabar Plain below were clustered in groups, talking with each other, probably about what had just happened. The Light of Fane was safely contained. Danger was finally past.

He leaned forward and took a deep breath. "*Ernith, somnaya* is evil stuff."

I swivelled to face him. "What?" I breathed in and smelled a trace of its scent. A telltale sheen of sweat shone on Cal's forehead. "What did you do?"

"I couldn't tell what was going on in your vision, but I could see it wasn't going well. I decided the best thing to do was to join you in it."

I stared at him. "*You* took it?"

Cal shrugged. "I did say we might need it one day."

"You drank *somnaya*?"

He wouldn't meet my eye. "I needed to get into your vision with you."

"But it's dangerous."

Another shrug. "I couldn't get you out of your vision, so what else could I do? I needed to see what you were seeing. I needed to be able to speak to you so I could get you out."

I remembered his voice. Heat rose in my face. He'd done more than speak to me in my vision. Did he remember it, too? He shifted, and I caught sight of the bottle in his hand. It glinted as he drew back his hand.

"Wait!" I was too late. He hefted the bottle in a powerful throw that curved an arc through the air. Once away from the balcony, it disappeared into darkness, although I heard it land, the snap of breaking glass reaching me from the ground below.

"Sorry." Cal faced me. His lips twitched. "You did tell me to throw it away."

"It's not that – it was half-empty."

He didn't understand. "Did you want me to save it?"

"No. That's a massive dose, Cal. You could have—" The thought was too awful to say aloud. I amended, "You could have done yourself some harm with that much. You saw what it did to me."

He shrugged, tipping his head up as though fascinated by the black sky overhead. "It was the only way I could think of to help."

"It was too big a risk," I told him.

His frown reappeared, big as ever. "Do I look as though I can't evaluate risk and make my own decisions? I wasn't about to leave you to face whatever you were facing alone."

"You should have done." I bit my lip. That wouldn't have worked out well. But still...

He faced me, angry for the first time. "Would you stop saying I should abandon you like – like an empty bottle or something. I couldn't do that if I tried. And I wouldn't try, not with you, Dee."

His cheeks were pink. That could just have been the effects of *somnaya*. Or it might have been something else entirely. "Do you— " I cleared my throat and started again. "Do you remember what happened in the vision?"

He was staring towards the horizon as though the moonsfall sky was the most fascinating thing he'd ever beheld. "It's a bit jumbled, to be honest."

It was what I'd expected him to say. I knew how *somnaya* made you feel. But I wasn't prepared for the way disappointment thrust a knife through my chest.

I nodded, breathing hard so I could trust myself to speak.

He looked at me. I thought the colour in his face was stronger, but I'd have to have looked straight at him to be sure and there was no way I was going to do that. Not now. My turn to stare hard at the horizon.

"I do remember one thing, Dee." He caught my hand in his. The rough ends of his damaged fingers brushed the soft skin beneath my knuckles. I looked up and the expression in his glittering eyes trapped me. "I remember kissing you."

I wanted to look away, but that moment might never have come again. "I remember that, too," I managed.

"I'd, er, like to do it again. For real. Would – er,

would that be all right?"

I smiled and reached a hand to his face, loving the feel of his warm, smooth skin. His hand tightened on mine, his scarred skin jarring. I pulled away. I was done with hiding, done with being frightened. I was the dreamseer and I would take responsibility for my actions – all of them. "I have to tell you something. It might change things."

Cal's expression clouded. His throat worked. "Go ahead."

I closed my eyes so I wouldn't have to look at him as I admitted, "It wasn't my mother who found you for Issaenaptra." He wasn't stupid. It wouldn't take him long to join the pieces.

I squinted at him, waiting for the anger. Waiting for him to finally turn away and leave me. He stood perfectly still, his frown etched further into his skin than it should be possible to go. He searched my face. His left hand was still in mine, the damage Issaenaptra put there – because I'd made it so she could – like a brand where it touched my skin. I closed my eye again. He hadn't said a word. Maybe he hadn't put it together.

I took another breath. "From the age of thirteen, I did it all. I'm the one who found you when you ran. I told Issaenaptra where you were. I'm the reason she... hurt you. I'm the reason you had to flee to Earth." I glanced at him. Was that anger in his mad eyes? I was sure there was fury in mine – at Issaenaptra and my mother for what they'd made me do, but mostly at myself. "So you really don't have any reason on Fane to like me." My chest hurt, as though I had heaved something out of me and thrown it at his feet.

263

There was a big, long silence. I wished he would shout at me. Or simply turn and walk away.

Instead, his hands tightened on mine. "Deena, it doesn't matter."

I looked up. "Of course it matters, don't you understand—"

"Yes, I understand. And I'm telling you it doesn't matter." He took a breath. "I knew there must be something like this."

"What?"

He dropped my hands, rubbing his cheek like he was trying to find the right words. "I know we didn't get off to a great start and I... thought some wrong things about you, but you were so twitchy around me I knew there had to be something more to it. I saw what Saldamia did to you and I know Issaenaptra would have been worse." He took a breath and looked straight at me. "Did you betray me by choice?"

"No, but—"

He gathered up my hands again. "That's all that matters. The war's over, Deena. Let it be over."

I searched his face. "Don't you care?"

His shoulders shifted, like he wanted to shrug but couldn't. Honest, straightforward Cal couldn't tell an outright lie. "Yes, but I care just as much for what she did to you as what she did to me."

"So – you don't hate me?"

He smiled and was beautiful again. "No, I don't hate you, Dee." His thumb lifted to stroke my cheek, coming to rest under my chin. A fingertip traced my bottom lip. I put my arms around him, revelling in his warmth and solidity. The strength I knew would always be there for me. He dipped his head to mine, his breath soft on my cheek before our lips touched for a single, tender moment.

"Dreamseer!" The call came from the other side of the flames.

Cal gave a grunt of annoyance and straightened. "The council had better be wanting to congratulate you, not demand something new of the dreamseer."

I smiled, giddy from the kiss. "Or they'll have you to deal with?"

"Yeah, that's right."

Together we walked around the balcony, squeezing past the flames, into the council chamber.

Gallia met us, her face sober. "Fane has lost its queen."

Saldamia had been brought into the palace. She lay quite still on the floor. She might have only been unconscious, except that the healer with her wasn't attending to her but standing to one side, pale-faced as she spoke to one of the councillors.

I nodded and waited for Gallia to claim the title. Sunrise was only hours away and a new queen had to be crowned because that was what had always happened on Fane.

Instead, Gallia straightened and addressed me. "Dreamseer, the council needs to know what vision you have seen for Fane – have you seen a new queen amongst us?"

The councillors fell silent, turning to watch me and Gallia – and hear what I had to say. For the first time, I didn't see judgement in their expressions. They would listen to what I said – whatever that was.

"I have seen no queen," I replied. "But we have all of us tonight seen a vision of fanes working peacefully together. We no longer need a queen, we simply need a council to work together for the good of us all and provide advice and guidance when we ask."

Gallia nodded, then turned to the other councillors. "We have heard the dreamseer. Do we all agree to abide by what she has seen for our future and work together for the good of Fane?"

"I agree." A councillor at the back spoke up first. I couldn't see who it was but the others followed, with greater or lesser degrees of enthusiasm. As they were making their promises, a familiar figure stepped into view. Keba moved silently to my side and patted my shoulder. Our eyes met. She smiled, acknowledgement of what I'd achieved.

"And just like that, Fane becomes a republic," Cal drawled.

The sarcastic tone was familiar. I'd have thought Cal would approve of self-rule, but it was always hard to tell with him. "We don't need a queen," I said again, reassuring myself as much as I was telling Cal anything.

"And now we're all agreed on that fact."

Keba added her view. "Oh, I'm sure it won't be that easy. There'll be plenty for the council to argue about. It's what they do so well."

"Let's bask for a bit," Cal countered. "You've got everyone to agree, Deena. That's something neither Issaenaptra nor Saldamia ever managed."

His smile was infectious. Relief warmed me. "Not bad for a useless dreamseer, huh?"

"You're not useless; you're quite something, Deena," Keba stated. "Don't let anyone tell you different." With a nod, she vanished into the crowd in the council

266

chamber.

Cal frowned. "I never thought you were useless."

"Yes, you did." I said the words without resentment. "And maybe... maybe I was. But I'm not now. And you did change your mind."

"Yeah," he conceded, a smile tilting his mouth. "You do know they'll be knocking on your door at the first sign of trouble, don't you?"

I smiled, because for the first time I didn't mind. This was what it ought to be as a dreamseer; a servant of Fane, but not at anyone's beck and call. "If I can help them, I will." Through the broken windows of the chamber, I saw the crowd outside disperse, groups of them bounding into the air, back to their homes where I had to hope they would tend to their crops, help their neighbours, and allow peace to flourish. As their lights went with them, the sky darkened so the flames burning high on the balcony seemed to grow brighter still.

"Is that going to stay there?" Cal asked.

I shrugged. "Easier than taking it back to the Isle of Fire."

"But what if someone else decides they can get it to work for them?"

I remembered Esta's hopes for the future. "Now we've seen where that leads we have to trust we'll make the right choices."

Cal huffed. "You're optimistic."

"And you're cynical. The truth lies somewhere in between." I smiled. "It'll be exciting to find out."

"So what will you do now? While you're waiting for a summons from the council?" Cal's eyes gleamed. His light hair was gilded by the flames.

"You know, it wasn't until you and Keba and Zan knocked on my door that I'd seen anything further than a league away from my home. I'd like to see it all. For real, not through visions. And in less of a hurry this time."

"You could go with Tullan, perhaps. It would give you some time to catch up."

When Cal said his name I looked around to find my father. Tullan was on the other side of the room, in a small group with two of the councillors, one of the guards and Keba. As though he felt my gaze, he looked up and raised a hand. I waved back. It was enough. I wanted to spend time with him, and I would, but we had plenty of time ahead of us for that.

"My father has his own things to do. I'm happy to go on my own."

"Oh."

My eyes jerked up to his face – was that disappointment? But he looked just the same as ever, entirely Cal. I had to be mistaken.

"Don't you want to go home?" I asked.

He smiled and his cares fell off his face. He was handsome when he smiled. "Dee, I've wanted to go home for about four years. Now's my chance to decide where home really is." He looked at me sidelong. "I wondered... maybe we could see if there are places we'd both like to visit. It's more fun to travel with company."

I looked at him, a smile pushing at my cheeks while a hundred futures bounced around my thoughts. The past was over and I didn't want to see the future before it arrived. Anything could happen, and I'd find out when it did. I let my smile go free. "Yeah, I'd like that."

"Just until you can't stand the sight of me."

My heart beat fast as I replied in the same tone, "That'll give us a day or so. If we're lucky."

Cal's smile widened. So did mine. He slipped his hand into mine, his fingers warm across my palm, tips curling to press firmly against the side of my hand. I stared at the connection where the two of us joined together, very aware of the heat of him where we touched.

"Is that all right?" Cal's voice was anxious, his gaze focused, like mine, on where our hands met.

I looked up. He was watching me carefully, head tilted, that ever-present frown between his brows as he waited for my response.

I wrapped my fingers around his warm hand to keep us connected. Daring, I boosted onto my toes to press a light kiss against his cheek. "Yes. Yes, that's good."

Do you want more?

Princess Witch

Princess, Pawn, Sacrifice. Step into a fantasy kingdom where Princess Jurelle's rebellion against an arranged marriage has results she could never have dreamed of...

Dragon Thief
Dragon Flight
Dragon Fury
Dragon Stone

The Four Kings series (fantasy)

Kyann hates mages and anything that reminds her of the father who abandoned her family. So accepting her own magical abilities might be difficult...

Awakened by Magic
Inspired by Magic
Shattered by Magic
Drenched by Magic
Ignited by Magic
Courted by Magic

A Clockwork War series (steampunk)
In an alternate England eternally at war with Scotland,
Clara only wants to keep her brothers safe. But her
decisions lead to betrayal and heartbreak.
The Clockwork War
An Airship from Ashes
The Tinker Queen
The Immortality Device

Post-apocalyptic Standalone
Socially-awkward Libby has her life turned upside
down when she helps her doctor father treat the
wrong patient. In the space of a day she's on the run
with a boy she has every reason to hate.
Rising Tides

Find details on all Katy's books on her website:
www.katyhaye.com

About the Author

Katy Haye spends as much time as possible lost in a good book. She has a fearsome green tea habit, a partiality for dark chocolate brazils and a fascination with the science of storytelling.

Acknowledgements

Cheers to my writer friends, the 10k Angels and the Paisley Piranhas for mutual support and cheerleading when things looked difficult-to-impossible. I'm so glad I have company on this crazy roller-coaster!

Thank you to Rachel Daven Skinner for insightful substantive edits that stopped me vanishing into my own plot holes, to Morgen Bailey for painstaking line editing, and to Icy Sedgwick for my beautiful cover.

And my thanks go to all my wonderful readers. Your enthusiasm is much appreciated.